THE PACKING HOUSE

ABOUT THE AUTHOR

G. Donald Cribbs has written and published poetry and short stories since high school. Donald is a graduate of Messiah College in English and Education, and holds an MA in Clinical Mental Health Counseling. Donald is a licensed professional counselor (LPC) with the PA state board.

He and his wife and four boys reside in central Pennsylvania, where he is hard at work on his next book, the sequel to his debut novel, *The Packing House*.

Having lived and traveled abroad in England, France, Belgium, Germany, China and Thailand (you can guess where he lived and where he visited), Donald loves languages and how they connect us all. Coffee and Nutella are a close second.

THE PACKING HOUSE

G. Donald Cribbs

Cherish
EDITIONS

First published in Great Britain 2022 by Cherish Editions

Cherish Editions is a trading style of Shaw Callaghan Ltd & Shaw Callaghan 23
USA, INC.

The Foundation Centre

Navigation House, 48 Millgate, Newark

Nottinghamshire NG24 4TS UK

www.triggerhub.org

Text Copyright © 2022 G. Donald Cribbs

British Library Cataloguing in Publication Data

A CIP catalogue record for this book is available upon request
from the British Library

ISBN: 978-1-913615-56-7

This book is also available in the following eBook formats:

ePUB: 978-1-913615-57-4

G. Donald Cribbs has asserted his right under the Copyright,
Design and Patents Act 1988 to be identified as the author of this work

Cover design by More Visual

Typeset by Lapiz Digital Services

Cherish Editions encourages diversity and different viewpoints. However, all
views, thoughts and opinions expressed in this book are the author's own and
are not necessarily representative of us as an organization.

All material in this book is set out in good faith for general guidance and no
liability can be accepted for loss or expense incurred in following the information
given. In particular this book is not intended to replace expert medical or
psychiatric advice. It is intended for informational purposes only and for your
own personal use and guidance. It is not intended to act as a substitute for
professional medical advice. Professional advice should be sought if desired
before embarking on any health-related programme.

To those who have found a pathway through their abuse, despite the kind or combination, and who continue to climb outward and upward toward recovery and healing, and to those special loved ones who stand in the aftermath, come alongside and love survivors, despite their many wounds.

CONTENTS

It has been said, "Time heals all wounds." I do not agree. The wounds remain. In time, the mind, protecting its sanity, covers them with scar tissue and the pain lessens. But it is never gone.

—*Rose Kennedy*

PART I

BROAD RUN HIGH SCHOOL

Home of the Panthers

PART I

BROAD RUN HIGH SCHOOL

Home of the Panthers

1

MONSTER

At the bell, I head to study hall, my last class. There's a substitute today. Cell phones come out. Someone has their iPod up way too high. In a way, I feel sorry for the sub; as a job, it has to be right up there with garbage collector. I prop a book between me and my backpack then close my eyes, which have been slamming shut all day.

The next thing I know, the substitute is standing over me, his hand on my shoulder, shaking me awake. Someone sniggers nearby.

"Wake up, young man. There's no sleeping in study hall."

Pushing my glasses back into place, I look up and try to get my eyes to adjust and stay open; I blink a few times and look around wildly. *What an idiot.* I even forgot where I was for a moment. A flush of warmth starts at my ears and neck before sliding across my cheeks.

"All right, I'm up."

Whispers erupt in various places around me as I sit up and rub my eyes. Someone laughs. My desk is askew. Something smells bad. *Sulfur.* Odd... the realization hits me hard.

A female voice remarks, "If I were him, I'd be so embarrassed!"

"What's your name?" the substitute asks quietly.

"Joel Scrivener."

The substitute leans down. "Joel? You might want to speak with a counselor about those dreams."

"What do you mean?"

He leans closer, lowers his voice. "You kept saying, 'Get off me, stop touching me, get off me,' over and over."

He gives me what he must think is a reassuring smile. Then he leaves.

The only thing worse than getting caught asleep in study hall: getting caught asleep *and* crying out from a bad dream in study hall.

There's more whispering, but this time it crackles nearby. A recording—presumably of me—replays the sound of me jerking around in my chair, desk legs scraping against the floor, then "Get *OFF* me!" and "Stop *TOUCHING* meeee!"

The bell rings.

Down the hallway, students gather in odd clumps, skittering away from me like I'm the monster. A cacophony of whispers follows a chorus of aborted cackles; I hear my voice playing over and over, like my life jammed on repeat. I'm too stunned to reply, even when Shampoo Girl, who rides my bus, tries to stop me. I'm not good with names. We move too much for them to matter. This girl is heavyset, plain, with nice hair. I like how it smells if I sit behind her on the bus. Shampoo Girl. She's one of the few I've caught glaring at my bullies when I'm dropped into the lunchroom trashcan or tripped with an armful of books between classes. She hasn't said anything to my attackers, like that punk from Algebra II, but her quiet defiance is at least reassuring. Not that I've thanked her or acknowledged her for that.

"Joel? Joel, are you okay?" I definitely don't deserve her sympathy; instead, I look back down the hall.

My own brother Jonathan is with his swim team posse and says, "I can't believe you dudes got this," before he sees me.

"Izzat rilly yer bro, man?" asks a blond-haired skater-punk friend of Jonathan's, pointing at his cellphone. They must be watching the video of me from study hall just like everyone else. *Man, that traveled fast.* On the far end, cackling like a fiend, my brother Jonathan laughs at his best friend Elias, who's doubled over and turning purple. Skaterdude is on this end, sputtering and waving his arms like he's imitating me from the video. Between the other two is Elias. *God, I hate him sometimes.* Why does he stick his nose where it doesn't belong?

"You still owe me a fiver for the Terror Bet," Jonathan says, slapping the back of his hand on Skaterdude's chest. He should've kept our energy drink bet private, between the two of us, but instead I imagine he thought he'd impress his posse and make a few bucks. *So he bet off me, did he?* Jonathan looks up and sees me staring right at him. He tosses up two fingers after bouncing them off his chest like a salute to his homies, although I'm clearly not one of them. I'm just his loser brother.

It doesn't matter.

He's right. Jonathan must think of me as another one of his casualties, just like *him*. I'm a cast-off, like Terror Man, my mother's latest boyfriend. To Jonathan, Terror Man and I are just accessories on his social status climb. Even after our most recent beating for touching the shrine of Terrors, Jonathan dared me to try to steal one without getting caught. I thought he was just looking out for me since I haven't been sleeping much, but I guess I was wrong. If I can't tell the difference between someone being nice or using me, I wonder how I will ever fix things with Amber Walker, the only girl I've ever wished was more than a friend.

No turning back now. My social life is officially over. I wonder how long it will take until everyone hears, and probably sees, a cell phone clip of my nightmare.

Only I can't wake up from this one.

***

I don't plan to collapse on my frameless mattress late that night. By the time I'm fully out... *I'm already drifting down a vaguely familiar set of stone stairs, before I realize the déjà vu—at first a cold tingle then a white-hot shudder that seeps down my spine. As it dissipates, I continue down, despite the thrumming in my ears.*

Firelight dapples across shadowed walls near the bottom. Cold air gusts past, chills me until my teeth rattle, and almost blows out the torches. The room opens to the right, but I can't see around the corner.

As I step into the guttering light, I'm knocked on my face so fast I barely get my hands out to break my fall. I gasp for breath beneath this tremendous weight. There's no getting away. Sharp pain bursts along my ribs.

From its grip, I get a twinge in my spine, sharp stings that shoot up my back and spread out across both shoulder blades. Whatever is behind me is huge. Its hulking mass presses me down into the ground. I sure as hell don't dare move.

"C'mere, Joel!" the deep voice snarls against my ear.

***

I wake up.

Sometimes I wake screaming. *How does it know my name?* My mother has found me a few times that way; about as comforting as getting caught jerking off under blankets.

When she finds me like that, I roll toward the wall and mumble about a bad dream. *I'll be fine. Go back to bed. Please don't ask any more.* I'll never live this down if my mother holds my hand and chases away some boogeyman. I've got to figure this out. Better to man up than be labeled a loser. At least Jonathan's still asleep. I don't need him betraying me any further.

If I could, I'd squeeze my eyes shut and will myself back to sleep. *What if that thing is there?* The stone stairs. The horrible, personal things it says. The sweat-rot stench of sulfur. I'd rather stare at the blurry ceiling all night. Besides, questions begin to swirl, threatening to keep me awake indefinitely. There are at least three hours until it's time to get up for school. I might have a test. Better not think too much.

Next thing I know, it's light; the roof of my mouth is sandpapery, I've got rank morning breath, and, if I don't get to the bathroom right now, I'm going to have a waterbed for sure.

I have to limp my way there, momentarily forgetting about our lecture at the hands of Terror Man last night. I don't like him. He's always in our faces. Always trying to prove what a man he is when he slams us against the wall or some shit.

He's nice enough when he's not railing on Jonathan and me for drinking his Terrors.

As I find relief in the bathroom, I start to wonder about this latest nightmare. Then I grab a shower, wincing when the tender spots on my back come under the flow. Maybe I should've let Jonathan take the brunt of it all, since he made the bet, but I couldn't live with myself if I hadn't intervened. I thought he was gonna kill Jonathan this time. What a nightmare. Which reminds me: I've got too many memory gaps to make sense of it all. I need to figure out their source. The root cause.

It's not for lack of trying.

I've scoured every book on nightmares I can find. One said the mind is a strange muscle that remembers every ache. Nightmares are a way we revisit each painful experience, circling back to make sense of what happened. That still doesn't explain how the creature knows me well enough to snarl my name. *Is it someone I know?* I glance at the clock. No time to dwell; the bus'll be here any minute. Time to get dressed and head downstairs.

My mother is at work, and Jonathan went in on the early bus for swim team. I grab breakfast and ibuprofen and then head for the street corner. My hand lands on the last two cans in my backpack. I'd forgotten all about the Terrors. *Jonathan.* I'd toss them back in the fridge if I weren't already at the bus stop.

Might as well. Chugging the first one down, I collect weird looks as I let the burp rip. Jonathan still got pretty roughed up; after all, he dared swipe from the shrine of Terrors on the top shelf of the fridge. Terror Man left no visible marks on me, only bruises, but I doubt Jonathan made it out unscathed. I wonder what Coach said to him this morning.

Was Jonathan trying to set me up? Guarantee a win for his second round of Terror Bets, so he could up the ante? It's never enough with him. Jonathan can't seem to leave well enough alone. Like he has to poke the bear or something. Everyone knows you let a sleeping bear lie. Not him.

The last stragglers come out as the bus pulls up. I'm the new guy. Technically, it's Redhead-Dude-With-Braces-And-Acne's stop.

I must space out the whole ride to school because it feels like only moments later when the bus pulls into the drop-off circle by the *Broad Run High School, Home of the Panthers* sign. Cheerleaders brush past in uniform, and the football team is sporting jersey hard-ons, strutting as we all press toward the door.

School's a bust. I doze through most of my classes, but at least I overhear that the history test has been moved to next week. Now I just have to make it through English class (easy for me), study hall, and I'm out.

We're reading this book *Fahrenheit 451*, where Guy Montag is an anti-fireman who burns books for a living. If I could talk some sense into him, maybe he'd lay off the bonfires and help me sort through all the bizarre shit in my brain. Yeah, it's a crazy thought, just like the ones about Amber.

I get flustered when I think of her.

Maybe Montag and I aren't as different from each other as I first thought. We both have problems we're running from. Beatty hunts him down when they catch Montag hoarding books in his air vent. I knew he was a reader. His own wife turns him in. *Betrayed by someone that close. Man.*

That's what set him off running.

My English teacher makes us write on the salamander or fire lizard. Is it a tattoo or just a uniform logo? I consider writing a story or a poem. According to legend, they're not lizards, which are reptiles. Salamanders are amphibians and have an affinity for fire. They can also regenerate lost limbs and tails. Remind me of an Escher tessellation. Patterns that transform from one thing to another. I should go for extra credit.

Speaking of extra credit, my grades have been nothing but toilet water, they're so flushed. Up until now, I've held tight at honor roll. But, just like that time in the closet with Amber, it, too, was a test I knew I was doomed to fail. Now I can't shake these nightmares. Neither could Montag.

If I don't do something soon, I'll have to repeat my sophomore year. Then I'd be in the same grade as Jonathan. That's reason enough to invoke my previous plan.

2

LOCK-IN

It's late afternoon and not the time for sleep. I manage to snag an hour on my mattress, the one thing between me and the floor of our room, before Jonathan's loud-ass banging wakes me. This is the only rest I'll get ahead of tonight's school lock-in. He crams contraband in his backpack and slams drawers. Still, he could be quieter if he expects me to help him pull off the booty call he's been lining up for weeks.

Like I'd want to do anything for him at this point.

Which is—of course—why losing the Terror bet obligates me to do crap for him now. Screw you, universe. Every time I see Jonathan, my mind fills with Terror Man and his belt and every word he slung at us in lecture mode. *You two are just a couple of punks, taking things that don't belong to you. It's time someone set you straight.* Well, that and the crap at school.

Jonathan had his posse in on the bet, too. They were settling up in the hallway after study hall. Why'd I have to go and lose the bet? Now I'm a slave to my younger brother and his list of girls for the night. At his beck and call. I'm an idiot for agreeing to any of this, but it's too late for should-have-knowns.

I stretch out the aches in my limbs and rub the remnants of sleep from my eyes. With any luck, I'll find somewhere private to crash at the high school, in case the nightmares come back. I was up all night with them again, filling notebook pages to keep from seeing that thing chase me down again. The shudder takes me by surprise.

"I had no idea you were trying out for a spot at the zombie prom."
Like Jonathan knows all the things that keep me awake at night. He
says that but knows I've been the recent target of locker-wedgies
and toilet-swirlies, thanks to Math Punk and his drones, just because
I carry a pocket-sized notebook to jot down ideas while I'm at
school. I guess that makes me an easy target. Maybe Jonathan knows
something he hasn't said.

"I'm not, doofus. You're cocky as ever." I glance with meaning at
his bulging… backpack. Must be tied to his booty-call plans. "You
can't be serious."

"A Boy Scout is always prepared."

"You're no Boy Scout."

Forcing myself to stand, I rummage through my bag to see what
else I'll need. *This time, I'll run away for good,* I promise myself, doing
my best to ignore the slew of images as they flash through my mind
from my latest nightmare. I grab a hoodie off the floor, cinch it
around my waist, and snag the book I'm reading off the milk crate
that serves as my nightstand. My eyes slam shut in protest. Jonathan
looks over and sighs.

"Dude, I'm serious. I've got a lot riding on your duties as
wingman. Don't let me down." He passes me several forbidden
Terror drinks he probably stole from the fridge. After last night's
beating, this is a new level of desperate, even for Jonathan. I hesitate
but take them anyway. Our mother has taken things with Terror
Man to the next level, letting him stash his drinks at our place, but
they're off-limits for us. I'm talking "police lights rolling red blue
from every reflective surface" off-limits. Doesn't mean we haven't
pinched a few.

A wave of guilt washes across my beyond-tired frame. I know I
shouldn't do it, but there's no way I'll survive tonight without some
serious help. I crack one open and chug its contents, gasping as it
burns on the way down. Just in case, I hide the empty can in my
backpack. I prefer to avoid any more collateral damage, if I can
help it. Jonathan's considerate gesture is highly suspect. If he weren't
thinking with his dick, I'd be more suspicious.

I shouldn't get so worked up over a drink that tastes like ass. It's wannabe beer, not even a legal issue; carbonated cough syrup. Why do I let it get to me? Because it's one more excuse my mother's boyfriend uses to thump the life out of Jonathan and me. He could threaten to take away the library from me for good... the hell if I'm giving up the one thing that keeps me sane, though.

That's why Jonathan started calling him Terror Man, the way he guards those drinks like they're his claim over our territory. If you ask me, he might as well piss on the refrigerator or on my mother's bedroom door. Clearly visible is that purple welt Jonathan earned from last night's Terror Beating.

I shudder. These images keep cycling through my mind on repeat, whether I'm awake or asleep.

It's the same with my mother. I used to call her mom, but that changed when we spent time in that homeless shelter because she was gambling away the bill money. I can still feel the roaches crawling over me in the dark, hear the crackheads screaming through paper-thin walls. They weren't supposed to be using while they were at the shelter, but sometimes they got away with it. Most adults don't think kids pay attention to details, like the exchange of pharmacy bags and money, the glazed-over look in their eyes, or the tools used to cook their meth and the marks they left behind.

I made the mistake of pointing this out to her. "We wouldn't be here if you hadn't gambled everything away. Now we have to check for roaches before eating anything and pretend we can't see or hear those other people shooting up in front of their kids."

My mother fired right back at me, "Let's get one thing straight. I'm the mother and you're the son. Learn your place. I won't be talked to like that by a child. You hear me?" You bet I did. To this day, I've stopped calling her mom, and only use "mother," now that I've learned my place.

Not that she's noticed.

Our mother's voice wafts up from somewhere below. "Joel? Jonathan. Get a move on, you two. I'm not driving you in, if you miss the bus. It'll be here any minute." I grab the pack of Amber's letters as an afterthought. We thunder down the stairs, backpacks and smuggled items in tow. Fortunately, our mother isn't one for a strip search or pat-down. Too bad I can't stop the belch from the Terror before it's too late. My mother raises an eyebrow.

"Sorry." Laughing probably doesn't help much, either.

"Please tell me that isn't what I think it is. You know how he gets when you touch his stuff. Give me a break, okay?" Like she sticks around to watch Terror Man dole out consequences.

"It was his idea," I say, tagging Jonathan on the chest before bolting out to the safety of the bus stop. Soon after, Jonathan comes out, hauling ass. He must've done some smooth talking.

When we get to the bus stop, my stomach pitches. *Elias Stone.* I couldn't care less; it's his sister I'm queasy about. I still haven't managed to figure out why she gives me the time of day, unless she's leveraging for something. Elise could pass for Amber's doppelgänger if she curled her straight hair and dyed it fiery red. I'm convinced everyone has a body double scattered in different parts of the country. That's what Amber and I are now. Scattered. Past tense. No longer a thing.

If Elias's here, Elise's already back at school, warming up for the pep rally on Bonfire Field. That's not the official name, just what everyone calls it. Every varsity player and cheerleader will be there rehearsing. In fact, the school lock-in might as well be a season preview. At least I'll know where to avoid.

My thoughts aren't enough to distract me from witnessing Jonathan's fist bump and one-armed hug fest with Elias.

"Elias, my man. What's shakin'?" They complete an elaborate handshake before full-on chest bumpage. That's when Jonathan's bag splits open, spilling an ambitious quantity of condoms at their feet. Elias doubles over just as the bus pulls up.

"Aw, yeah, that's what I'm talking about." More high fives.

If they were any friendlier, I might second-guess their orientation. Jonathan's straight as a line and completely at home with his sexuality. He doesn't even mind it when other guys, including Elias, check out his junk in the pool locker-room. He and Elias are both on the swim team, but I don't think Jonathan knows all there is to know about Elias, despite how he's fronting now.

"D'you bring your gear for the show? The honeys I've lined up got game."

"Sa-weet."

I slug my backpack over my shoulder and climb aboard.

***

The universe has it out for me. When we arrive at school, not only does a hole fail to open and swallow me whole, but Elise meets us at the drop-off. I can't help but eye how high her cheerleader skirt rides up as she bounces around, apparently excited to see her... brother? *Ah, of course.* She's practically panting for *Jonathan.*

He slides his arm around her waist as she flings her arms around his neck. She's all over him. Still, I ogle every flash of Spankies, even though I can't actually see anything, until the thought of Amber seeing me check out Elise makes my stomach contort. I duck behind Elias and Jonathan and slink away, muttering something about catching up later. Or never. Besides, I have plans that have little to do with lock-ins or making good on this debt thing with Jonathan.

The universe has other plans.

"Leaving so soon?" Elise grabs me by the hoodie, using sleeves to steer me back around. I look up at the splash of sunset scattered across the evening sky, unsure how to speak popular.

"Pretty much," I reply.

"That's too bad."

Dare I ask? I'm distracted by the uniform and how much Elise reminds me of...

"What did you say?"

"I said, 'That's too bad.'" Her eyes wander over to where my brother is amassing a small crowd. She emits an excited squeal before turning back to me.

Yep. Too bad every girl I know looks right through me at Jonathan. "Have fun with pool boy."

"I was hoping we could finish our conversation." Elise sidles up next to me. "From last time."

I shake off the urge to place my hands on her hips.

"Your lips moved, but I don't recall words."

She doesn't deny it. At Jonathan's last at-home meet, Elise had pulled me over to her while we waited outside the locker room, but it'd felt wrong, like I was just there for her practice or amusement. We'd been so close to kissing…

And now, even though Elise is standing in front of me, Amber is a hundred miles away. The confusing part is how much they look alike. I do a double take every time I see Elise. I want to do things I shouldn't, things I never got the chance to explore with Amber.

My brain engages, and my gut screams for me to get out of there, picturing how we stopped short.

"Sorry, my plans for tonight are—see you around."

Before she can protest, I dive for cover inside the school and press through the crowd. Most of the students greet their friends in clumps and check the schedule of events. I keep glancing over my shoulder to see if I gave them the slip. The images slam through my brain, reminding me they're still there. Like I could forget.

When I see the flash of pompoms, I don't hesitate. Pulling on my hoodie, I duck into the auditorium where they're showing slasher movies. I pick a seat on the far left end, near the exit door. Just as a door opens in the back, I slink down in my seat. *Please don't let them find me; please don't let them find me.* The door closes again. I let out a slow breath. Realizing I'm in the dark and somewhat horizontal, my eyes scrunch shut. I fight to reopen them. I could knock out hard. As I exhale, sleep tugs me down until the realization hits me, and my eyes pop open, darting left and right. I can't let that happen. Not ever. Especially here.

Then I remember the other Terrors in my bag. I pull one out and down it. The auditorium is not safe. I'd better find somewhere else or get going on my real mission. Sneaking out the side door and up the dim hallway, I can already see a commotion underway.

"Five bucks he croaks before his fingertips touch water."

"Isn't this the third or fourth time he's tried?"

"Not a chance he'll break the record."

"He's gonna do it. Everybody to the pool!"

Jonathan mentioned a "show" when he greeted Elias, but I didn't know it would draw a crowd. *What an attention whore.* The mass of bodies shoves toward the Panther pool. Heading in the opposite direction, I'm met by a wave of pompoms and cheerleaders surging back toward the crowd I tried to avoid. When I look away, an arm slides around my bicep and steers me back toward the natatorium.

"You're going the wrong way. I thought you two were close."

"What's this about, Elise? Why are you even slumming with the likes of me?"

She gives me a look and then continues. "You disappeared before I could tell you earlier. Johnny's gonna try to break the district record. If he gets it, he'll land Regionals."

When we stop, I turn to face her.

"First of all, his name's Jonathan. Not Johnny. Second, he's been trying to break that record since summer tryouts. I've got better things to do than watch another one of his shows."

"Well, I want to be there when he does."

"Don't let me keep you." A huff escapes before I can stop it.

Elise leans in toward me, catching me completely off guard. Heavy-lidded, her eyes cast down toward my lips. When they close, I freeze, unsure if I should kiss her back. Her presence reminds me so much of Amber—of when we were together in the basement closet not long ago—that I struggle to think of anything except anticipating the taste of her lips and tongue, my hands on her skirt, pulling her close. Some part of me fires off an alarm, a warning, an interruption.

What is *wrong* with me? She's obviously using me to get to Jonathan. I bolt.

Cutting through the open gym, I pass clusters of students playing basketball and volleyball. I run. The divider wall has been opened so students can move between stations. A few lucky teachers are directing from the sidelines. What must Elise think, expecting our lips to meet and instead being startled when her eyes open and I'm gone?

Running is my go-to response, especially in a situation like this. Without thinking, I did it, like putting on one pant leg and then the other. One step always follows the other. It was easy. Nothing messy; I just took action.

I stop to catch my breath once I'm out of the building, my eyes adjusting to the night sky and glittering stars as I overlook the field. Everyone's probably at the pool, basking in the glory of Jonathan's show. Which is why I'm here, making the most of this opportunity.

Even though I didn't think it through, didn't discuss it with myself, I know where I'm going. In fact, I planned this all along, when I packed extra clothes and Amber's letters and my toothbrush. I never planned to stay at the lock-in or play wingman for Jonathan or run away from Elise all night. My plan was to leave—something no one will see coming until I am long gone. I promised myself and told no one: *this time I'm running away.*

"Where have you been?" *Shit. Jonathan.*

"Look, I'm gonna hafta reschedule. I'm busy."

I hope the look on my face somehow helps to explain enough so I don't get sucked into twenty questions. Too bad his brain is otherwise occupied. If he could, he'd formulate a question. Instead, he just stares at me.

"Jonathan, I've got problems. Elise won't keep her hands off me." There's no time to talk. I head for the tree line at the edge of the field.

"Woah, bruh. Good for you."

"No, not good." I turn to face him.

"Oh?" There's something weighted in his reply. Like he's holding back some part of what he's thinking.

The sound of the band and the crowd surging out of the school for the field coincide with the realization that my plans have failed. Now I'll never get away before someone spots me. I can't ditch Jonathan if he sees me leaving. The adult staff is busy lighting the bonfire.

"My first rendezvous should be here any minute. I need you on point. Circulate and prep the next few girls. Check your list, but try not to be Captain Obvious. Capisce?"

I'm exercising great restraint not to deck him in front of his entourage.

"You sure upping that bet was legit?" He'd won the first round fair and square, but still, my kingdom for a loophole or an escape clause.

Elise arrives in a flurry of pompoms and skirts. Not that I was looking for her.

"What are we discussing? Is this about the current Terror Bet or that video thingy?" She smirks, crossing her arms over her chest.

"What the hell?" I look from Jonathan to Elise and back.

"Uh, I can explain." Jonathan lifts his hands and starts to back away.

He betrayed me?

If he blabbed about our bets to Elise, what other embarrassing or private family stuff has he told her? Certainly not who gave him the shiner last night. *Or would he?* My mind floods with images of the study hall video clip aftermath: walking down the hall, all those eyes drilling into me. Everything explodes, tinged in red. I'm shoving Jonathan with both arms before I even realize I've downshifted into action.

"No need. Elise has caught me up plenty, asshole." I take a swing and shudder as my fist clashes against his raised arm. Cue the posse.

"Brother fight!" someone shouts as the crowd encircles us. I miss the next few punches, but a kick sends him reeling, and then I've got him pinned to the ground and my fists are pummeling him before I feel myself floating away, and it's like I'm watching someone else turn his brother's face to hamburger. Guys from the football team and the swim team pull us apart as teachers engage, barking orders. I feel something hot dripping down my face. I can't open my left eye. Both hands hurt like hell. If my right eye is working, I'm in far better shape than Jonathan.

When we're escorted to the principal's office, they call our mother to come get us. I must have nodded off longer than I realized in the auditorium. It's close to three in the morning, and our mother is not a fan of losing sleep. I can't believe he'd betray me like that. If Elise knows, then half the upperclassmen know by now. What a douche.

This whole thing was a set up. What business is it of hers? And why did Jonathan feel the need to share it with Elise Stone? Neither of us speaks. I doubt we could stick to words at this point.

My mother's voice slams into the tiny room before the rest of her catches up. "I've a mind to let you two spend the night in jail for the stunt you just pulled. I cannot believe you'd do this to me at three o'clock in the morning." From the way she's digging in her purse, I can't tell if she's searching for car keys or cigarettes.

"Jonathan's the one who started this whole thing. He—"

The back of my legs bang into the chair. It lists across the floor.

"Joel threw the first punch. He tore into me for no good reason." He grabs his bag from the chair at the other end of the room.

"Hey. Cool it. Not interested in who did what. I've a mind to let Samuel talk some sense into you two when we get home. Until then, zip it."

A hush falls as the weight of her words and the realization sinks in: Samuel only lectures with a belt in his hands. Jonathan glares. I flex my hands and wince. Our mother signs us out, and we head to the car in heavy silence. There go my plans.

3

STRAINED

The dishes are a mosaic of broken shards on the tile floor, bits of food still clinging to some of the pieces. I halt in the kitchen doorway. My mother's boyfriend may have noticed a few of his Terrors missing.

I'm the one Terror Man will pin it on, thanks to Jonathan spilling the fact that he should check my bag. But Jonathan stashed them there, not me. I got played by my own brother. I can feel the weight of what's coming. It's familiar. My mind buzzes through these thoughts like a fly, angry and unable to land.

Moving through the room in slow motion, I might as well be underwater. My stomach drops out from under me; it feels like I kick it across the kitchen floor, along with the debris. The stench of day-old food mingling together cloys at my nostrils. The house is too quiet. I follow the trail into the living room, where I can breathe again. Maybe he didn't notice.

The railing is ripped off the stairs and hangs like a limp arm out of its socket. My hand instinctively slides up to my shoulder. I must be the first one home. *Should I go upstairs?*

Not that I have a choice. I've got to sort this out. *Did this happen because of me?*

"Not again," I say and sigh. No, it's not the Terrors. It's not me. Before I reach my mother's bedroom, I already know what I'll find. She's not here, and we'll have to move again.

I enter her bedroom. This time there's a huge hole in the bathroom door. A bed rail protrudes from the hole, pointing oddly at the ceiling. It looks so strange—the way a needle lances a blister—that I start to laugh.

Water gushes everywhere, soaking into my sneakers.

The toilet and sink must've overflowed. Stepping back onto the carpet, I hear the slap of water beneath my feet. This'll probably rain down through the living room ceiling. *Will I have to change schools this time?* Guess it depends on how far away we have to move. I hate moving. It's like running away on someone else's terms.

I should have run away when I had the chance.

All these places we bounce between are like the shimmer trail a snail leaves on the ground. A few summers ago, I used to trace their squiggly lines across sidewalks. Now I'm the snail, dragging myself shell and all through another day I never asked for. I don't get to choose which part remains: me or the iridescent line like a shadow behind me.

Coming to my senses, I realize I've imagined the water. But I'm sure I heard the slap under each footstep. *Was I... dreaming?* Nightmares are bad enough, but seeing things that aren't there while I'm awake is even worse. This can't be happening. Just like last time.

I know the drill. I've done this before. Punching in the numbers, I dial the police and tell them who I am. A crackly voice answers.

"Please hold."

After a minute, they get back on the line to tell me my mother is there, *at the police station*. She's been assaulted.

Which one was it this time? In the past year, she's seen a couple different guys, like the black dude who rides a motorcycle from a few doors down. We might have to leave the state. *Oh, boy. There goes high school.* I'll be a nobody. That guy with no name. Hiya, No Name.

My mother comes on the line long enough to tell me to stay put, she'll be home soon, blah, blah, blah.

I hear myself saying, "But Mom, there's a bedrail sticking out your bathroom door—"

"I'll explain it when I get home."

I come to when I hear dial tone in my ear.

Then I realize I haven't seen Jonathan yet. Nor have I heard mewing from the stowaway fuzz ball he snuck in off the street, right after we got nailed for the lock-in. It's like he can't be in enough trouble already? I head to our bedroom. The closet door is shut. There are muffled sounds. Well, he's here, but I have no way of knowing whether he saw what happened or if the kitten is okay.

"Hey, uh, Jon," I say as calm as I can muster. "Everything all right when you got back? With the kitten, I mean?" My stomach lurches while I wait for an answer.

Pause. Then, "Yeah. Sure. Why?" He says each word stilted, probably trying to figure out what I'm getting at. I hear suppressed giggles. Jonathan's not alone in there. Guess he got lucky after all. He must've just come in and gone straight up to our room with one of his lock-in booty calls. Missed the kitchen. But how would he have missed the railing? It was still dangling when I came upstairs.

"No reason," I begin. "Well, there's a reason. Something you'd better see. Mom's on her way home. From the police station."

The door flies open. Two bare legs disappear into the closet. Jonathan's head pops out from behind the door to join the rest of his body. All he's wearing are boxers, and they're on inside out. More snickers. An arm pulls at him and starts sliding the door closed.

For a moment, I'm reminded of Amber and me at her place. *Damn it.* Why does it work for him and not for me?

"What did you just say?" Jonathan holds the door, distracted.

"I said, 'the police station,'" I repeat.

"What's the matter? Why is Mom coming home from the police station?"

"I'm not sure, but the house is pretty smashed up. Didn't you notice the railing was off the lower stairs?"

"Come here," a female voice interjects.

"No, I was in a hurry." Laughter erupts in reply. "To check on Meshach. I kinda like Abednego, too." He turns back to his girlfriend, and the door slides shut with a bang. I guess they came in the other way, through the front hall and up the stairs. But the railing... He's got balls to bring her here.

"Well, if you planned on getting it food, the kitchen's a mess. Don't go through the living room, and be careful where you step. I'll talk... when you're done."

Guess he isn't that worried about the kitten, just what it can get him. Now that Jonathan's preoccupied, I head downstairs, relieved my spot on the couch remains unscathed by Terror Man's path of destruction through the house. My throat tightens; a lump forms and tastes like metal.

My own thoughts keep crowding in. I wonder if I'll ever be worthy of Amber's attentions. I don't mean it in the way Jonathan plays them. There's way more to a girl than that. Swallowing hard, I retreat to the safety of pages. Everyone's after Montag. He has to go to this hermit guy for help to mask his own scent. I lose track of time.

"...'Meaningless! Meaningless!' says the teacher. 'Utterly meaningless! Everything is meaningless.'..."

Words sting like salt as tears streak down my face. My nose runs. Eyes bleary and red, I take off my glasses and wipe at them. Don't let anyone see me like this. No one cries over a book. Maybe it's not just that.

Montag got away from the robot hound to memorize Ecclesiastes? *No way.* No. Way.

"...The sun rises and sets, ... the oceans are never full, ... there is nothing new under the sun..."

I get that, but I need answers, not this shit.

Not sure if I like this or not. I wish it could help me decipher things with Amber, like the secret decoder rings in cereal boxes do. Maybe if I revisit it later, the meaning will be clearer.

Should I care what comes next in English? I'll be long gone by then. Then it hits me: *why the hell should I stay put or wait for my mother to come home?* Jonathan'll be fine. After all, his celebrity status is more important than blood.

He made that clear with the Terrors.

Getting up to leave, I watch Jonathan and Elise come barreling down the stairs. *Elise.* Why am I not surprised? Guess they ran out of condoms. Turning away, I wipe my face. Their feet thud at the landing, and their staggered gasps peel through the silence. I turn around to find them witnessing, apparently for the first time, the mangled railing still dangling.

"Whoa, when the freak did this happen?" Jonathan leans over to touch it like it might disappear. At least they're both dressed.

"It was like that when I came in, and you were already here."

"I don't know how we missed that—"

Elise pulls him in for a lip lock. "I think I can refresh your memory."

"Oh, yeah," Jonathan says with his mouth full. "I wuhmembuh."

"Gross. Get a room."

"We already did," Jonathan proclaims.

"Wait, he's in that YouTube thing, right?"

"That's right," Jonathan says, wagging his finger at me. "Did you know your study hall slumber party is an online sensation? Everyone's talking about it."

I want to say something, but I can't do it. This isn't like the lock-in. How would they like it if I filmed them and put their closet rendezvous online? I can picture their blanched faces, but I won't follow through. Not with her here.

I take a ragged breath and let it out. So, now it's online. My mother's trips to the police station are bad enough. Anyone can look up police records online. I can't get away from a video.

"Look. I fell asleep. I couldn't help it." My eyes begin to well up.

"What will everyone at school think?" Elise is talking to Jonathan as if I'm not here. After the lock-in, I doubt if anyone could separate us, given our epic brawl in front of the whole school.

This can't go any further. It's too personal. I've got to get out.

I can't leave it like this, either.

"I can always count on you to stick up for me."

Grabbing my bag, I aim for the door and head to the library. I use my sweatshirt sleeve to wipe my face. Walking into a strong wind, I work my way out of the development and onto the road, away from the direction my mother will come in. I cross the field and speed up.

"...No one remembers the former generations, and even those yet to come will not be remembered by those who follow them..."

Nothing makes sense anymore. Nothing but running. I keep my head down, collar up, and shove hands into pockets. My backpack bounces rhythmically against my shoulder blades.

I keep going and lean forward into a biting, unforgiving tailwind.

4

LECTURE NOTES

Just my effing luck. I don't even make it to the library before the
skies rip open. Clouds clatter, tossing thunder and lightning in a
game of cosmic catch. Rain joins the party. Not the gentle spring
kind; the soak-your-clothes-to-your-skin kind of rain.

By the time I reach the entrance, my sweatshirt looks more like
a dress than something to keep me warm. Forget warmth. My teeth
bang together so bad, I make a grand entrance to the normally quiet
atmosphere I love. Twenty pairs of eyes glare in unison. Not that I
can see much through wet glasses.

Great.

Withdrawing to a back corner, I pull my sopping-wet sweatshirt
as tight as I can around me. Maybe if I sit here long enough, I'll dry
off and feel my feet again. All men are created equal in cold weather.
The same is true for cold water. My 'nads retreat so far back, I doubt
I'll ever have children at this point.

I think I've found the quiet corner, but a family comes in and
makes camp in the open chairs next to me. The mother and father
help each of their sons out of matching raincoats and hang them over
an empty chair.

When the chair dumps, spilling coats, a flash of a memory slices
across my eyes between blinks...

...He shoves me from behind. His weight presses me to the floor...

"Daddy, help me find a book about pirates," the younger boy in
front of me says.

"*…You had this coming. Make a sound and you're dead…*"

"Mom, I'm going to find the next book in this series," the older boy says, before heading to the young readers section.

"*…Not a word…*"

"I can help you with that, honey," the mother replies. The father and his son return and begin looking through their books together.

Time for me to bail.

"Didn't know this was your spot," I mumble as I exit.

"Oh, we're sorry. We can move somewhere else." Too late.

"*…Make a sound and you're dead…*"

I'm still shivering, anyway. I hope they have a bathroom with a dryer. That could help me regain feeling in my extremities before winter sets in.

My vision is blurred before I reach the bathroom. I don't care. No one here knows me, so what does it matter? I already stick out like a foster-child reject. Probably couldn't even find a family dumb enough to take me in. The only small concession I find is a push button dryer in the men's room. I must hit the button at least 500 times until my clothes are dry-ish.

My eyes still burn from the family on display back there. Must be nice to have it all. Our mother and father split when I was young.

Who pushed me down?

All I remember are the fights and the yelling. Doors slamming, pictures falling off the wall, shattered glass. Maybe if my parents had been together longer, the words of each fight might still buzz around my head. Fuzzy bits of memories linger, like my father's smell on a plaid shirt. Old Spice.

It couldn't have been him, could it?

I wish I could choose which memories to erase.

We don't have the money it takes to flaunt ourselves through the library in coordinated raincoats, galoshes and umbrellas.

What do I have? Nothing. And no memories to go with a big fat zilch on the side.

Why can't I recall large portions of my childhood? I remember I grew up near the ocean, but that's it. I guess I've been back a handful of times since we moved away, now that I think about it. Amber lived nearby. Her family wasn't perfect, but neither was mine. Her mom rode her pretty hard, like a bad dream you can't escape from. Her father seemed nice enough, not that I know much about having a father around, someone who cares about me over his own agenda.

But now, my mother has these different guys she sees. They come over and try to "be a friend." I don't want to be friends with any of them. Who knows if they'll even stick around long enough to remember our names? Why bother?

The most recent one is a tough guy. He gets along pretty well with my mother. They've gone out for a few months. At least they did until he tore through the house. Jonathan and I've been calling him Terror Man for so long, I might've forgotten that Samuel's his actual name.

When I leave the men's room, the family is gone. Good riddance. I am determined to stay until the library closes, so I have less awake time when I go home.

It's peaceful again, but I can't bring myself to read. When I don't want to read, I write. It's the charged atmosphere I love, everyone in their own solitude. I pull out a notebook and pens. Somehow I think I can coax words to help me out of this mess.

Maybe it's just another way to run away.

When I write, I'm closer to finding myself, the edge of my soul held up like a reflection. Words begin to orbit, almost tangible around me. Time to get them down on paper.

I've filled at least ten notebooks with stories and poems. Not sure where they all come from or why I can pour words out like water, sometimes like flames. When I write, not even a book distracts from the empty page before me.

The librarian's voice startles me before I look up and realize it's closing time. I grab my stuff and head for the exit. At least the rain has stopped, and so have my tears.

I'm in for a lecture when I get home. All I did was delay the inevitable. No rush to get back to that. The weather outside gives me a false sense of security about my mother's word tsunami when I arrive home. She precipitates at full-force when I walk in the door. I should have seen it coming.

"And just where were you, young man?" she demands. "Who do you think you are, running off when the house is torn up like this? I need to be able to count on you."

Right, this crap only happens to her all those times we have to move.

"Okay, I get it. I lost track of time," I say instead.

Then she hits me with, "I cannot believe you'd leave Jonathan. He's too young to be left by himself for that long." This is laughable.

"Jonathan can take care of himself just fine. Trust me."

Geez. I didn't know she wasn't going to come right home. Maybe she told me that on the phone, but all I heard was blah, blah, blah. She doesn't look hurt or anything. Another flash flickers between blinks.

...He shoves me from behind. His weight presses me to the floor...

"Where has this attitude of yours come from lately? You think you can talk to your mother like that? I will not tolerate anymore..."

"...You had this coming. Make a sound and you're dead..."

After a few of her best zings, the rest drifts into the background. I've gotten so good at hiding behind my eyes, I can absorb it like a sponge and squeeze it out later. I could probably draw the blood back into my veins if I had a cut. An inaudible grunt or two, followed by an *"uh-huh"* here and there, and she can talk for hours.

"...Not a word..."

Without a father around, my mother vomits whatever words are pent up. I just half-listen, nod a little, and she's off for a good 37-minute clip. No, really—I've checked the clock, even kept a record, and she averages out to exactly 37 minutes without a pause or coming up for air.

Where do I go during all that time? I read in such a way, it doesn't look like I'm doing it. She continues with a "when I was your age," followed by a "kids these days." *Does she think any of this helps?* Probably makes her feel better. It's hard to tell if she's more shaken up than normal, or if this is her playing out the drama.

My mother doesn't understand what it's like. She sure as hell doesn't get what it means to be me. Letting her boyfriends issue consequences to us doesn't equal love. I'd rather have a father than a long line of Samuels.

I pick up a few things that I have to know at school, but not everything I need.

One thing I need is for these flashes of remembered conversation to not be my father. *Was that why he left?* I've heard PTSD come up in conversations, but I just thought he was screwed up from some war. My mother's no better. They should've had their shit together before bringing me into the world.

By the time she's done with her lecture, I might as well be a pile of bones looking back.

***

I wouldn't make it through school without reading as my out. Most of my teachers are duped, just like my mother. But my Algebra II teacher won't fall for it. He's too literal.

First off, he's got me in the purgatory front row, dangerously close to the designated call-on-me seat. I have to give him all my focus or, the minute I drift, he calls on me. Students who don't give good answers have to write the problem on the board. Then the boy behind me starts in. He puts something in my hair and talks smack but low, so only I hear it.

"I heard you're one of those *fag*-gots, aren't you? You know how to go down on a guy, right?"

More fallout from the YouTube thing.

"You would know."

Jonathan's been funny lately. I wonder if he's behind this. The heat chugs up my back, my neck, to the tips of my ears, jagged tongues of fire lapping upward until I'm engulfed in flames. I'm not gay, but I've dealt with Math Punk's kind before. That's not what pisses me off. It's the crap he throws in my hair. Math Punk needs to stay out of my personal space.

"Cocksucker."

This time I don't hesitate.

Just as quietly as he whispered to me, I whisper back, and while the teacher puts a problem up on the Smartboard, I mutter-growl, "Keep it up, jerkoff, and you'll regret it."

This is what he wants. I don't have to look at him to tell he's got a huge smirk smeared across his face. Maybe his buddies egg him on.

"Is 'at right? I bet you swallow, too. You gonna do something about it?"

"That's two," I fire back.

"Looky here, pretty-pretty princess. No one's impressed you can count. Word is you've sucked off half the swim team, including Elias Stone's big dick." This is the last thing he says before I pull the 30-pound Algebra II book from underneath my desk, stand up and pivot, all in one choreographed, smooth movement. My arms go rigid. My hands grip tight to either end of the book. I watch frame by frame in slow motion as the book crashes into the left side of his face. He staggers forward and then topples like a ragdoll out of his desk into a puddle on the floor.

"Leave. Me. The *hell* alone!" I shout, thrusting the book down and seething in great gasping huffs. Everyone freezes. We're playing a giant game of freeze tag. I must be "it." I'm the only one who moves. I pick up the textbook and toss it on my desk. Guess I schooled him. Or I've become what I've feared: I've become *him*.

I'm panting. The wave seeps out of me like a deflating balloon. Mr. McKinley comes to his senses. "Guidance office. Now!" His eyes lock onto my trajectory and follow me with a heavy bead until I'm out of his classroom and on my way to get some "guidance."

I spend the next 18 minutes waiting in the small seating area just outside a cluster of offices, while an antique copier is serviced by a man who does not seem to know what he's fixing. I stare at the wall to avoid the stereotypical butt crack. I've no interest imprinting that in my catalog of images that can't be scraped off my mental picture file.

There are no windows where I sit in guidance-waiting-room hell. I keep checking my hair to see if I got all of the spitballs. Friggin' jerk.

How will Ms. Truman lecture me this time? Will she take the obvious route and say how she's disappointed in me, not living up to my potential? Will she tell me how my actions forced her hand? My muscles tense, thinking out various scenarios.

Some teacher must have had a birthday; there's fresh buttercream-frosted cake in the teacher's lounge. Did all the adults suddenly make a beeline for their early afternoon cake fix? Who knows what teachers do in there?

I look up, but there's still no one back here. My theory may be right. That's where they all must be—the teacher's lounge. When the bell rings, I slink out to the flow of students heading to class and get lost in the crowd. I never hear anything else about the Math Punk incident again.

Maybe my luck has turned.

Dear Amber,

Remember our trip to the lighthouse? I think my shoulder still hurts. Ha! Will we ever go there again? I heard it fell down—the ocean reached up and swallowed the lighthouse whole or something. Are they going to rebuild it, do you know?

You asked me to write you a story, so I'll include my latest with this letter and a poem. I don't know if it's any good. I wish I had more to say, but things aren't great here right now.

Signing off for now,

Joel

BENEATH THE DOCK

From the journal of Joel Scrivener, included in a letter to Amber Walker

I sleep. The beach,
with the moon seagull-perched
over my shoulder, presses
against the last stars clinging

like sand on chilled skin.
I slip into the sleep of shells
making their way to shore,
discoveries beside the dock at night.

In the space between thunder,
the red pulse of the lighthouse
confounds me, blinks back rivulets.

Under waves of sunlight sliding
beneath eyelids, the tide unalterably
rises, proclaiming a loneliness,
a distance only gulls understand.

5

BATHED IN FIRE

When my parents were still a couple, they took a trip to a lighthouse up the coast with one of the other young families that had moved into our neighborhood. I met Amber for the first time on that trip, despite our living near each other by the shore. We were young, maybe four or five. Her parents introduced themselves, and that weekend we all went to the beach together.

Amber and I held hands as we crossed a long bridge. At the other end, I raised our hands so they were stacked, one on top of the other, like two dancers at their first waltz. My father snapped pictures with his camera. Now that is just a frozen moment of memory, lost to time and circumstances.

The lighthouse rose up hundreds of feet nearby the two of us, white on the bottom and red on the top; our parents were lost in adult chatter just ahead. It's one of the clearest and earliest memories I have. I was happy. The sun sparked off Amber's brown hair in fiery red edges. I noticed the smell and spray of the ocean and how she'd brought a book with her to read.

"I might get bored," she said, a challenge.

"Wanna go chase seagulls?"

"Sure."

Amber shoved her book in the back of her sash that was tied around the waist of the dress her mother had insisted she wear, something with purple flowers. We ran across the scrub grass and rocks while seagulls shrilled. They swooped down among the shells and washed-up muck, scrounging food. Of course, our parents called out, "Come here, Joel," and, "Stop that, Amber, you'll ruin your lovely dress." On our way back to the bridge, Amber nailed my shoulder out of nowhere. I didn't see it coming. From that day on, I was blown away...

My mother, brother and I moved after my father left. Letters were how Amber and I stayed in touch. Sometimes I included a story or a poem. After our blowout from the basement incident a few years ago, I had to write many stories and poems for weeks before she even responded again. I don't know what I would have done if she had stopped all together.

***

Despite my best efforts, I give up on sleep after 1am. Reading fails me. Writing what I want to say to Amber fails. I need to call, but we don't have long distance, and I'm positive her parents won't accept the charges.

I couldn't take it if she turned on me. Amber's the last person I have to depend on. She's my anchor, my strength.

I close my eyes, praying rest comes.

Instead, it's choppy and restless, crashing waves of sheets and blankets on the shoreline of my bed. I can't get comfortable. At some indeterminate point, I drift into ink-black waters where I'm pulled down into torpid darkness.

***

I descend again, down achingly familiar stone stairs. Why can't I stop? Fire flickers near the bottom. Around a corner, the low rumbling timber of a strange voice sniggers.

My hands and feet go numb. I don't want to find out what's down there. My gut contorts. Go back up the stairs. Run the other way.

Still, I continue down. I might as well be perched on my shoulders, watching. My stomach muscles clench and flip. I wipe clammy hands on pant legs.

Light dances across my face, bathing me in flames. I turn where two darkened rooms remind me of a crypt. When a quick burst of light flashes across my back, something luminous and fiery notices, and then pursues me. I run away toward the left into darkness.

The guttural rumbles pick up. The heat and flames lick at every stone, throwing light and shadow jaggedly in front of me, and I flee with all my might away from the massive presence bearing down. I can't get away. I feel myself losing ground.

I press on toward a slim passage between two stone walls, only a few more steps in front of me. This thing chugs and fumes, hot sulfuric breath beating at my neck, a freight train on top of me. I stumble forward and push off from the walls wedged on either side of me.

I can't get away. I can't get away. The passage narrows. I have nowhere to go.

***

I jolt awake in my bed like I'm bursting out from under churning waters. The sting of air hurts as it hitches and burns down my throat. My chest rises and falls. I'm okay… for now.

"Dude, d'you have another nightmare?" Jonathan sounds out of it. *Must've woken him up.*

"Sorry, man. Go back to sleep."

Errggghhh. He rolls over and starts symphonic snoring. *Fantastic.*

My whole body is drenched in sweat; it rolls down my back in beads before bursting in a pool and soaking the sheets. I wipe my face. Our room is humid and sticky. Every nerve ending prickles as I pant.

I am grateful for air and that nothing is devouring me in flames and heat and sulfur and darkness.

"Jon, you asleep?" No answer.

I haven't figured out where these nightmares come from. They're going to kick my butt if I can't stay above the surface. I squint at Jonathan. *How much does he know?* He's not letting on. I can't ignore these dreams. They come from somewhere. Maybe they're trying to tell me something, but what exactly?

I must be losing my mind. This would never happen to a normal person. Everyone can't have nightmares with demons lurking, so why me? My heart jackhammers in my chest. A flash bursts behind my eyes.

...He shoves me from behind. His weight presses me to the floor...

Why does my demon have to come after me like I'm the only meal he's had in ages? I don't even know what time it is. I can't see anything without my glasses; the clock's a bunch of red-number blurs.

"Jon?"

Nope, nothing.

"...You had this coming. Make a sound and you're dead..."

I could be up all night. I sit and wait for something to tell me what comes next. Nothing comes.

"...Not a word..."

Shit. Shit. Shit.

"...Make a sound and you're dead..."

My breathing slows, and I slump back in damp bedclothes. I spread out my palms and lie prone against the mattress, expecting the surface to crumble away and drag me back down like the video for that Linkin Park song. Instead, it feels solid, mattress-like, real. I lie there for some indiscriminate length of time and stare at the ceiling. The words to the song pound in my head like an ear-worm. The urge to run presses against my temples. I breathe and breathe until my eyelids grow heavy, and sleep draws me back down into dreamless darkness.

6

STOWAWAY

At least sleep is a break from the shit with my mother.

It's always about her. Somehow she always makes everything about her, even if it's something that happened to me. I can hear her on the phone as I come downstairs, reliving the near-fatal tragedy with her friends, our family, anyone who'll listen. This was after I had an asthma attack while running my mile for gym a few days ago. I nearly passed out, couldn't see, and puked between the track and the nurse's office. Mrs. Adams called my mother, of course. Then we saw the doctor, and I got my inhaler.

I attempt to grab breakfast and sneak out while she's on the phone. When I step into the silence of the dining room, I realize I'm too late. The phone is on its cradle, and my mother's gaze has me trapped.

"Did you remember your inhaler?" I nod. "Let me see it, Joel. Do you remember how many puffs you need if you have another one of your flares?" Cursing my luck at being caught, I flash it before sliding it back in my pocket.

"I remember."

"Honestly, Joel. You don't need to start in with the attitude this early. I've been sick with worry since you nearly…" Her words trail off like she can't bring herself to form the word "died," which is still an exaggeration, but somehow it makes her the poor single mother with an ailing son whose recent brush with death gives her license to whatever street cred adults have with each other.

"Look. The doctor went over the instructions, several times, and the nurse makes me practice using it when my peak flow lands in the red zone. I got it."

"Make sure I'm called right away if anything else happens. I made sure the nurse has my number."

"I'd better get to the bus stop before I'm late."

***

Looks like I'm the first one home. I don't hear anyone, even though I stopped by the library first.

Jonathan has kept the kitten (and this round of sexual escapades) a secret for ten days. It's his longest record for a stowaway. I've gotta give him props. What's-her-face is probably happy to oblige, though. A thousand graphic possibilities converge in my mental picture frame.

Guess he's got his own way of dealing. Not that I agree, but I wait for the fallout when my mother catches him, and she will. I just wait for the crap to hit the fan.

Speaking of, I haven't figured out how he takes care of the poop and pee. He doesn't have kitty litter. My mother won't nail me for Jonathan's pet, but if it goes all over the carpet, we'll both be grounded.

I'm all for watching my brother's demise. When our mother started talking about another mid-year move to get away from Samuel, aka Terror Man, Jonathan begged her to stay for the sake of his swim team. I doubt that's the only reason. He and Slut Girl have been at it every chance they get. I refuse to call her by her former name. I'm practically living at the library now. This online thing about me is also out of control. Not only did my study hall nightmare get posted, but the one from my gym class attack is even worse. I've spent way too much time checking hits and comments. We can't afford a computer at home. I know I shouldn't read them, but I can't help myself.

The day after I nearly passed out running laps, I found confirmation I had indeed been recorded looking pathetic and throwing up during gym class. The pelvic thrusts made by the guys who carried me in were even worse. It's like my life writes its own disasters for the amusement of Broad Run High School, and I can't figure out how to derail it. I've flagged the clips as inappropriate every time I've checked them, reported them as a legal issue even, but they're still getting hundreds of hits and comments every day.

I watch the clip again where the guy snort-laughs, "Stop TOUCHING me!" Others behind him make motions with their fists by their cheeks, poking their tongues to simulate a blowjob. Laughter ensues. Each new comment stings or burns as I read down the page. What does Jonathan expect to gain?

I've got to put a stop to this, and I know just who to start with.

I head upstairs where I find Jonathan holed up in the closet again. This time it doesn't involve the girl kind of pussy, just the kitten kind. I click the bedroom door shut. He and FuzzyClaws are down on all fours, eye to eye, playing with an old, ratty sock. One of mine, I think.

I blurt out a knee-jerk response. "Hey, could you ask before you turn my stuff into chew toys?"

"Oh, it's just you," Jonathan replies, looking up briefly. The kitten dives onto the sock, tugs at one end, and tries to break my brother's grasp. "Didn't think you cared about an old holey sock." He turns his attention back to the kitten. *Perfect.*

I take advantage of his distraction, hook my arm around his throat and under one arm, then drag his ass out of the closet and throw him down on a mattress. I pivot around, fists raised.

"This shit ends now."

"What the hockey sticks? It's just a sock."

"I don't give a fuck about a sock. This is about the shit at school. The videos on YouTube. I know you're the ringleader."

He puts his hands up and scoots across his mattress to the floor. Pretty boy has a meet soon and doesn't want me to rearrange his face. He already had to play off that bruise he got from Terror Man with his coach. I know I should've said something earlier, but I'm not good with confrontation. I tried to stop it on my own, but this is out of control.

Jonathan's eyes go wide, and his breathing quickens. "I had nothing to do with it, bruh. Get your facts straight." His words aren't lining up with the rest of him.

"I saw you and your homies in the hall right before the first video went up. Now there's another. Both posted by PoolStud69. You're just using this to get laid."

Jonathan scrambles to his feet and backs away. I move in closer, fists at the ready.

"Believe me, bruh, I don't need any help getting girls—"

My fist collides with his jaw. He stumbles back into his mattress. I glance over my shoulder at the door, in case our mother has arrived home from work and heard us.

My hand throbs like I slammed it into a concrete wall instead of Jonathan's face.

"Get those videos down, or I'll kick your ass for good. And don't think I won't tell Mom about your stowaway."

He glances at the closet as the threat sinks in.

"I read your thread comments. What were you implying when you said you noticed me checking out the swim team? I was there to support you, not watch anyone getting dressed in the locker room. The shit you're saying is making it worse." When he looks up at me, I stare hard, clenching my jaw and flexing my fist.

"All right," he says with his hands up. "I'll lay off the comments thread. We cool?"

We drift into an uncomfortable silence.

Jonathan looks at me a few times, like he's deciding whether to say something else. "You know, I've heard those rumors for a while now. Part of me wonders if there's any truth to them." He stares at me.

"What the hell do you mean by that?"

"It's not like I haven't noticed you looking sometimes."

"Dude. Everyone's junk is out in a locker room. I might as well be looking in a mirror. You know we've got the same stuff. So what?"

"Well, did you give Elias a blowjob?"

"What kind of question is that? Are you fucking kidding me? Who the hell are you to make it any of your business? Who I fuck is between me and them. Just because you make all your private business public doesn't mean I have to." I cross back over and stand with fists ready. "Stay the hell out of my business and I'll stay the hell out of yours, asshole."

Jonathan swallows and nods.

My thoughts scatter, a gathering storm. I pace back and forth. My brain clouds and then dissipates. I don't want to hear the thoughts in my head. *What about the stuff with Elias?* When the kitten starts mewing loudly, I remember the other reason I came to check on Jonathan.

"So, what are you doing about its poop and pee?" I ask him, checking the closet for evidence. Self-preservation wins out over the rest of my thoughts. "Mom'll have a canary if you let it crap on the floor."

"I took care of that," Jonathan replies, hand on his chin, pointing toward the closet. I think he's steering clear. "I set up a box next to his bed with torn up newspaper and coated it with duct tape. When I change the box, I just wipe it out with the kitchen wipes. They smell like orange, so it kills most of the stink."

I'm surprised to find myself impressed. I should still be pissed, but I've started to calm down. "Guess you thought of everything. How often do you change its box?"

"Well, only when Mom's not home." He sits up and rests on an arm. "I've only had to change it twice so far." This conversation will be over soon enough, just as quick as one of our fights.

It's enough of an answer, but I'm still pissed. I need a distraction. I plop down on my mattress and read Amber's latest letter.

Dear Joel,
Ah, the lighthouse! I haven't thought about that in forever. I'd love to go again. For the record, I don't even punch that hard. When can you come out? I hadn't heard about the lighthouse being damaged. I'll have to check and let you know.
Thanks for the story and the poem. The story was a bit dark. I don't think I like the demon ones as much as the others, but the poem was nice.

*I know what you mean. Don't we all feel alone? I've included a copy of Psalm 91. Remember, you're never alone. God is always with you.
Amber*

My reply sounds desperate, too much like a stalker to send. It lands in the circular file. *Two points.* That's the only score I'd make. Instead, I find my spot in the current book. I'm about done and due for a library run, despite coming just home from there.

Without warning, our mother opens the bedroom door. *Nice knock. Glad I wasn't naked.* I glance up then over at the closet where Jonathan slides the door behind him. So far, so good. Our mother looks tired and distracted. She clutches the cordless. Something is about to go down. I stop reading and sit up, marking my page. She looks from Jonathan to me and back.

"Do you remember what I told you boys about Samuel? How the police held him for questioning? Well, they finished their investigation, and as it turns out, they did not bring assault charges against him. He has to pay for the damages, but since he lives in another unit, they just added them to his rent. Which means—"

"—which means what?" I ask.

"It means he's being released within the hour. We need to leave right now."

Panic sets in. Both Jonathan and I register that if we want to keep anything, we'd better get it packed. We both leap up. Jonathan shoots me a look. He doesn't know what to do. I'm sure he thinks he should spend all his time sneaking the kitten away. He can't make arrangements with his girlfriend without warning ahead of time.

"Get some bags and pack up your clothes, your things, your toothbrush, and your bedding and bring it down to the car. We're leaving in 30 minutes."

There's no time for arguments or discussion. Our movements are automatic, almost rehearsed. We grab bags off the closet shelf and pack everything we own, which isn't much. Having moved often, it has become useless to keep much. The only thing of lasting importance to me is a stack of letters I keep from Amber. Her most recent letter arrived a few days ago. I've got to try again to write her back. I put the bundle in one of the crates we use as furniture and shove all my clothes in the bag. Jonathan stands, looks to the closet and then to his bed. He rubs his neck with the back of his hand.

"What am I gonna do?" Jonathan asks. "I can't just leave him." I gather my bedding and shove it in the crate on top of the letters.

"You could tell our mother, see if she'll let you keep it," I say. "Or just leave it behind. Maybe you can get it to your girlfriend if we come back. I bet one of our neighbors would take it in. You could visit it then."

I throw the last bit in to give him an out. We don't have time; flight is essential. Samuel's gonna be pissed. Might as well paint a big bullseye on the bathroom door. It still hasn't been fixed.

"Guess you'd better figure out what's more important—getting the hell outta dodge or holding onto a mangy kitten. It's like your dream car debate all over again—Camaro Z28 or Firebird Trans Am? Either pony car is a sweet ride in my book, but you still can't decide, can you?"

I hope this sidebar conversation will distract Jonathan long enough to decide the thing for him. If I keep him going, he won't have time to formulate a viable plan, and we'll be on the road in ten minutes. I wonder if our mother has any idea where we're going. I can hear her on the phone downstairs. She's gotta come up with something. Jonathan's a statue. He can't move. I punch him solidly on the shoulder. He winces like I'll start up again.

"C'mon, pony boy," I say and pick up my crate. "Let's bring a load down while you think on it."

Jonathan knows our time is up. We'd better get the lead out or say goodbye to everything we own. I can see the look in his eye as he yanks his bedding off in a heap. He starts to grind his teeth as we descend the stairs and head out to the car. Signature move: grinding his teeth. I've seen it a hundred times at swim practice. Which reminds me: this totally sucks we're moving without getting to say goodbye to anyone we may have considered friends. It's always like this, though. I know how I'd finish things with Elias... Damn, I may actually miss the guy.

No time for that now.

We're in an old Ford Pinto hatchback. It's no pony car, even though it's named after one. There's a hole in the radiator. We have to add water before we go anywhere, or else we'll overheat and end up stuck until it cools off.

We drop our first load and head back. Our mother has a bunch of bags and stuff by the door. Jonathan goes upstairs for the rest, while I start on her things. I could pack the car with my eyes closed. I have it all down to a science: I've moved more times than I care to remember.

I press the boxes against the back seats, and it fills up pretty quick. Soon, I load up the empty seat and the floor behind the driver's seat. I ride shotgun, while Jonathan climbs in behind me. Probably so he can grind his knees into my back. I slam my elbow as hard as I can into the seat. Maybe he's holding a grudge. Just like him to choose now to get back at me.

My mother comes out and sends me for one final once-over. For a moment, the world flips, and I imagine being awake as the nightmare and my sleep as my life. Not sure which one's worse.

I grab my backpack and shove the book I'm reading on top. We always leave a few things behind, and if Samuel comes over, he'll know. I hope we can come back to get the furniture. That would at least give us a head start. We'd be that much farther ahead.

I have no hope this will be the last time.

STRAINED

From the journal of Joel Scrivener, included in a letter to Amber Walker

The hiding place beneath stairs is boarded up,
flesh remembering each slash scarred over.

Immersed in a quiet field of thought, I've drawn
blood back in, straining for each drop.

Those frantic moments I reeled through the empty
house: a mosaic of dish shards on the kitchen floor,
furniture overturned, the stair railing's limp arm dangling.

Upstairs, I see the bathroom door speared
by a bedrail. The telephone sirens off the hook.

The police station *expects* my call—astounding, isn't it?
The complexities we can live with. Moving again,

displaced by boxes, a packing house—we leave
precious things behind. Rising again, we lay
our bodies down among the broken things, tiny shards

fitted firmly to the tile floor, straining for beauty.

7

TRAILER TRASH

Jonathan and I get in the car while our mother locks up. The sun is an orange smear pulling us toward the main road. We run through fast food for burgers and fries and then head west out of town. Crap food seems to fit. It's almost funny. Almost.

Following along with our route, I notice the mountain ahead. I finish eating and open my book. I need something to distract the alarms firing. My mother must have found a place; no reason to be freaked out. But something lodged has broken loose and is rattling around in my thoughts. The electricity that kept getting shut off at the homeless shelter; my mother's empty promises, "It's just temporary," or "Until we're back on our feet." I don't want to remember any of these thoughts. Instead, I read.

Next thing I know, we're off the highway and entering a trailer park that looks like a bunch of metal coffins sliding down the slope. I clearly overreacted. We left pavement back by the highway.

I hate being the bastard child of Poor and White Trash.

Residents stare as we drive in; gravel crunches beneath our tires. A dirty girl looks up from the pothole she squats in, covered in filth. She goes back to digging with what used to be a spoon. I glance at Jonathan. He stares out the window at the rows of dingy trailers, but I've seen too many of the signs already: bits of needles near several trash cans and bandages in obvious places.

I stifle the urge to scream or gouge my eyes out.

We've arrived at the Meth Lab Mothership. Too many vacant eyes to be a coincidence. Nearby, a dog's barks echo, their clipped bursts bouncing off the outside trailer walls. We drive partway down the first row and turn in next to a yellowed, browning trailer. Something smells awful, like gasoline. It wouldn't take much for one of these to go up in flames.

"What's that smell?" My face contorts.

"Kerosene," my mother says. "Most of these are heated by outside tanks." She points to ours, a rusty tooth in a gravel yard. There's a wooden stoop going up two steps from the dirt. My mother has reached a new, all-time low.

"I just saw your girlfriend," I jibe at Jonathan. "She thinks you're kinda cute."

"Screw you," Jonathan fires back, muttering below our mother's radar. "At least I've *had* a girlfriend."

We get inside just as the rainstorm tears across the sky, hammering the roof and sides of our tin-metal trailer in a hail of stray bullets. Now all we need is a burlap sack and baseball bats to lighten the mood.

My mother snaps at everything. Even mellow Jonathan oozes a few too many F-bombs. Maybe his brain completed the equation that he's gonna lose swim team with this move. I sound the retreat. The role of my bedroom is to be played by a closet. Tiny doesn't even begin to describe this space. At least I still have my book.

As we enter each room, we have to duck under the doorframes. The air is musty and damp. Already, claustrophobia sets in. The acrid smell of kerosene seeps into every piece of clothing, every pore, and reminds me of sulfur. I can't stop imagining fire licking these walls. I start to cough and continue late into the night, losing count of how many times I have to use my inhaler.

There is no furniture, and everything is dingy brown. It's like a time warp. Inside the front door, there's a small kitchen, the living room, and a narrow hallway that leads to two miniature bedrooms with a tiny bathroom sandwiched between. The place ends with a master bedroom at the back. There's an exit door leading out of our mother's room, but it feels like there aren't enough escapes.

The walls begin to press in.

After an hour or so, the rain subsides, and we make a break for our bedding and a few essentials. Luckily, there's the weekend to try and get our furniture. We're paid through the end of the month.

Our mother wants to avoid another confrontation with Samuel at all costs, it seems, although we haven't heard many details about the fight that left our townhouse pulled apart and gouged in places. All signs point to her wanting to end it and him not being ready. I doubt his response will get him anywhere. We've seen crazy before.

I've already claimed the first bedroom so Jonathan takes the one closest to our mother. We set up pallets on the floor, and I read until we have to try to sleep. If all goes well, the coast will be clear tomorrow, and we can make a run for our furniture. I go to our mother to dig up more information.

"Think we can go back?" I ask in her doorway.

"I have the neighbor watching for signs when he comes and goes. He'll probably go in and look around. Once he realizes we're not there, maybe he'll look elsewhere, which is why I left papers by the phone for him to find so he'd think we're moving back to the shore, near your dad's family. Once he's on that trail, we can go back," she concludes, triumphant.

"Foolproof," I say. "Unless he sees we left our furniture and decides to wait us out." My mother doesn't like the sound of that. In response, her bedroom door slams in my face.

"I guess we slum it for a while," I say, poking my head into Jonathan's tiny bedroom.

"*Umph*," he replies. No one's talking. Forming a pallet with my bedding, I read until my eyes are so heavy I begin to drift. I startle a few more times before shoving a bookmark in and climbing under the covers.

Here in my miniature bedroom, the shadows are new and ominous, bent at funny angles with jagged teeth. I try to think of something to avoid the inevitable dream and stone stairs, but I know damn well it's pointless. I tuck in as tight as I can, but covers offer little protection. I'm bombarded by strange new noises: the dog on its chain leash; an animal digging through the trash; someone yelling, "Shut up, will ya?" I drift off before I know it.

In the morning, I jolt awake, anticipating the visit from my demon again. Only it doesn't come, which irks me. These nightmares have too much influence. I can't go on night after night and wonder if I'll wake up screaming again, running from some fiery terror.

Then I realize where I am; I smell kerosene instead of sulfur. My head pounds. I hope our mother brought aspirin. I don't hear anyone up, but that could just be the lack of furniture.

Jonathan's up, eating a donut from the open box on the kitchen counter. Our mother leans against the counter and sips a gas-station cup of coffee. I nab a donut and grab some carpet in the living room near Jonathan. He gives me a nod before finishing his.

"They're not bad," he says.

"They look good," I say.

"We're gonna head out soon, so grab what you're gonna eat now, but keep it short. I'm still working on coffee," our mother says. She grips the cup with both hands and sips with long intakes.

"Any juice?" I ask, turning to our mother in the kitchen. My tongue works to find every bit of donut still stuck in my teeth. She shakes her head. I can already tell this is going to be a bottomless food day. No matter how much I eat, I'll still be hungry.

I finish a second donut and grab my backpack, making sure my book is inside. We could get stuck, if Samuel surprises us. This bites. It's like we're walking straight into a burning building, trying not to notice the smoke. Everywhere there's smoke, there's fire. No way we won't get singed.

"Can't we go to the Salvation Army, the thrift store, or a church?" I ask, claiming shotgun in the front seat before I realize the words have already left my mouth.

"Joel, he's not going to be there. He'll have come and gone. Sam thinks we're headed back to the shore. He'll check there first."

That's where Amber lives, by the shore. Except for short visits here and there, I haven't really seen my dad's side of the family since I was young. They live there, too. It's been nearly a decade. The urge to return begins to rise.

As we head back to civilization, I read, but I can't ignore stomach growls that shove me back to reality. It's going to be a long day. I dig around my backpack and score peanut butter crackers. Jonathan perks up.

"Help a starving brother," he pleads.

"Fine," I say, tossing a few back for him to scrabble after. I haven't forgotten about our fight from earlier, and I'm not entirely over it yet.

It's nowhere near enough. I'm looking for more when my mother breaks the silence. "I'll stop for food once we check on the house." We cheer loud and long. As bad as a confrontation might be, I'm almost willing to hope Samuel is there, so we have to go some restaurant that doesn't have a drive-thru to avoid him. I try to read. It's futile. I go over the same sentence three times before noticing I still don't know what I've just read. My mind stalls out. I need a jumpstart.

We enter through the east side of town. My mother makes the turn onto Locust and heads into our development. Our *former* development, I remind myself. Off to the right, the wooden playground sits, and bulldozers and road equipment prepare to encircle the structure in black tar sidewalks.

They've already started on the side closest to the road. I'm mildly intrigued, but my thoughts wander back to Samuel. I don't see his car, but that doesn't mean much. He could have parked and walked over. Another thing, Samuel's a big guy. I doubt Jonathan and I could take him, if it came to that. Plus, we've seen what he can do to stair railings and bathroom doors.

My mother turns into the parking lot and finds a close spot. One of the neighbors a few doors down, that black guy Mom's dated, has a truck; he said he could help us move the big pieces. He seems nice, but I don't remember his name. He's been over a few times. I always ducked out. I didn't want to know more than that. I took my book and ran.

The coast looks clear, so we head in like we're not trying to sneak away. Maybe we should have done this at night. The house is too quiet. I wonder if the kitten is still okay. Jonathan's edgy. He makes a beeline for our bedroom.

My mother heads into the kitchen, so I start with the dining room table. How many times have I taken this thing apart? Loosen a few screws and it's in pieces; the top comes apart and can just clear the back hatch. Jonathan will have to sit on the table, or he'll ride shotgun while I follow in the truck with whatshisname. We have the car loaded in no time. Jonathan tells me the kitten is okay. A bit shaky but alive. He decides to come clean. I pull up a front-row seat.

"Mom, I need to show you something," Jonathan says, heading up the stairs. "I'll be right down."

"What's this all about?" she asks me. I shrug. Jonathan comes back down with the box. I can tell it needs to be cleaned out.

"Mom, a friend from school asked me to watch this kitten for her. I didn't know we'd move this soon, and I was afraid you wouldn't let me keep it. I'm sorry. Can we keep it until I can work out other arrangements?"

"You should have asked permission."

"I know that now. I'm sorry, Mom. I saw other pets at the trailer park. Can we please keep it?" I can't believe she doesn't see right through his pathetic performance. If it were me, I'd be nailed to the wall.

"If it's just a short while. You're in charge of upkeep."

"You've got it." Jonathan beams.

"It's a small trailer. It wouldn't take much to smell up the place. You'd better keep that box clean."

"I will, I promise."

"We can get food and litter, but don't get any ideas. We're not keeping it."

"I can live with that," Jonathan says. We head over to check on the neighbor with the truck.

His name is Mr. Davis. He's also the one who rides the motorcycle.

"Any chance you could help us with our move?" my mother asks, leaning in his doorway. My stomach twists when I realize she's flirting.

Ew. I do not need to see my mother this way. It's like walking in on her having sex, which has happened. I taste stomach acid.

"Sure, I've got time." He moves in close, placing a hand on the side of her arm.

"We don't have a lot, mostly mattresses, a couch and a dresser. I'll owe you one, big time," she says, twisting so her hip rubs against him. He smiles. I'd better get out of here.

We don't have much to move. What we do have will make the trailer seem more cramped than it already is. At least there will be furniture. I'm not complaining, not about that.

"Let me get my rigging, and I'll be over. You can have the boys bring down their mattresses."

"Thank you," my mother says, tossing a broad smile over her shoulder. "I couldn't do this without your help. It's just, with the police involved…" She trails off abruptly, like she's going to cry. Reminds me of the way she's talked to everyone about my asthma.

Oh, boy. Here we go. Instead, she takes a deep breath in.

"Okay, boys. You heard Mr. Davis. Let's get those mattresses downstairs." I get the hell outta there, Jonathan trailing, before they start doing it right in front of us.

Just as we're coming up the sidewalk, Samuel opens the door of our townhome and walks out to meet us. He looks pissed off, probably at my mother. Maybe he needs a Terror. On second thought, maybe not.

8

CONFRONTATION

"I see you've come to get your things," Samuel says to my mother where she stands several doors down, pulling the door of our townhouse shut. When she and Mr. Davis head around the front end of his truck to get away from Samuel, he steps out into the parking lot to intercept them, stopping just in front of her. Jonathan and I stay on the sidewalk, unsure what to do. Samuel's eyes are flames licking down every inch of her; his serpentine head bobs side to side. I can't stop myself from shuddering. Something so familiar...

He steps closer, his focus on my mother.

Now she is going to lose it. I can't help it. I find myself inching forward with Jonathan, our instinct to protect our mother outweighing the need for self-preservation.

"Listen, Sam. I have a restraining order. Leave, or I call the police. You'll go in for at least six months." She pulls out her TracFone to underscore the warning, but her hand trembles despite the firmness of her words.

No one moves.

"You think you can just get rid of me? Dismiss me and threaten me like that? I will not let you go that easy." He sounds pretty serious. Moving forward, he toys with a strand of her hair. I'm reminded of the furniture knocked over, the broken dishes, and the bedrail piercing the bathroom door.

I try to slink back, out of his reach. Mr. Davis steps forward right into the silence, realization blooming across his face. Samuel stands unyielding. He grips her hair, yanking it forward while glaring at our neighbor. My mother stumbles forward, crying out and reaching up to break his grip.

"Let go of me, Samuel. What kind of monster are you? Where is all this—"

Monster...

"Not a word," he snarls, cutting her off.

"...Not a word..."

Each word is punctuated by another vicious yank. "Not another damn word outta you!" My mother shrieks, her hands scratching against his to pry herself free. Since Mr. Davis seems stuck on his next move, eyes darting back and forth between them, I step forward with the plan to kick Samuel's shins when I realize it could be *him*.

"...Not a word..."

Shit. The voice. It's him... Is it him? Is he the voice from my nightmares? I try to swallow the fear back down before he sees it all over my face, the recognition. The knowing. The thing that will make him do something about it, like hunt me down and devour me in front of everyone I know.

I'm ready to make a break for it if Samuel comes at me. "What's all this?" Mr. Davis demands, stepping toward our mother. Samuel shifts his attention toward Mr. Davis.

"So, is *he* why you're ending it with me?" Samuel asks, balling his hands into fists. My mother breaks away, eyes locked on Samuel.

"Mr. Davis is helping us move our furniture. We're friends."

"I see," Samuel says. "You're friends."

"Don't read too much into it, Samuel. Leave now, or I hit send," my mother says, typing 9-1-1 and hovering her thumb over the button.

"...Make a sound and you're dead..."

I bite the inside of my mouth until I taste blood. Panic thrums in my ears.

"Oh, is this the guy?" Mr. Davis asks my mother. "You'd better leave." He moves between our mother and Samuel.

"...Make a sound and you're dead..."

"It's not over," Samuel declares. He glances away, and then takes a sudden swing at Mr. Davis, who somehow anticipates his fist, grips his wrist, and ratchets Samuel's arm way up, behind his back, the momentum from his punch turned against him. Our mother starts to cry. Her face is all red and blotchy. Tears tip over the edge of her eyelids and splash down her front.

"You're lucky there're kids present," Mr. Davis growls, as he releases Samuel with a shove. Samuel stumbles, takes a few steps and grips his arm.

"*...Make a sound and you're dead...*"

Mr. Davis moves closer to my mother, opening his left arm to console her. Samuel starts across the parking lot. Either he was waiting for us when we arrived, or he came after we did.

"Hell if I don't come see you again, Carrie," Samuel says, turning back to face us. "I won't just let this go." He turns, shakes his head, and crosses over to his car. As he peels away, tires squeal, somewhat muffled by the playground crew.

I hear the phrase repeating over and over in my head: "*...Make a sound and you're dead...*"

I dare not make a sound.

No one speaks. Instead, we turn back and load mattresses in Mr. Davis's truck. We finish with the couch and climb in. The day is long, but it's not even 11am.

The drive out is quiet. Jonathan rides with Mom, and I ride shotgun with Mr. Davis. I dive back into my book, relieved to be lost in the pages, happier to ignore the thoughts buzzing in my brain.

Is Samuel serious? Will he come after my mother? Will we have to move over and over so he doesn't find us? That restraining order seems like a waste of paper, an empty threat. I wish I could ignore our other problems.

Most often, it's money. We never seem to have enough to pay our bills and keep from getting evicted. Other times, it's any number of men. I don't think my mother knows how to free herself from their hold. Maybe she likes the attention. Before it all went south, she sure seemed to like it. Too often, Jonathan and I get the fallout.

We reach the trailer before I look up from my book, not that I can remember what I read. More like going through the motions. It's still there. The trailer hasn't managed to collapse or burn to the ground while we were gone. I guess that means we sleep here tonight, then.

Now that I'm all cheered up, I get out and wait for directions. My mother and Mr. Davis discuss how they want to move the furniture in. The queasy feeling returns, along with the kerosene smell. I tie the door open to the railing.

Perhaps the trailer park residents are done with the current batch of meth and await fresh supplies. That would explain why everyone stares. I'm surprised when no one pulls up lawn chairs. We're the entertainment. They should have signs that welcome us to the Mothership. I wonder when we'll get our brain implants.

We haul the furniture in. It doesn't take long to get it inside. *All right people, show's over.* I close the door with relief.

My mother thanks Mr. Davis, and we say our goodbyes. Then we slink to separate rooms.

I can't stay cooped up in this tin coffin all night, so I tell my mother I'm going for a walk. I invite Jonathan. He doesn't have anything better to do. I kick gravel as we walk.

The road bends to the right, and we follow it. An old guy works on his Camaro, someone sponges a motorcycle clean, and a girl with lavender hair and piercings takes her dog for a walk. Each row has a half dozen or so trailers before a turn boxes us in completely. It's like a maze that spirals inward. Eventually, you're stuck in the middle and can't find your way out.

We head downward. The ground continues to slope. I can't see the river, but I hear water, so I know it's there. I take a deep breath and exhale.

Green leaves, brown bark, dancing shadows, forest stillness.

As I lean into the silence, forest sounds rise up. A branch falls with a thud in the underbrush. Something moves, scuttling across the green and dead-leaf ground. A bird chirps sharply, up and to the right. I can't see it, but I hear its incessant call.

I head into the woods. With a glance at Jonathan, I duck in. He follows. At first, we're all wobbly, like the first time we went fishing. It takes a few minutes to find our forest legs. Then we're up and over fallen branches, downed tree trunks; we easily steer around divots and dips in the uneven ground.

We're stopped in our tracks by a young deer. It drinks water from a rivulet coming off the stream below. It lifts its head, sniffs the air for our scent, and pivots its ears back and forth, trying to catch the noise it just heard. We stay frozen, waiting to see if it will run off anyway, just in case. Instead, it dips its head back down to take another pull from the water at its hooves.

I focus on its tail; a muscle at its rump twitches. Must be a bug or something. Jonathan shifts his weight, breaks a branch, and it's off like a shot, legs following its body, as it bounds effortlessly back into the safety of the woods.

"That was friggin' awesome!"

"Yeah," I mutter, unsure what else to say. The edge of fear is much closer to fierce than I realized. I saw it in the deer's eyes. Fear and fierce colliding.

The magic from our stolen moment has gone, returning me to the sounds of people going in and out of trailers. Children laugh as they play in the gravel street. A car drives by and parks. We are down the slope, but man-made sounds bounce off the trunks and tumble over to where we stand.

"C'mon," I say to Jonathan. "Let's get back." And we head up. Our mother is unpacking when we return. The door claps shut like a screen door. The walls are so thin, they might as well be made of glass. It doesn't lessen the fishbowl syndrome rising, like we're living in an aquarium. This has us all out of whack, as if we're on some kind of bizarre reality show.

"Need any help?" I ask as we tromp through the front door into the living room. The trailer is lined in fake, dark, wood paneling, making the already small spaces that much tinier and cramped. My headache thuds back to the forefront, right on cue. I sure didn't miss the smell.

"I'm just about finished," our mother replies, looking up. She puts the pantry stuff away in the upper cabinets.

After dinner, Jonathan and our mother try to get the television to work. Fat chance in a metal box. They try tinfoil and wave the antenna like they're landing an airplane.

I retreat to my shoebox of a room and read. At least that gets me somewhere. I hear laughter in the background, but soon, all I hear are the characters.

When I read the part where Ponyboy and Cherry discuss the differences between Greasers and Socs, it reminds me of me and Amber. We always understood each other, even though we weren't in the same circles at school. I think that's why she liked hanging out. It meant she didn't have to wear a dress. Her mother kept her to a brutal schedule. I can imagine Amber saying what Cherry said to Ponyboy: "...'Things are rough all over.'..."

Amber once confided the pressure she felt from her mother, who insisted she take ballet and violin lessons. "There's no pleasing her. If she could, she'd cram her toes in my shoes and string my bow herself." Our mother never made us do anything close to what hers did. Amber's father and my father were friends from work, back when we still lived near each other. Come to think of it, when Amber and I used to be together, it was always her father who was over.

I had forgotten how hard she was on Amber and what she thought of me.

9

LAUGHTER ISN'T ALWAYS THE BEST MEDICINE

I startle awake sometime late, sensing someone standing over me, their eyes cutting through me. Bile rises in my throat. I focus on slowing my breaths until I no longer see those flickering eyes staring back at me. When I look around, no one is there.

I must have drifted off thinking about Amber's hair pulled back except her one long bang in the center. "Things are rough all over," she says, tucking her hair behind her ear.

My heart beats grasshoppers all over my chest.

The bedroom light is still on. My mother and brother are asleep. As I search to find a clock, the trailer is completely dark. It's the middle of the night. I hear the jangle of a dog chain as I get a drink of water. Since I'm still in clothes, I strip down and head back to bed.

Eventually, sleep comes.

***

This time I'm already in the room at the bottom of the stone stairs. I'm alone. The ceilings vault upward toward a center point like a tent. This is no circus. In front of me are two cells about the same size. They remind me of a jail. I want to leave before something shows up.

Turning behind me, I head toward the crack in the wall partway down. Actually, it's a narrow passage. Since nothing is bearing down on me, I look more closely. I must have missed it before. Passages jut off to the left and right. If I run straight, it does dead-end, but there are several offshoots before I run out of passage.

Behind me, lights flicker. There's a distinct intake of breath, and I feel those horrible eyes studying me. I turn. A deep, booming voice chuckles, almost playful—a resonating rumble near the two cells—a laugh stretching back down the passage where I stand. A chill pings like a tuning fork up the center of my back and around my neck. My skin prickles down my arms and legs.

The air around me is sucked out like a vacuum. My throat slams shut, jagged from the absence of air. I try to swallow. How does it know? The booming gets louder, pounding against my head, all the way to the edges of each hair and the tips of my fingers. I've got to run, but which way? I head back toward the fiend who knows too much and falter.

"You'll have to face me eventually. Run if you want. It's better that way." I try not to hear the rest. Instead, I pour all my energy into moving forward.

Partway up, I turn left and make a break for it.

I run away from the light, so the path darkens with every step. Behind me, a large form blocks the remaining light, filling the space from floor to ceiling. I stop to catch my breath and lean on the wall to my right. The surface is cold. I run and hope for an opening, up and out.

It knows it has me. I run out of passage and slump against the wall, palms flat against the clammy surface. The air is chill, or is that me? Hot, chugging breath bears down, filling in the enclosed space. Its laughter slows like a heartbeat, thudding in my skull. There's no way out; I might as well let it do what it wants. It grips me hard in its claws, one on either side.

I feel a sharp prick in the middle of my back.

Searing pain tears my insides. It radiates out in every direction.

***

When I wake, I gasp while my hands grasp frantically for the middle of my back, fingers slipping around an old, bulky pair of headphones. Flipping over, I lay prone on my stomach, panting, until my senses adjust, and I know I'm back in the trailer—it was just another one of my stupid nightmares.

Breathe. Breathing is good. That's about all I can handle. I close my eyes and pray it's morning soon.

When morning hits, light slants through the blinds, cutting past my eyelids and bringing me to an upright, awake position. Whatever dreams I had are whisked away by harsh light. I've got to get curtains up or turn my blinds the other way.

I feel like I've been run over by a Mack Truck that backed over me again for good measure. My head throbs, and my back is still sore from the headphones. Every vein hammers the insides of my skull and begs me to turn over and go back to sleep. But sleep isn't a comfort. Not after last night.

Swinging my legs over the side, I sit up on the edge of the mattress, rub the heaviness of exhaustion from my face, and push my blankets back behind me on the bed. Today is a day for coffee. I've gotta do something to pull myself out of bed. Thankfully, my mother set up the coffee pot the night before.

We might be poor—we may not have cell phones or the latest tech—but we always have coffee. I pour a cup and then concoct some mixture of chocolate syrup, creamer, coffee and a few turns of caramel, like I've seen done at coffee shops. I succeed in masking much of the coffee flavor and enjoy my morning joe while the others sleep. Sitting at the kitchen table, it's nice to have the place to myself. With hands wrapped in warmth, I take my time drawing in sips.

My mother has stacks of bills out in various piles. I flip through a few and notice something. Most of them have 30 days, or 60 days past due stamped on them in red.

It looks like Samuel isn't the only reason we moved.

Then I see something I missed, tucked under one of the piles. One of the casinos she frequents sent her an itemized sheet listing her recent transaction history—she's gambling again. Mostly losing. Those weekends we thought she was with Samuel, she must have been at the reservation, and she was using bill money. Now she's way behind. Talk about nightmares. But these don't go away when morning arrives.

As I stand from the table and back away from all those papers, I catch a glimpse of an envelope sporting Amber's curlicue handwriting. Did she write me again? I grab it and head for my room.

I'm not going to stick around and find out what happens next. I've had it. I don't care if she's a single parent. I've got too much going on myself to worry about the electricity being turned off and running out of food. I don't want to be a part of begging at local churches for food money or end up back in some roach-infested homeless shelter, when I know she had the money but gambled it away.

I'm a kid and I get this. You go to work, you get paid, and you pay your bills. Adults are supposed to be responsible. Why the hell am I the one who has to manage things? Screw her. I'm not taking any more of this shit. Enough's enough.

While everyone's still asleep, I grab my backpack, clear it out, add a few books, Amber's letters, my deodorant and toothbrush. Dressing in jeans, I tuck in another pair, grab underwear and socks, some T-shirts and a hoodie. I have toothpaste I keep for after lunch at school. I tie a windbreaker around my waist.

Heading to the kitchen, I gather snacks to last a few days. I grab a small jar of peanut butter, a few sleeves of crackers, the last Terrors Samuel had at the townhouse, and a few apples. I'd better get going before someone wakes up and I'm trapped. The last thing I nab is a twenty from my mother's purse.

I'm gonna do it.

10

RUNAWAY

I open the door and close it behind me as quietly as I can. Jonathan would stay, anyway. He's too chicken to take off like this, too much of a momma's boy to break free. He wants to know what's for dinner.

We went through this before, and I didn't like it then. We were at the shelter, and my mother was at work. It was my job to get us breakfast, so I poured Jonathan and me bowls of cereal. It was as I poured the milk that I saw them rising to the surface, and not all of their bodies had drowned on their way up. The bowls clattered out of my hands, spilling onto the countertop as I watched the roaches climb over flakes, and I'd screamed. The lady behind me had suggested I just flick them out and eat the cereal anyway. I grabbed Jonathan and dragged him out of there. He couldn't understand why we weren't eating. I just couldn't. And I have no intention of staying this go-round. Besides, she can't afford to take care of one child, let alone two.

I can take care of myself.

I haul ass for the main exit and out to the road. Instead of going left toward the highway we usually take, I veer to the right as far over along the tree line as I can. It's a one-lane road, going in both directions. The posted speed limit is 45mph, but I'd guess the locals go 50 or 60.

The sun creeps up the sky and throws shadows down from the branches that sway gently overhead. Keeping my focus on the ground, I watch the wind blow in the outline of gray splayed across the blacktop. My eyes begin to water. Must be my allergies kicking in.

I try not to think about it too much, but I'm so effing mad, I can't even see clearly. If I thought it would help, I'd scream, but attention's the last thing I need out here on the road. I want to disappear.

Why can't she just… grow the eff up? She's so friggin' selfish. Maybe Jonathan will finally wise up and follow my example. I wonder if she could take care of herself if she was all she had left.

Seriously doubt it.

This reminds me of Montag's wife, the same self-destructive spiral. Funny, I'm on the run like him. At least lethal robotic dogs won't hunt me when they notice I'm gone.

What a mess. My mother is a train wreck, I'm effed up, and my brother screws anything with boobs and a pulse. At school, I'm the butt of the joke—hell, all the jokes. What will this next school be like? How long until it starts all over again? I can't get away from these damn nightmares. I don't want to face where they're coming from or what's made them come back recently. It makes me tired.

Amber is the only thing that's right in the world. If I didn't have her to hold me down, I'd uproot and let go of the earth, floating off into the sea-colored sky.

I stop to hitch my backpack, retie the coat at my waist, and keep going. I won't be anywhere nearby when my mother and Jonathan get up. If they follow me, I want to be far enough away that they can't figure out which direction I went. I'm not going back there with her. I'd torch the place first.

The road crests at the top of a hill and curves to the left up ahead. Tall trees line either side, with pastures and farmland sprinkled here and there to break up the monotony. It's a nice walk. I should flee more often.

I gulp at the kerosene-free air, the loser-mother-free air. At least I won't end up on YouTube. I walk faster. Silence, except for my teeth grinding and the pop of my jaw clenching.

Maybe an hour goes by. It's still early. Not many people are out yet on a Sunday. I must not be near the church-going crowd. Sunlight dances across my arms and clothes, even my shoes. I'm reminded of the path of freckles Amber has spattered on her smooth cheeks and how I'd like to kiss each one. I shudder. Would she let me, if she knew all I've kept from her?

11

THE OFFER

There are no cars on this stretch of road. I stop to adjust my pack.
To my left, trees are clustered more densely. To my right, a sign says
there's a town two miles ahead: *Sanderville*. I head in that direction
and hope it has a bathroom.

A rumble sounds behind me coming from what must be a large
vehicle downshifting in my direction. It rounds the bend, the word
"Mack" on the front of its shiny silver grill. I turn back around and
keep walking. He's gotta be making a delivery nearby. Maybe he's
looking for a gas station. I know I am.

Feeling downward pressure and the need to take a dump, I clench
my cheeks together and hope two miles goes by fast. As the truck
passes me, it shifts gears; the brakes release with a hiss. The passenger
window whirs down.

"You headed into town, son?" the driver asks loudly and kind
of slurred.

"I'm fine," I say back, loud enough for him to hear. "Thanks." I
turn and start walking.

"Now, wait a minute," he hollers.

"I'm not from around here, if you're lost."

"Help a fella out and I'll make it worth your while."

Hell to the no.

"Sure," I say. "Only, my mom needs me right away. Love to help,
but I can't."

"Why don't you get your ass in this truck, and I'll give ya a ride into town?" He's practically shouting. Maybe he's hard of hearing. I don't know. But my "creepy-old-guy" radar is sending me a signal loud and clear: *get away now.*

I don't think twice. I dive for the cover of the woods. He lays on the horn, and then, after a minute or so, I hear him drive off.

I run, sufficiently weirded out. I didn't get a good look at him, but I saw his white hair and saggy face. I don't know what he wanted, but I sure as hell wasn't about to find out. Now I'm shivering and sweating. Maybe running away wasn't such a great idea. Damn. I was this close to a bathroom and a hot meal. Another wave passes. I reconsider the woods. *Nope, not happening.*

I should call my mother. She has a prepaid TracFone. It's a wannabe cell phone, but I could call her. What would I say?

Maybe I can tell her I went to find the library. I asked someone for directions but got lost somehow and ended up in Sanderville. She might even buy it. I could tell her I was bored and didn't want to wake anyone, and I just needed a new book to read. I'd probably get into some trouble, but not "I decided to run away" trouble.

What is it about that guy that creeped me out so bad? It wasn't his plaid shirt. He could be someone's grandfather. Why do adults think they can talk like that? Something's not right.

A bell rings in my mind, too distant for me to put my finger on. Something tells me there's a connection to these nightmares. I need to talk with Jonathan to figure it out and hope he doesn't catch on. I may have to give up on running away.

I cup my hand at the river and take a tentative sip then decide to fill up. After a good ten-minute wait, giving the scary truck driver time to get what he wants from Sanderville and leave, I head back up to the road.

I'm not ready to go back home just yet. I am serious about the gambling thing, not wanting a part of that again. If I say something, though, she'll know I looked through the papers. But then, if she knows I looked through her papers, she'll be less likely to continue, knowing I'm watching for it. She could hide it from us better, but there are other giveaways. Maybe we can reach a stalemate. But where do I begin?

It's got to be afternoon by now. I head up to the road as the sun continues a downward arc toward the horizon. I keep a close watch for every vehicle and make sure none are of the Mack Truck variety. I don't want to end up on the evening news. I just want to get away from my mother's gambling and her constant turmoil that's pulling me down.

Maybe I can get her to trade up to smoking. I don't want to kill her—well—she does infuriate the hell out of me. Still, she's my mother. I don't want her dead. I just want her to keep her shit to herself.

12

RUNAWAY REVISITED

As I come into town, I pass the end of the tree line and see a gas station up ahead. Better yet, no sign of a vehicle bigger than a pickup truck. I try to appear as inconspicuous as possible, like I belong here. I adjust my baseball cap and head into the gas station. It's not one of the commercial ones, just a locally-owned unnamed gasoline and convenience shop. The door jingles as I enter and scan for a bathroom. The male clerk is of the extreme-tattoo-and-multiple-piercings variety. He looks up with disinterest.

"Where's the men's room?"

"Back by the water fountain," he says in the automatic staccato of someone who answers this often.

"Thanks." I head for the back. Part of me is relieved to have a real bathroom. Part is a whirlwind of muddled thoughts that swirl together like a flushing toilet.

Now what?

I passed a pay phone on my way in. You don't get much more small-town than that. I wonder if it even works. Still, not everyone has a cell phone. I sure don't. If I'm going to make my move with Amber, I've got to just do it. Call her and find out how she really feels.

I wash my hands and face then check myself in the mirror. My water bottle is empty, so I rinse and refill it before putting my backpack back on. When I head out, no one's using the pay phone, so I wander over and pick up the receiver. Feeding it some coins, I trigger the familiar sound of dial tone that changes after a few seconds to an automatic message, "If you'd like to make a collect call…" I follow the instructions and wait for Amber to answer.

When the call picks up, I hear a man's voice answer, "Hello?" The automated voice responds, "Will you accept charges for…" and inserts the recording of my name. After a pause, the male voice says, "Yes."

My hands are sweating, and I drop the receiver. Scrambling, I pick it back up and place it against my ear. The man is repeating, "I said, hello? Is this that punk Joel kid I found my daughter with in the basement closet? What is it you want with her? She's my daughter."

"Sorry" is out of my mouth before I realize I'm speaking. Then I hang up. That could not have gone any worse.

Behind me, the door jangles, and I dart behind the dumpster just in time to see Jonathan enter with a white piece of paper in his hands. Moments later, he's back outside, heading toward our mother's car. The paper he held is gone. *What the heck is that all about?* I can't see the Pinto from here. She must be parked around the side.

Before I made the call to Amber, I had planned to call my mother, but now I need to rethink. They woke to find me and my backpack gone. I left my school books out and didn't leave a note, so their conclusion had to be I ran away. I'm an idiot. *Way to cover my tracks.* I can't remember if I put the papers back or not. I was in too much of a hurry to leave.

Jonathan probably told Mom about the walk in the woods and the nightmares. Would they have discussed why I might run away? Maybe while I was in the woods today, Jonathan retraced our steps, just to see if I'd gone down the slope from the trailer again.

I head back in and try to act casual. The clerk glances up then stops. A quizzical look crosses his face. Keeping my head down, I glance around until I see a flyer with a picture of me posted by the register.

It's a Xeroxed paper that reads, *POSSIBLE RUNAWAY: Joel Scrivener, 16, brown hair, hazel eyes, 5'11", last seen at Cumberland Trailer Park, off Highway 91,* printed with marker. The picture is my last school photo. At the bottom, *Please call*, and my mother's TracFone number. Without thinking, I turn and make a break for the door.

The clerk sees me and calls after me, "Hey, you didn't pay for that!"

I stop in my tracks, look down, and realize I'm still holding the candy bar. "Oh, sorry." My face is hot as I reach in my pocket for the twenty and return to the counter to pay. I hand him the money and look down, hoping he doesn't realize I'm the runaway from the flyer. Nearly stealing the candy bar, while embarrassing, is at least a good cover. I shove the change in my pocket, grab the bar, and head for the door without looking back.

Behind me I hear the clerk again, "Hey, kid. Is this you? Are you the runaway they're looking for?"

When the jangle of the door sounds behind me, I know he's following, and I make a break to cross the road, aiming for the first side street I see. I don't look back until I'm halfway down the block.

Thankfully, he's not following me any further. I slow to a walk and try to catch my breath, concentrating on my breathing. A few old houses with front porches and weathered furniture line either side of the street.

I need somewhere like a barn or shed to lie low. A bus or train station could get me out of the area that they're covering with flyers, but it's too risky, since I'm sure my mother will have a police roadblock up by now. I haven't even been gone that long.

Shit.

I guess it's good they care, but I don't like where this is headed. I ran away to leave my problems behind, not to have them hunt me down and force me to face them. I don't do well with that, which is probably why I'm having these nightmares again in the first place.

Double shit.

13

NIGHT SCHOOL

They say that when a person kills another person, the likelihood the murderer will make errors is astronomical. I don't remember the statistics, just that dozens of mistakes are made. All I did was run away. Still, my mind crunches the data and compiles a list of likely slip-ups.

The stuff I pulled from my backpack and left on my bed; the papers I may or may not have put back; the money I... borrowed, as payback for all the birthdays she couldn't afford. Still, I can't stand here, thinking about possible errors. Movement is the only thing I can do about what-ifs. Slowing down and getting sloppy are sure ways to get caught.

There's a side road to the left with a smattering of houses. It's off the main street and out of direct eyesight. My stomach growls like an angry, cornered cat.

I had visions of a hot meal, but now I can't risk it. There's no telling if they're still searching for me or have given up the chase. I'll eat again when I have a hiding spot. I pick up the pace like I know where I'm going. A car passes me and heads to a stop sign before making a right and disappearing.

Trees line the street on both sides. Each house has its own neatly manicured lawn. A few have children's toys, bikes, a basketball hoop—signs that a family live there. Running away was supposed to help how I feel. Instead, I'm developing the sense I don't belong.

I cross at the corner and see grass and trees ahead that might be a park or playground. Once I'm closer, I see a large brick building up a low hill. The sign reads, *Sanderville Area Middle and High School.*

This might be the place where we're supposed to transfer to. I'd know for sure if I'd stayed home. I wonder if there might be a door open, a way in. No one would think to look for me here.

I don't notice anyone driving by, but I feint toward the sports field just in case. There's a playground at the far end of a single-story building that I think might belong to the middle school. Closer to me is a larger, two-story structure—presumably the high school. It's massive, like two buildings morphed together. The high school ate the middle school and is slowly digesting the remains.

I follow the path around, hoping to find a way in. Behind the school are smaller buildings and a few dumpsters then some fenced-in ball fields and a track. Since there's no one out there, I continue along the back of the school to check doors.

The first few are locked tight around the high school, which seems newer. I head along the hallway that seems to connect it to the older-looking middle school. Still no door unlocked. *But one of these has got to be open.* Still, every door at the back of the middle school is locked tight, too.

So much for that idea.

Then it occurs to me to check the windows. Peering into each classroom, I see the typical desks grouped together, bookshelves filled with bins, walls decorated with bright posters, classwork hanging from strings. I keep scanning each window for an opening, but I'm rewarded with zilch.

That is, until a car I wasn't expecting turns the corner. My heartbeat quickens like I'm in a bad horror flick.

At the end of the building, a set of windows goes behind a large bush. I duck out of sight before anyone in the vehicle can get a good look at me. Inside looks like a teacher's lounge with tables, chairs, a counter behind with microwaves. I see an old, gold fabric couch and a refrigerator; the couch is probably as old as some of the teachers. A copy machine stands in the corner under the last window, which looks like it's open just a crack. *Bingo!* But when I tug on it, I find it locked like the rest, just bent away from the frame. An image of my mother flashes in my mind.

I should keep a better lookout for my mother's car, I think. From behind my bush, I can see that the car has parked and strangers are getting out. But it's not my family.

I climb back out, exhale and head back toward the high school. There's a storage shed there, a bit away from the building with a green dumpster next to it. If I climb up on the dumpster lid, I could shimmy onto the roof of the shed. The space between the shed and the roof of the middle school isn't large. *I wonder...*

A blue car comes flying around the side of the building. It's the same color as my mother's, but I can't tell what make it is. As it gets closer, I realize it's a Corolla not a Pinto. Still, I'm pressing my luck if I don't get out of sight fast. They could still be searching for me.

Despite wedging my foot on the side of the dumpster where the garbage truck would lift it, I still can't get a good foothold. I slide the door open, and I'm hit with the warm odor of Friday's lunch. *Ugh.* Grabbing the top, I use the opening as a step and swing up onto the plastic lid. I keep glancing back to see if any other cars have followed the now-parked Corolla. I don't see any but have lost sight of the driver. Staying to the outside edges, I stand and reach the lip of the shed roof. Good thing no one sees me looking foolish up here. The weight on my back doesn't help. Sweat has transformed my shirt into an oversized moist towelette.

I swing my backpack up, keeping it near the edge in case I can't make it, myself, then I try to pull my whole body up. Fail. Looking at the dumpster lid, I flip the right side open to give me better leverage. I always sucked at pull-ups.

"Lose something?" a female voice calls out of nowhere.

My body convulses. My hands were up, reaching for the ledge. *This is the police, put your hands up*, runs through my mind as I lower them and turn.

"Funny thing, this looks worse than it is. I was tossing my backpack around, and it got caught up there." I point at the shed roof, hoping the lie rings true. The woman before me is in her late twenties, early thirties? Mildly attractive…

"As long as you're not doing something foolish, like attempting to break in, I won't have to call the police. Try and be careful up there, okay? You wouldn't want to get stuck up on the roof." She smiles and turns back toward the track; I notice now she wears a running ensemble. Is *she the type who would call the police? Was she the one driving the Corolla?* I can't help but notice the way Corolla Lady's outfit accentuates her curves… My brain is already imagining her as a cougar.

Once she's out of sight, I shake off my muddled thoughts, grab the edge, and scramble up the wall to push myself off the side of the lid. It takes some effort, but I manage to get over the edge to my waist and then swing my legs up. At least I've regained my backpack, but I'm standing pretty high up. *Great, now my stomach freaks out.*

My kingdom for a burger and fries.

From the shed roof, I can see most of the top of the middle school. It's flat with a lip around the edge and what looks like gravel scattered over the surface. Various metal tubes and A/C units protrude along the center. Where the middle school meets the high school, I see an access door with a bucket near it. *Do the custodians come up to the roof to sneak a smoke?*

The gap between the school building and the shed looks too wide for a safe jump. I'm not about to try it; I'd end up as road pizza. Looking down, I spot two wooden two-by-fours. This must be how they clear the garbage. I use them to cross over.

On the roof side are two more boards. I cross back, retrieve my backpack, and then put the two boards back. I also close the lid to the dumpster with one of the boards. After returning to the building, I pull down the second set of boards. No sense leaving a trail. Heading to the door, I finally find an unlocked entrance. *Score.*

I'm in a stairwell that leads down to a door. As it shuts behind me, I'm in pitch black darkness on a staircase. This is way too familiar. I'm struck with a flash of flickering eyes, but only off to the sides, not when I look straight ahead. Using the railing, I guide myself down in the dark and open the door's push bar. Now I'm in a small, dark room. Feeling along the wall, I kick something metal. It seems like the janitor's closet; there's a noticeable musty smell.

With my hands out in front of me, I take a few tentative steps, searching for a door or light switch. A flash of rancid breath at my neck jerks me right back. I shudder. My hands find the cinderblock wall and a door. I fumble for the handle. It turns but doesn't open. I'm trapped in the custodian's closet of Sanderville Middle School. This is just great.

Will I ever be free of these nightmares?

I search until I find a light switch. Once the lights are on, it's clear the room itself isn't very large. My hands are shaking. There's a mop sink framed in the back left corner, like a white plastic sandbox. The bucket I stumbled into is on my right. But there's no monster or flickering eyes anywhere. Along the wall, a metal strip with rubber clamps holds mops and brooms. When one clatters into the sink, I startle again.

On a metal shelf with cleaning supplies and rubber gloves, I zero in on an open pack of Marlboro Reds and a lighter. *Rock on.* Maybe my theory about the janitors' smoke break is right. I tuck those into my backpack.

Back by the door, I see a few hooks with rings of keys. *Aha.* Maybe these are the room keys. My luck has turned. I take a set and pull the deadbolt, escaping the closet. I find myself in a school hallway, which sure beats the flash of memory my mind recalls: being dragged up the stairs, scrambling for footing, and praying Amber's dad doesn't rough me up on the front lawn. *Fun times.*

I take a look around, trying to get my bearings. *Where's a map when you need one?*

I head down the hall to the left, hoping to locate the teacher's lounge. I find it on the left, not too far from the main office. The door is locked, so I get out the keys and try them all. *Click.*

It's the same as the one I saw from the outside; I notice it also has a small sink and kitchen, plus a vending machine behind the door. My stomach immediately jumps. *Down, boy.* I decide it's time to find the cafeteria. Near the exit door, taped on the cinderblock wall, is a floor plan. *Awesome! Now I can find food.*

After eating and grabbing a shower in the locker room, I check out the teacher's lounge couch. The sun has almost set; the room is much darker now. I can see a few people throwing a Frisbee on the football field, while others walk their dog around the track on a leash. No sign of Corolla Lady.

Throwing some change in the vending machine, I grab a candy bar then get comfortable on the couch. The sky grows dark, and shadows blanket the room. The exertion from the day plus my lack of sleep after the recent run of nightmares finally catches up with me. I'm all but wiped out.

I sink into the comfort of the couch and ponder whether I should read. Once I lie back, though, I'm a goner. I don't remember any dreams at all; I don't even wake once during the night.

Who knew the couch in the teacher's lounge could be so comfortable?

14

CORRESPONDENCE COURSE

In the morning, when the sun begins to peel back the darkness, I jolt awake. It could be the smell or the brocade texture of the ancient couch, but something familiar hits me as I sit up. *I know this couch. Or one like it. And that's important.*

Realizing I'd better find a better place to hide, I hurry back to the janitor's closet. I hang the keys inside but leave the deadbolt unlocked. The noise I hear next catches me off guard. A low thud threatens behind me, and I jolt, recalling the way Amber's dad wrenched us from between coats, hauling me up and out with a slam and a growl. I've heard that growl before. Uneasiness roils in my gut. There's something about Amber's dad that I can't figure out. Understanding flickers right at the edge of all I can remember. I've got to shake it loose somehow. The wind shifts outside, raking through trees and pressing the building so hard, it creaks like an old house.

I'd better move before people show up. If someone asks, I'll just say I'm new and got lost—too many turns in a big building. Someone will take pity on me.

Sneaking around the school makes me bold. *Why hasn't anyone ever thought of this before?* I've gone to a lock-in but never thought to stay at school after hours on purpose.

Seems counter-intuitive. Everyone I know wants to get *out* of school when the bell rings. I guess that's because they have a home or friend's house to go to. Not like me.

I hear footsteps and singing long before I expected to, and almost don't make it down the hall and into the bathroom before Lunch Lady whistles her way into the kitchen and turns on lights. I don't know how she misses seeing me. I was standing right out in the open. I sneak a peek from the bathroom and catch her from the back as she crosses into the kitchen.

I've got to sneak out and head up the back stairwell. From there, I'll try to work my way toward the high school. At the bottom of the stairs are stacks of chairs and some other storage items, so I duck behind them and settle in.

There's one problem: I'm probably not registered yet as a student. So I can't go to school until at least tomorrow, after my mother transfers our records. I'd better come up with a Plan B.

I need something to do that will take up the time until school starts. I absolutely don't want to have a run-in with my mother or Jonathan until I've figured out what I'm going to do. If I had access to a phone, I could call her. I decide I'd better write Amber and then find the post office. I pull out the bundle of letters and reread her latest to me.

Dear Joel,

You seem even more distant than usual. Is everything okay? I know it's been tough with your mom, but it will get better soon, trust me.

I just got back from a week at camp. Our youth group always does a trip this time of year. Maybe you could come with us. Wouldn't that be fun?

I liked the story you sent me. I wish I could write like that. You should write more. I'd love to read anything you wrote. Send me something, all right? I'm so bored here!

I shouldn't say bored. I'm always busy with school, chores, and stuff my youth group does. We have so much fun—it's not just a church thing, don't worry.

Well, I want to get this in the mail. Don't wait so long to write me back. Seriously. I miss you. I've been thinking. It's been so long since we've hung out. Promise me you'll fix that.
Amber

It has been a long time. My grandmother and aunt and uncle live nearby her, where I grew up. Sometimes, I get such an urge to go to the beach that I entertain thoughts of hitchhiking my way there. Maybe I should consider that.

The "promise me you'll fix that" from the letter reminds me of a conversation I've long since forgotten. Amber had found out a friend lied about her. That same friend then lied to her face, and Amber called to tell me about it. She'd needed to vent. Her tears were fresh, staining each word as she spoke. She told me what happened and then pointed the conversation toward me.

"Too many people have screwed me over, and I couldn't stand it if you were one of them. Promise me you'll never fail me the way she did."

"I promise, Amber." I hadn't thought much of that promise until her letter reminded me of my commitment. I just hoped it wouldn't come around to bite me in the ass.

I finish my letter to Amber and fill out the envelope. *Wait a minute.* I realize I've totally forgotten about the new letter I grabbed off the table back at the trailer. It was mixed in with the mail and the bills. *Why did she write me again before I wrote her back?* Panic claws at my insides. I dig through my backpack three times, even dump and repack it piece by piece, but still no luck. *Shit. Did I imagine it?* No, it was there. I remember putting it in the front pocket of my backpack to read later and never did. *Damn it. This could change everything.* I've got to find it, but I can't waste any more time.

I decide to sneak up and see if any other staff or teachers are here yet. I'd better get back into the neighborhood so I don't look strange, walking down the street. I'm just mailing a letter before school starts, right? That, and I've gotta eat something.

My food is pretty much wiped out. I've got to plan this better, if I'm going to stay at the school. I'm such an idiot. Last night I was so hungry, I didn't think straight. I should have grabbed food for later.

At the top of the stairs, I check the halls for signs of life. The lights are on in the main office. If I'm quick, I should be able to get out the side door, down the hill and head up a side street. I scan outside to see if anyone else is coming. So far, it's clear. I bolt for the front door and don't look back. My heart thumps in my ears as I run and jog in alternating bursts, unsure how to appear "normal."

I lope down the front lawn, watch for cars, and keep it up until I'm safely on the sidewalk. A car pulls in the drop-off area of the high school just as I reach the sidewalk nearest the middle school. Hope they weren't too close.

That road the car came in on seems too direct, but I don't think they paid attention. I don't want eyes picking up on the fact I don't belong. I slow my pace, adjust my backpack, and walk as if I've just left my friend's house and want to get this letter mailed before school. Unfortunately, I channel awkward like a champ. The way I did in the closet with Amber.

If she knew the way I think sometimes.

I've thought about her way more than I admit. Sometimes I imagine things I shouldn't. This doesn't line up with who Amber is— so involved with church and God and youth group. *What would she say if she knew?*

I think she's scared. Afraid love is reserved for fairytales and books, not real life. Maybe God and youth group are a shield. She made me swear we'd never go there when we were younger, never cross that line between friends and benefits that could only end badly. We spit-shook on it.

Then we hit puberty and ended up there anyway. I got pulled into a version of spin-the-bottle that landed us in the closet for seven minutes of heaven on the first round. I can almost taste the kiss that never happened. We'd never done anything like that before.

I'd known her since we were young, but not like this. She acted so strange. That was the year her breasts became cleavage, and my hands itched to know how they felt. Until then, I'd tried to fight it. When she pulled me into the closet, I couldn't stop myself. Between the coats, our lips barely skimmed each other, a tangled dance in private darkness. The heat smoldered in that space, before our air hitched at the sound of her father's staccato footsteps on the basement stairs.

I didn't care. I returned to complete the kiss we never finished.

The thudding drum of my heart pounded mercilessly in my ears, blocking out every other sound. I thought it would rip through my ribcage. But I could feel her trembling there in the dark. And I knew. I fumbled for the knob in a confused swirl of panic that he'd find us like that. Then came the abrupt halt as I beat back my desire to finally kiss Amber Walker on the lips, and the painful reminder, a bulge pinched uncomfortably between my legs.

After that, my memory gets murky. There was a flicker followed by the door flying open, and Amber's dad must have seized me by the collar, because the next thing I knew I was scrambling for purchase on the stairs, and then I was out the door—*slam*—and blinking in the yard, trying to see in the harsh slices of sunlight.

Sure, he tossed my ass out of his house, but it didn't change what happened in that closet. That was something I could keep. A tangible exchange and something… more.

Amber didn't talk to me for a solid month. She was scared. But of what, I kept wondering? Her mother had labeled her the equivalent of a whore. I was a bad influence. Her father turned his back on me. Sure, we were making out in her basement closet, but I can't believe he actually physically threw me out of their house. Makes me wonder if there wasn't something else going on there with her dad.

Still, she keeps writing me. She's the only one who hasn't bailed yet, and she's shared things with me she hasn't even told her dad.

Like why her mother runs her so hard, which I'll never understand. The woman demands too much. Last I heard, she was pressing Amber to take college courses already, though she's just started high school. I wonder if Amber will ever live up to her expectations.

I reach the end of the street, wait for the car to pass, and trudge across the road. I haven't really told Amber about the nightmares, but even she has picked up on something in my letters. I didn't tell her when I replied, either. *Should I?* If I could, I'd kick myself for not being real to the one person who matters. I could write a new letter and tell her everything—but I can't even figure out how to sort it out, let alone how to put it in writing.

Would she understand? At this point, I could lose her, too. My insides are a jumble. I haven't eaten, and nausea sucker-punches me. I start to burp, the kind that comes up from stomach acid burbling over. I taste rancid chocolate pudding.

Why can't I be normal and have a cell phone? I'd call her right now.

My head starts to spin. I think I'm falling apart. *Where did all of this come from?* I managed all day in the hot sun, through the woods and along the river with no food. Now I'm a mess. *Was that just yesterday?* It has to have been a week I've been gone.

I stop under a tree and try to breathe. There's more air here. My heart pounds against my ribs. It's not all that far back to the entrance of the woods. I need some time to think and maybe rewrite this letter before figuring out what to do about food or school.

There's a breeze as I near the edge of the woods. I look over at the last house at the end of town. The yard is well-tended. Whoever lives there must take their time; everything is in its place. I spot a leaf tumbling end over end in a small pocket of wind.

That's me, a cold leaf blowing against the door.

15

FISHING

I pass the welcome sign, only this side reads, *Thanks for visiting, come back soon.* It's just as well: I don't belong. Since it doesn't matter if I'm on this side of the river or the other, I head right into the woods and put layers of trees between myself and the road. It's time to get my head on straight and finish Amber's letter.

Being back in the woods is where I belong. The sound of birds and animals fills the air. As I head in the direction of the river, I notice water flowing in the background. I can smell it in the air. It rejuvenates me.

Finding a shady spot on a fallen trunk, I plunk down and lean against the tree. I pull out the letters and a notebook, then read Amber's letter again and decide to tell her the truth. She hasn't betrayed me; why should I do that to her?

Lost in thought, I begin to drift and imagine I'm sluicing down the river on a boat or raft. Then a flash of memory startles me... There was a lake—it was hot and muggy, like summertime—and we were fishing. There was a blue two-tone pickup truck, two shades of blue. I can't see who I'm with, but I remember how I felt. I feel the same stomach churns and knots as I did when I headed back to the woods.

"C'mere, Joel!" echoes from somewhere—past or present?

I tried to take a worm, lance the side of its flesh with the hook, and shove it through so I could cast my line into the water, only—I couldn't bring myself to do it. I chickened out. I looked at the worm and thought it didn't deserve to die. Not like that.

It didn't have any choice.

Instead, I watched the worm wriggle in my hands and then let it go in the grass at my feet.

I jolt. A chill shoots up my back, breaking me from my reverie. I can't remember the last time I'd thought of that trip to the lake. I know I was young—five or six—but I remember bits of it like pictures emblazoned in my mind.

Something unsettling pulses around in my mind. I can't put my finger on it, can't make it come back clearly, or fill in the gaps from so long ago. *Who brought us to the lake?* I know I wasn't alone, but I can't remember who it was.

I turn back to the notebook. I need to finish one task. Since I can't make sense of these bits of memory, I focus on my letter to Amber. It will be good to share all this with someone. Maybe I won't go crazy if Amber knows. Plus, she might be able to help. More than anything, I want her to know the truth.

Dear Amber,

You're right. I haven't been good about keeping up with our letters. You've guessed it has something to do with my mother. Right again. One of her boyfriends tore up our townhouse after they had a fight a couple days ago. We moved into a trailer to get away from him, and I haven't started at the new school yet. In fact, that's why I'm writing you.

I found some papers that showed my mother is at it again—gambling. You know what happened the last time. You were there. I can't go through all that again. And my nightmares are back. So I stuffed my backpack and took off. I'm all right. I wanted to tell you so you wouldn't worry. I'll be fine. In fact, I'm thinking of coming out your way. Would you like me to?

As soon as I have an address, I'll let you know. I'm sorry I didn't write a new story this time. I'll work on that, too.

Joel

I close the notebook and tuck everything in my backpack. Hunger sweeps over me. I scrounge and find an apple. It's better than nothing, so I eat it and then dig around until I hit gold: a pack of

Pop-Tarts I'd forgotten about. This takes the edge off, but I'm still hungry. Junk food never satisfies hunger. The only thing left is the last Terror, but I'm saving that for a real emergency. I have a little water to drink instead.

I wish I knew what that other letter from Amber was about. *Could I have dropped it somewhere? Damn it.* I've been in and out of my backpack, through the woods, the gas station, and Sanderville. It could be anywhere or nowhere. Either place is just as far away from here as possible.

Fu-uck. Fuck it.

I have no idea what time it is, but I guess it's before 8am. I still need a distraction. Pulling out the book I started, I read about a boy named Jerry who stood up to this group of bullies, determined he wouldn't sell their chocolates. I can relate, except I'm not as athletic. If I were crushed at try-outs, I'd stay down on the ground. You couldn't pry me up with a crowbar.

"... Do I dare disturb the universe? ..."

I don't know if I have what it takes to stand up, to fight back. Overcome. I need a motivation beyond myself. What is it that this kid Jerry has that I don't?

Thirst nudges me, so I refill from the river, drink most of it down, and refill again. Just as I tuck the bottle in my backpack, a bunch of birds squawk and chirp as they tear out from a clump of trees a few hundred yards downstream.

Then I hear it—*Bang!* A rifle or a gunshot for sure. *Great, now I'm being descended upon by hunters. Or maybe a SWAT team.* It's my own dumb fault for not keeping an eye out for my mother. Guess I won't spend the morning in this shady spot I found. I hitch my backpack up on my shoulders and hightail it out of there. I'm not looking to get any closer to gun or rifle shots than that. Another bang—much closer this time—and I scramble up the hill as fast as I can go.

THE DUST OF WORMS

From the journal of Joel Scrivener, included in a letter to Amber Walker

My words rise like a worm to the surface.
I devour earth, minerals, filaments of light,
pass these through a fiery, ribbed body.

Down in the stalks of gathered water
I posture hands, bent to the hardened womb,
and turn to eat the placenta now worn at my feet.

Perched atop dark pines, crows tear flesh.
Hell is not much farther than their feathery
darkness, gorged, clinging to a dead tree.

What will come next, but the distance
of rivers which worms move between;
flesh stirring flesh, spirit stirring spirit.

Through water, the glimpse of light passes
between the bowels.

PART II

SANDERVILLE AREA HIGH SCHOOL

Home of the Ravens

16

HIDING IN PLAIN SIGHT

I keep up the frantic pace until I burst out from the trees and can pause to catch my breath. As I stand, hands on knees, sucking in great gasps of air, an image flashes in my mind. For a moment, I'm displaced. I can't tell if the image is from that fishing trip years ago or is more recent, like from yesterday.

I'm standing in roughly the same spot where the trucker offered me a ride into town. For a second, I see a glint of steely eyes piercing through me. Not the kind of eyes you want staring at you, *ever*. The kind that make you heave from your toes.

What's one got to do with the other? My mind races, thoughts scattering like a thousand birds shooting up from the security of trees. I'm still not clear of those gunshots. It's late. I'd better head back.

Since I ducked into the woods just outside of town, it's not long until I'm closing in on the gas station again, where I stopped before. I don't want to stay on the street, so I decide to risk it. I pull my baseball cap down and head to the bathroom inside. I glance at the clerk on my way back, the door jangling behind me. This one's female, not the guy who recognized me from the flyer last time.

I wash my face, fix my hair with my fingers, and shove my hat back on. I pull the brim down and brace myself. Even though I know they've likely changed trash, I still check the can and floor for the lost letter. Nope.

I don't notice the flyer this time. Maybe it's been thrown away. I've eaten all of my spare food, so I need to restock: a Gatorade, chips, a candy bar, and a few hot dogs from the roller grill. I go to check out, and the clerk motions me over.

"I'm on this register, hon."

As I put my stuff down on the counter, I freeze. The poster is right in front of my face. I look right at myself. It might as well be a mirror. I cover by saying, "Oh, I forgot something. Be right back!"

I dart around the corner as my heart threatens to charge out of my chest through my throat. *Get it together.* If I panic, I'm sure to be caught. *Stay calm. I'll be out the door in a few seconds.*

I take a deep breath and freeze, my hand gripping a bag of trail mix a bit too tightly when I hear the clear sound of the door alarm jangling. Someone's just entered. *It couldn't be them. The sign is already posted.*

I risk a glance but don't see anyone. Instead, I hear the clerk talking. *Damn, I'm stuck.* I need to get going but I can't while someone's on the other side of the chips display. The chances of it being one of the two family members I'm avoiding are slim. I need to relax.

This is just my head playing tricks. I step out and duck behind the motor oil and road maps. The clerk has moved over to the front register. I catch a whiff of hotdogs, and my mouth waters. I'm briefly tempted to move out and buy them when I hear, "My mom said you can call day or night. Thanks for your help." *Shit. I know that voice. Jonathan.*

I had started up the next aisle but pivot back behind the maps, not sure where he's at. If I make for the door, my mother might be waiting outside. If I stay, Jonathan might find me and turn me in. I've got to think of something fast.

"We'll check back tomorrow. Thanks."

I go to the only place I can think of: the bathroom. Once I'm behind the locked door, I let out the breath I didn't notice I was holding. The handle jiggles violently. Someone taps on the door with double knuckles. *Signature Jonathan move.*

"Can you hurry up, please?"

It's him. I don't answer. He'd recognize me for sure, even if I tried to disguise my voice. All I can do is wait him out. If I don't, he'll find me for sure.

"C'mon, dude. Seriously." I can hear him hopping around. *What if he just stands there forever? How long until the clerk comes in after me?*

I'm saved from the least likely of places. The unmistakable blare of a Ford Pinto car horn. When I look in the mirror, I see an ashen face staring back.

"That was too close," I whisper back.

After several minutes, I risk returning to my purchase, which is still sitting on the counter at the far register, inches from my poster. I grab a bag of random candy before swapping it out for beef jerky.

"That's everything," I announce a bit too loudly.

"All right," the clerk says and rings up my purchase. She looks at me funny. *Oh great, here we go.* "Shouldn't you be in school?"

"Oh, right," I say. "Doctor's appointment. My mom's taking me." I hand over the cash and wait for change. I slide the bag towards me. She counts it out and I bolt, throwing a "thank you" over my shoulder. I slam my weight into the door and then I'm back in sunlight.

I downshift into my least conspicuous speed and watch for my mother's car or my brother, who may pop out from who knows where at any given moment. From side streets I can keep a better look-out as I head back to school. I make tracks, aiming to get off the main road.

Since everywhere else is out, I'd better find somewhere at school to hide. The letter to Amber will have to wait. Maybe I can mail it after school.

I cross the street and head up a block. I still don't know what to do about Jonathan. He might know things from the fishing trip that would help me, but involving him has blown up in my face in the past.

I hope I can figure out where to hide. The biggest problem is— besides not having a hall pass—I don't know anything about the high school, and that's where I need to be. It's one thing to sneak in the building, and it's another to navigate the side of the school I've never been in before without getting caught. If I do get nabbed before I'm registered, how will I explain why I'm here?

I can picture the headline now: *"Runaway Found in Wrong School, Story at Six and Eleven."* Of course, I could be completely wrong. This may not even be the right school. It could be in the same district. I guess I'll have to risk it and see.

I go in the double doors and find myself in almost the mirror image of the middle school. To the right is the main office beside a hallway that connects the schools. To the left are the classrooms. It's the same layout I discovered in the middle school.

Since we moved twice last year, this will be my fourth high school already. I've stood in one spot too long: two girls carrying planners walk past me and giggle, tittering at one another. I guess the planners act as hall passes here.

I make a mental note and steer away from the office before someone sees me. I head through the closest stairs and find myself in an identical hallway upstairs. The only difference is there are no main office and entrance to the auditorium. Down the front hall I see the library. *Home.* Right outside the door is a lost-and-found box. Near the top, I spy a planner and decide I'll borrow it until I get my own.

It's been several days since I've been to a library. The last time I went was the day of the thunderstorm and the fight between my mother and Samuel. That's also the day I almost walked in on my brother and his girlfriend.

Any time I enter a library, I'm comforted by all the shelves and rows of books. I usually make friends with the librarians and become often recognized, but I don't want that here. Not yet.

I navigate my way to fiction and find a nook at the end of a set of shelves where I sit on the carpet and lean back. I pull out my book. Somewhere in the background, I think the bell between classes rings a few times.

I don't pay much attention.

Then it occurs to me that no one has even noticed me here. When I came in, I flashed the planner as my pass, and the librarian assumed I had a signature from a teacher to be here. Since I'm not a student here yet, no one realizes I'm not supposed to be here, either.

This is great. I can spend the whole day and not even get in trouble. I keep reading.

A new wave of students enters. Some of them work alone or at computer stations in pairs. I look up at a few students gathering around clusters of tables in the reference section. I can't believe I haven't been caught yet.

I sit in my nook and eat the book. I think I read about half of it before I realize it must be near lunch time. I flip through the planner and find a class schedule for Samantha Coolidge. She has a schedule B lunch, which is coming up.

How will I figure out where the cafeteria is? Most likely it's downstairs. When the bell rings, I'll watch what direction everyone goes in for lunch. I have a few dollars left, so I can buy. At our previous school, I was on the meal plan and had a lunch card. Hope I can get one once we're registered. I've got to be more careful or I'll run out of money.

The sucky thing about hiding is you have to come out eventually. I don't know how long I can keep going. The bell rings, and I head into the swarm of students. There's a definite difference in the air when it's lunch time. Everyone pushes when they're hungry, vying for a closer spot in line.

It amazes me how similar students are, even at different schools. They aren't the same people—their names are different—but one looks like that girl who dates a different guy each week; the huge guy looks like someone who must be on the football team, or half the team himself; there's a girl who talks so loud you can hear every word she's saying all the way down the hallway; and the hippie with dreadlocks in a cloud of patchouli oil.

There are others: sporty jocks, the popular crew with a posse of friends, those who haven't figured out who or what they are yet, and, bringing up the evolutionary rear, social outcasts. I fit best into the last category.

Since I don't know where I'm going, I don't move as fast. I find myself getting shoved on my way to the stairs and again as I head down, then I take a hip check into a string of lockers as we head *en masse* toward the cafeteria. I fit right in.

I follow behind the group in front of me and watch as they queue up at the end of one of several lines going in and out of the kitchen. I stay where I am and hope I can get something decent. After I grab some food, I go through and pay at the cashier. Now the harder part: *where to sit?*

Then, I see him.

Jonathan. He looks like a stray in a sea of pedigree students. I take the first opening away from his side of the lunch room and eat with my face in my tray as much as possible. I get a few funny looks, but I don't want my brother to notice me here. The sooner I finish, the sooner I can duck out and head back up to the haven of the library. That is, unless his class goes there, too.

I eat, but I could be gnawing sawdust. I can't distinguish a flavor. What if Jonathan has to come back up and he notices his runaway brother sitting at a random table at the same lunch as him? I wonder if the lunches are divided by grade. I could be eating at freshman lunch and not even know it.

I concentrate on chewing, horking it down as quickly as I can without puking all over the strangers around me. I ignore the "slow down, dude, no one'll take it from you," as I gulp the milk and pitch the rest, then clear my tray and head for the bathroom. I've got to slip back up to the library.

I hope the stalls have doors here. I head into the bathroom and am relieved: all three stalls have doors. Some schools ban them due to drug traffic. Two are available, so I take the one farthest from the door. They must be light in street-dealing here. I hang my backpack on the hook and take care of business. Lunch is only a half hour, so I figure it has to end soon. Maybe I'll wait out the rest of the time in the stall.

I guess I got my answer about this being the right school, since Jonathan's here.

If all goes well, I can go to the main office tomorrow and ask for a schedule. Tell them I lost mine. Hopefully they'll issue me a locker and a planner of my very own. All I have to do is make it through the rest of today without getting caught. Then, I can put Samantha's planner back. She might need it. You never know what kind of planner thieves lurk around here. I can vouch for her. Someone stole it right out of the lost and found.

The bell rings. I wait a few more minutes until it's quiet again. I pull the planner out and find today's date. I scribble the initials of my English teacher from Broad Run High School. *JCH*. It looks authentic enough to work as my hall pass.

Could the librarian recognize me? I figure I might have to show a signature. I'll say we have a research project and our class is meeting in the library. Maybe the librarian won't even care.

I head back up and keep the borrowed planner handy. Someone different is at the counter. It doesn't even matter. I beat a path to my nook and reclaim my spot.

Keeping a close eye on those coming in, I don't see Jonathan among them. I wish school was more like this. Come in a few periods late, read in the library, go to the wrong lunch, read some more. I even finish my book within the last 30 minutes.

The buses pull up outside. The bell rings for last period. It won't be long until Jonathan leaves, and then I can go. There's one thing I didn't finish today.

17

AFTER-SCHOOL SPECIAL

When I returned from lunch, I noticed an empty office with a desk and phone. Now, as the last class of the day arrives at the library to work on a research project, I take advantage of the chaos to slink in and duck behind the desk. After a few glances to make sure I'm in the clear, I pull the phone down and hold it in my lap.

My fingers shake while I dial an outside line and the number. After a few rings, she picks up.

"Hello? Who is this?"

"It's me. Are you still in school?"

"Joel, it's you! No, I'm out. Why did you call? You never call. What's wrong?" Her tone dips from curious to alarm.

"Nothing, I just wanted to hear the sound of your voice." *Lame.*

"Why are you really calling, Joel? Did you miss me? Speak." She's on to me.

"Okay, look. Don't get mad or freak out. Promise?"

"That's not funny. Quit stalling. You know how I feel about that."

I take a breath and then get it all out. "I ran away. And I've got to come see you."

"You—what?" I can't help but smile when I hear a twinge of hope in her reply.

"I left yesterday. Listen, if I came out there, would you help me?"

Pause. "Joel... what are you not saying? You're not making any sense."

Maybe this was a bad idea. I consider hanging up. *Damn it. I wish I knew what she wrote in the lost letter, and what she is thinking now.*

"What's gotten into you? Are you in trouble? Did you do something illegal?"

I can't answer any of these questions because, honestly, I'm terrified. This was wrong. I should have thought it through first.

Amber interrupts my thoughts, saying "Quick, call me back on my cell." She hangs up after giving me her digits. *What is that all about? Does her father monitor every move she makes?* I know exactly what his opinion of me is, given our last phone conversation from the gas station pay phone. Scrambling for a pen from my backpack, I write the number on the front envelope of Amber's letters.

Then I panic.

I'm not sure it's the right time to do this, but I want to call her back. I've put too much hope into where this could head next—or not—which is why I'm panicking. My heart thuds hard against my ribcage; I'm light-headed and may pass out.

I must've pondered a bit too long, since the phone vibrates in my lap, sending my heart into my throat. I scramble to tilt the phone to read the display and not drop it. *Shit.* It's her cell phone number. She's calling *me* back.

Fumbling the phone, I grab the receiver after it jangles against the cradle, inadvertently hanging up on Amber without meaning to. *Fuck.* I mouth the word to myself. Now she's going to think I hung up on her.

Picking up the receiver, I bang it against the cradle several times as if that will help reconnect the dropped call. Then I hang up the receiver, place the phone back up, and head out into the library among the other students. *What the hell am I doing?* While visualizing kicking myself for botching the whole conversation, I dart back in. What I say in these next few minutes of conversation is all I have within my control. Any more screw ups and I'll lose her for sure.

Before I lose my nerve again—which is clearly on life-support at this point—I dial Amber's number and try to breathe. She picks up.

"Joel, was that you just now? Why did you hang up on me?"

"That wasn't me, it was someone else. I mean, I dropped the phone. Sorry."

I hear her chuckling in the receiver. I swallow and start talking.

"I need to see you."

"I need to see you, too—"

"—before you object... Wait. What?"

"I need to see you, too, Joel. I'm pretty sure I'm being followed by someone, and I need your help."

"What makes you say that?"

"A feeling in my gut. Besides, I don't trust anyone else. The last several nights I haven't slept much. I keep waking up with the strangest feeling someone is watching me. When I get up to check, all I find is my Dad up, smoking one of his nasty cigars, zoned out in front of the computer screen down the hall. No stalker anywhere. But..."

"But what?"

"You'll laugh. It's stupid."

"Trust your gut, Amber. It's what keeps you safe. But *what?*"

"I can't put my finger on it, but I could swear I've seen flickering eyes somewhere. Not when I look straight ahead but off to the side, you know?"

Holy shit. I don't answer. Instead, I sit in stunned silence. *How does she know about the flickering eyes?*

"Joel, I know you didn't hang up on me again. I can hear you breathing. Say something."

I don't say what I'm thinking. Instead, I ask, "Why did you ask me to call you back on your cell? Is it your Dad? Wait. Don't answer that."

"I've gotta go. Bye." Dial tone thrums in my ear.

***

I return to my nook. *Stupid, stupid, stupid.* I hope she's not mad at me for insinuating anything with her Dad and the stalker. It's not like I think he's the one with the flickering eyes. After all, he's her father. That doesn't make any sense.

I wait a few more minutes to give my brother time to catch the bus, and once I see buses begin to leave, I head down. I want to get

Amber's letter mailed before I come back for the night. *Is there any point?* Beyond my mother's gambling, I never explained the reasons why. She'd understand better if she knew. The next time we talk, I'll plan better. Just like the next time I stay in the school overnight, I'll load up on food. I have to stay a few steps ahead.

A train could be hurtling down on me, just around the corner, although I suppose it's more like it's about to derail off its tracks. I've almost lost it a few times. Once at the gas station. Twice in the woods. Taking a deep breath and letting it out barely helps. Still, I've done well for a first-time runaway, but I wonder how long I can pull it off without getting caught.

Instead of leaving through the door I came in, I go down the first floor hall, past the office, and on toward the middle school. Two sets of doors lead into a small atrium. Two more sets of doors mirror the high school.

Between the buildings, I'm locked in from both sides. My only choice is to leave out the front or the back. All the doors have push bars, but only on the sides leaving the school. If I had tried to get into the high school this way, I would have been locked inside the vestibule.

As I head out the front door, I glance over to where students are still waiting to be picked up. The buses have gone, so my brother must be gone as well. I shoot across the front lawn toward the side street I came up earlier. Startled, I hear my name.

No one knows me—who could be calling my name? I turn around and see Jonathan heading right for me. As I try to make sense of this, my head fills with suitable expletives.

"Joel, it *is* you. Why are you here? I thought you'd be halfway to Grandma's house by now."

"I haven't made it that far," I reply. "I haven't figured out a plan. So… how was your first day?" I'd better steer this off me: deflect and divert or get a face full of train.

"About the same here as the last one. Plenty of new girls, though." He glances toward the crowd.

"Yeah, I can see that." Several pairs of eyes follow us. We're far enough away, they can't hear anything.

"We spent the entire weekend searching for you. Mom went crazy and put up flyers. You owe me," he says, tagging my chest. I can feel the weight of that debt.

"It must have been hell."

"She can't make up her mind whether she's more pissed or hurt that you left. Why'd you do it?" His eyes dart up, harpooning me momentarily. I can see how he gets the girls. I try to play it off.

"I figured she'd be like that. I saw the bills. She's gambling again."

"I knew you were up. I was too tired to see. But I heard thrashing. Our rooms are sardined together."

"No joke." No arguments.

"Last night was so quiet. Was it another nightmare the other day? What's that all about?" He's looking at me again. I have to look away.

"I wish I knew. Things lately… losing sleep on top of it all sucks."

"So you bailed?"

"I didn't want to stick around and go down in flames, no offense. I figured you wouldn't go with me, so I left. I can't stand her like this."

"You do what you have to, bruh. Just wish I wasn't alone. It's better with some of the heat on you. We carry it better together."

"Look, I didn't mean to leave you to deal with it alone, but you'll do fine. Soon you'll be busy with a new girl. Anyway, don't you have to catch the bus?" This has gone on long enough.

"Yeah. What's the plan?"

"I've got it under control. I might even go to school tomorrow."

"You know I told Mom you've been having nightmares. She asked if I knew why. She pressed me about what's been going on."

"That's just great. Well, at least I have a heads-up to prepare for the fallout."

Jonathan shrugs.

I probably shouldn't ask this, but I have to know.

"Remember the time we went fishing at the lake? We had the bamboo poles we got for Christmas? There was a blue pickup. Two shades of blue. Who took us? Dad, right?"

"I don't know. That was forever ago, but I don't think Dad ever took us."

If it wasn't Dad, then the only other person those penetrating eyes could have belonged to was "Uncle" Steven. He wasn't really our uncle, but our mom made us call him that anyway. He worked on our grandparents' farm after Grandpa's stroke. Then, he up and left when that boy from the neighbor's farm went missing. Later, the boy turned up: at least, his body was found in the barn. I shudder at the memory. The neighbor said he choked or something. My grandmother's seen "Uncle" Steven since then, but I forget where or when.

The bus arrives, and Jonathan turns to join the others. A few of them look familiar, like the girl with lavender hair. I step back from the bus.

"You coming or going?"

"I've got a letter to mail. See you around."

"What should I tell Mom?"

"Tell her you've heard from me. I'm okay, but you don't know anything else, all right?"

"All right." I can't tell if he'll go along with it.

I turn back and head toward the side street. My mind swirls. When we stayed at the farm with Grandma, it was a hard winter with a ton of snow.

I remember the neighbor's farm, too. The boy who died was their only child. His parents never had another child after that. Finding his body destroyed them. We were all shaken. How could I have forgotten about this, or the fishing trip, for so long?

An emptiness in my stomach rises, and I swallow back the lump. That boy didn't have a choice when he died. Neither did the worms. A sharp pain jabs me in the side like the prick of a hook.

18

PITCHING THE TENT

At the post office, I buy a stamp for Amber's letter and drop it in the slot marked "Out of Town". I don't even remember walking here.

As I sit on the bench outside, I can remember going up the side street to the main road and turning left. After that, I kept walking, but my mind went blank and I ended up here.

I look for water but the bottle is empty. Then I remember my second trip to the gas station. *Gatorade.* The hotdogs didn't last out of the parking lot. The Gatorade's warm but I don't mind. Fluid helps.

My mind is still running, as if it could get away from the rest of me. Sometimes you have to go backward to move forward. I can't get myself to zero in on one thing. While I sit and sip, I watch cars and people pass.

My mind whirs. A kind of numbness creeps over me. I can feel myself slipping away from center. There's a chill. Maybe I've sat here for too long.

Although I don't want to move yet, I force myself to stand, put on my backpack and head back. The way here was uphill so I'm almost propelled down the sidewalk from the pitch of the slope.

The post office was just past the hill I saw when I first came into town. I slide toward the school as though pulled by an invisible string. Oddly, it reminds me of the staircase leading to the crypt in my nightmares when I can't stop myself going back down, even though I know what's around the corner.

The walk is quiet and eerie, like the moment before an earthquake or storm. I wouldn't be surprised if tumbleweeds rolled past me. Did I stumble into a ghost town? I look around. There's no one else in any direction. Sanderville weirds me out.

A car comes from behind and heads down the hill, its engine breaking the silence. Someone turns out of the side street ahead, their dog on a leash, then heads in the same direction as the car. I've heard Amber describe the rapture, but I didn't think it was real. Even though this was just momentary, it still seems weird. I must be losing my mind.

I turn down the side street toward the school. There's a slight breeze. The street has trees on both sides, including a willow, my favorite. Its swaying branches shimmer, pulled by the same force that pulls me. Maybe I'm not alone—I just think I am...

I wish that were true.

Then I wouldn't be crazy or a runaway or someone who breaks into a locked school building. What other choice do I have? I am not going back. I can't. I've got to see this through, no matter what.

I wonder what other boys my age think about. They're sports fanatics or homework fiends—if they even do it. I'd say most guys obsess over working up the nerve to ask out the hot girl from history class. Their biggest worry is how many sit-ups and push-ups they should do before bed. Me? I'm a whole other animal.

The school looks deserted. I don't see any rapture piles of clothing left behind. Sounds echo from behind the school. Since I'm closest to the middle school, I head around the side.

Drum beats bounce off the back of the school. The marching band practices what looks like their halftime show on the football field. Reminds me I used to play trumpet one year.

The drums lead the students in groups, everyone trying to learn how to march sideways and play at the same time. They look small from where I am, but I can see enough to tell what's going on. I come up behind the shed and dumpster and take a seat on a set of metal bleachers behind the baseball field.

I remember I have that pack of cigarettes I swiped from the janitor's closet. The lighter was shoved between the clear wrapper and the packaging. Pulling one out, I tuck it between my lips and fumble with the lighter. Cupping my hands the way I've seen others do it, I tug on the filter, hold the lighter up, and watch the end smolder then dissolve into flame.

The sudden intake of smoke takes me by surprise, and I cough and sputter. Maybe I'm bringing something up from deep down. My hands shake, but I want to try these out, hoping they may take the edge off the recent craziness. I take a smaller pull and hold the smoke in my mouth. The taste reminds me of a campfire.

I take in a bit more each time until I'm used to it. I cough here and there, but not like when I started. Light-headed, I float away... drums in the background. The band repeats the same section over and over—eventually they get it—and so do I.

I take slow, deep breaths and try to hold the smoke as long as I can before I exhale. It's like air on a foggy day. I can feel it as I blow out. Am I ready to face what it brings up? My heart beats too fast, like I just got off a roller coaster. I may throw up.

I get up from the bleachers. Maybe fresh air will help. Flicking my finished cigarette, I twist it with my foot. I might as well meander to the other end of the high school. Before I can get in the usual way, I need the band to finish and leave.

Partway down, I stop and lean on the fence. I'm on the paved side. My thoughts drift back to that time in gym class, a few months ago, when I had been thinking about breasts bouncing beneath a shirt and a redheaded girl I had seen a few times who caught my eye. I started to go hard. I was so focused on the thought of how her nipples might look, I'd forgotten I was in the locker room shower, in front of all the other guys.

The next thing I knew, the tent pole went up, and I flushed crimson.

I tried to explain to the guys gathering around me how I'd imagined this whole thing with a girl, but they still gave me a hard time all the way up until we moved. They would call me Tent Pole (or Boner) and whisper, "*Sproing-oing-oing*" when we passed in the halls.

That never happened to the other guys, so I figured I was on the horny end of the scale. As usual, I'm some kind of freak.

It's like what happened between Elias and me—completely blown out of proportion. So what if things got heated between us? What's wrong with a bit of experimentation?

It makes me ashamed—racked with guilt even—for jacking off when I can't stand it anymore. I just need relief. Most guys don't start chasing girls until their voices drop and pubes grow in. These urges hit me much earlier than that.

There was an outhouse I used when I was very young, out past a corn field. It could have been at the neighbor's farm, the one where that boy died. I had never been in an outhouse, but I couldn't make it back to the house once when I needed to take a serious dump.

It was on this platform. The toilet seat was just a big hole, and in the dark sludge below was a foulness that knocked me over. I held my breath and sat down as quick as I could.

Then, I saw it. *Porn.* Someone had tacked up four laminated pages of naked people having sex. *Why here?* They hung right in front of me. I couldn't look away. I was mesmerized. There were naked men and women from the front, from behind, on top of each other— their mouths on everything. They looked like they were building up to something.

After I finished, I stood up. My eyes flicked across each naked body, taking a mental photograph to remember later. I felt an explosive wave tingling down my arms and legs. I pulled my pants up and left, feeling like I would puke if I stayed another minute.

I don't think the nausea came from the smell. Such a weight—like I committed a crime—hung around my neck. I buried it deep down, but every time after that… it didn't stop me for long. What is *wrong* with me?

There's still guilt, but now I'm not alone. Plenty of other guys do it. Hormones rage and up it goes. I think that's why guys hang their arms between their legs. Any time I've had that happen, I've got to think of something gross, like the deer we hit one time while driving.

It had such a fierce look just before impact, trailing the edge of fear when it struck us. I heard the weight of its sickening thud smack against the front window. It tumbled down the passenger door—a bloody inkblot—followed by trails of red running down the glass. The car swerved, and our mother slammed the brakes, fishtailing until we stopped further down the road. I tried to muffle the sound with my hands. My heart was in my ears. All of us were breathing in and out like we had just run a marathon. After a few minutes, Jonathan and I got out, although I had trouble opening the door. The deer had crushed some of the metal and so it stuck.

That was back when we had a station wagon. I think our parents were still together, but I don't remember my father being there. Maybe I have it wrong and he wasn't around. I thought that was back when we went fishing all the time, too.

We walked back and stared at the bloody body. My mind took copious notes then, too—a picture frozen in time, just like of those naked bodies screwing. I could go limp just thinking about the broken bones sticking out, the tendons and slick blood. Uncle Brandon came and got the carcass, and we ate from it for months.

The band starts to head in from the field. I wander back to where I left my backpack and think about road kill. Already I picture the locker room where I'll shower later—and what I'll do. I wish I could stop. My balls shift in anticipation. Most times, once I'm finished, I'm a little calmer, like I can resist for a while until the next one.

I'm hungry, too. I hope they leave soon. My stomach and my privates have declared war in my gut. Both sides assert demands. I catch snippets of conversation from the band as they file into one of the back doors, a helpful distraction. I wait a few minutes. When no one's looking, I make for the dumpster while I still can.

Once I'm on the roof, a thought flashes in my mind. If there are still students inside the building, I'd better not show myself to the front end. I look up at the second floor of the high school.

Last night, the buildings were empty. It wasn't a concern. Today, there might be people still inside. What if the janitors are still there doing nightly rounds? I rush over to the door with the help of two by fours and duck behind that end so no one sees me. From what I glimpsed through the windows, it's either the art studio or the library. I'm hoping it's the library.

The blue of the sky deepens, and the sun dips into the lower half of evening sky. It's that strange time of day where you can't tell whether the sun's coming up or going down. Stupid blue, I've heard it called. The clouds are brushstrokes with wisps of pink and orange along the edges. I'm reminded of Amber, of her absence. I can't tell where this feeling comes from, how exactly it surfaces or why it pierces so keenly in the center of my chest. I know I can feel it, though, one memory's sharp-edged blade, slicing me to the core.

The sky casts a reflection on the windows like slick magazine paper, and I can't get a good look, even though I peek around the corner several times. If the sun shines, it looks bright enough for lights to be on. I've got more waiting to do and have no book to read. A barrage of images fills my mind, mostly from the outhouse. It's suddenly clear. *Someone planted those pages for me to find.*

KNOWLEDGE OF GOOD AND EVIL

From the journal of Joel Scrivener

"For God knows that when you eat of it your eyes will be
opened, and you will be like God, knowing good and evil."—
Genesis 3:5

I stumbled upon pornography in the outhouse,
a standoff at the cornfield's boundary,
stunned by the taste of fruit in my mouth.

Serpents whisper when pants, a peeled
casing, sprawl behind the door latch smelling
of shit and piss, the rind at my feet.

Scaled eyes record each naked morsel
in a rush of blood, like God, shadowed
by the darkness breathing beneath me.

Repenting to the field, I fathom the firmness
of corn, hardened by its proximity to
acres of snake skins sloughed off, discarded.

Do I put on corn husks, or let light scald me into the sun?

19

LOCK-IN REVISITED

Now that I'm up on the roof of the school, it may not be safe to enter. The longer I wait, though, the better the odds. Besides, I'm still recovering from the mental parade that flicked across the shiny bank of windows as the sun sank. *Why did someone want me to find the naked pictures in that outhouse?* Glad I was near the bucket. I feel sorry for whoever finds the vomit.

I look over the roof's front edge to see if there are any cars. Staff parking spots are in the middle of the drop-off circles. I don't see any vehicles on this side, but there are a few on the high school end, where students wait for rides. Just as I pull my head back, a car comes into the high school circle.

Time to move.

I crawl back to the door and reach for the handle. It's locked. *Now what?* All this effort and I'm stuck on the roof. Maybe I should try again. I jiggle the handle, and this time it turns. The darkness of the stairwell swallows me.

I close the door behind me. At the bottom of the stairs, I listen for sounds. The hum of the A/C unit reverberates through the vents. I don't remember that from the night before, but I wasn't careful. I wait a few minutes and then steel myself to enter. The lights are off, a good sign.

Even in the dark I know to cross to the door and feel around until I have my bearings. I retrieve keys, turn the lock, and start to open the door when I remember there might be people. The door opens inward, so I pull and check for life. All the lights are off. I guess everyone here leaves early. The high school is where I need to take extra precaution.

I don't see anyone through the front windows when I step into the dim hall, but I stay close to the walls and try to blend into the darkness. When I near the front corner, I glance to the right. Since it's deserted, I make a break for the teacher's lounge, hugging the inside of the hallway as I go.

Once the door clicks shut, I'm wiped. I reach the couch and collapse. I'm so tired, I could sleep until morning were it not for my growling stomach. My loudly growling stomach.

An odor wafts up from the carpet. It takes a few moments to realize it's smoke. My clothes must be covered. Still, the couch is much more comfortable than metal bleachers or the rooftop any day. I linger and think about what I need to do before sleep. I should make a plan. Don't want to be caught off-guard.

Sneaking down for food, I plan to get enough for dinner and breakfast. I find leftover pizza and chili fries. The chili and the fries are separate, but I put them together anyway. I grab fruit, milk, and cereal for later. After I eat, I clear my stuff and head to the locker room.

I remember to pass by the shower room, where I find the towel in the bin right where I left it. I strip down and hang my clothes outside the shower to remove some of the smoke. The steam makes me cough. I do have fresh clothes in my backpack, but I'd like to get the smell out of these before I change.

Standing beneath the water, my mind wanders, and I'm consumed by the urge. I'm at the boiling point. Vigorous, explosive, and way too quick. As another wave rises, my mind flashes with images. Naked men and women in every position imaginable. I shudder. *Why am I thinking about men? Does this mean I'm...?*

I pull on clothes and put the rest in the backpack. Clearing the evidence of my presence, I head back to the teacher's lounge.

From my backpack, I pull the milk and store it in the refrigerator. I just have to remember to grab it in the morning. Feeling better, I call it a night. The sun's already set, and there's no one to watch through the windows, anyway.

Using my backpack as a pillow and my coat as a blanket, I stretch myself out. My attempt to read ends when I drop my book on the floor. When I reach over to retrieve it, I see an envelope sticking out from under the couch. *The lost letter from Amber!* From the way it's poking out, I can't tell if it dropped out of the book or is there from the day before.

Snatching it up, I tear it open as fast as my fumbling hands can manage. My fingers won't work and my eyes go wide. It's not at all like the one before. I don't know what's gotten into Amber.

Joel,
I know we've been close for a long time. While I have fond thoughts of our friendship over the years, my father suggested I focus on investing in the relationships I have locally. He thinks this has gone on long enough between us, and who are we kidding? This isn't much of a friendship when we hardly ever see each other in person. Maybe we should focus on the friends we have where we live and stop wasting time sending letters back and forth.
  Take care,
  Amber

This isn't like her. Something must have happened. She's not making any sense. Had I known this beforehand, I would never have made the call in the library. This is all I need right now.

A million sit-ups and push-ups mostly calm me down, at least enough to attempt sleep. My first day of school is hours away. The teacher's lounge couch eventually wins.

***

When I wake, it's much lighter than the day before. I glare at the clock like it must be lying. Sunrise was just after 6am yesterday. The clock reads 6:38. *Shit. I overslept.* And I forgot to return the keys again, damn it. I wish I had an alarm clock or a cell phone. *Why did*

I have to find that letter? I know the kitchen staff is already downstairs, so my best bet is the back stairs.

I grab the milk and my things and head to the door. Teachers may be in already, but I can't see out. The windows are covered in posters and announcements. The teachers must want privacy when they're in here.

After listening for sounds, I glance out into the hall. I don't see anyone, but I'm right near the front entrance. Across from me stands a wall of windows. I'd better make a break for it. If I run, I'll be noticed. Surveying the hall, I walk out with a purpose toward the stairwell. Once I'm further down, I glance back. Someone comes in. I'm not that far from the stairs, so I keep going and hope they don't notice.

As far as I know, all these classrooms are locked, and I concentrate on closing the distance to the door. My feet grow roots. The door stretches farther away. Whoever came in has got to be behind me by now. *Are they close?* I can't risk looking back, but I don't hear anything, either. If a teacher's behind me, they'll ask why I'm in this early. This is the middle school, and I'm pushing six feet tall. They can see I'm too old to be here.

I reach the door and no one calls out from behind. Starting down the stairs, I get partway down before I stop and make a 180 to see if anyone is behind me. The hallway is empty, thankfully.

Spiraling down, I reach my spot behind the stacks of chairs. I should have enough time to eat before heading over to the high school. After adding the banana, I turn the cereal boxes into bowls and eat. I don't have a trash can, so I tuck trash in the corner and make a mental note to take care of it later.

What would I have done if someone'd found me sleeping in the teacher's lounge? Damn, that was close.

20

FIRST DAY OF SCHOOL, TAKE TWO

I survived the dress rehearsal, now on to the main event. Since I hid in the library the first day, I'll have to take today as real as it comes. When it's close enough to 7am, I figure I can make my exit without trouble. At the top of the stairwell, I look out. Partway down, my exit is blocked by two teachers talking at the door of a classroom. I spoke too soon.

I hover at the upper landing, checking every minute or so. When they step into the classroom, I skulk into the hallway and aim for the side hall with the janitor's closet. I've got to ditch these keys.

I don't see anyone, and the closet looks dark from under the door. Carefully and quietly, I turn the handle and duck into the safety of darkness. The scrape of a chair across the floor startles me.

"What the hell are you doing here?" The voice reminds me of the demon from my nightmares. A barrage of images careens around the inside of my head.

I shudder. The smell of sulfur mixes with the chemicals stored in the closet.

"Do you hear me, boy? What are you doing in here, interrupting my morning nap?" This time, the voice is much closer to my ear. I drop the keys with a start, turn to grab the doorknob, and get the hell out of here. The janitor grabs me by my shirt collar.

"Let go of me!" I yell, twisting hard against his grip, grabbing the handle, and yanking as hard as I can. He lets go, and I hear the keys scraping across the floor, as the door closes behind me. A moment later, the door bursts open.

"Come back here!"

I hear the jangle of keys heading right for me. *Who cares if anyone sees me? I've got to get away.* I run for the front door, and slam into the push bar. Warm air from the outside washes over me.

"Damn punk kids," I hear as the door closes behind me.

I hightail it toward the high school entrance. I focus on looking indifferent, guessing the janitor gave up. No one else notices. If I had Jonathan's curls and clear blue eyes, they'd notice. But I evaporate from existence and arrive at the high school. The doors are open, so I head to the office.

I wait for the secretary to look up to introduce myself.

"My name is Joel Scrivener. I just transferred from Broad Run High School. My mother registered my brother and me yesterday, but I've lost my schedule. May I have another, please?"

"Give me just a minute. You can have a seat over there."

I'm directed to a row along the back wall. I take a seat at the end. A few minutes later, the secretary calls me back up.

"I printed a new schedule for you, and I can have someone show you where homeroom is. Do you need anything else?"

"Uh, I never got a meal card or a locker. Will I get textbooks from the teachers?"

"That's right. Your teachers will issue books. As for the lunch card and locker, give me a sec. You can have a seat again."

I wait like a good little student, not like a student who smokes out back or sneaks into the middle school via the roof.

A few minutes later, I'm being escorted by a girl named Amelia Hargrove, who talks nonstop and asks me at least a thousand questions, none of which I'm sure I can or want to answer. I just smile and hope this will all be over soon. Amelia's hard to understand, both for her speed and the fact she snaps her gum in between every few words. I focus on the edges of my mouth that are desperate to curl up and bust out laughing right in her face.

"So, you'renewhere, huh?" (*Snap*) "Myfamily's (*Snap*) beeninSanderville (*Snap*) allmylife. Where didyousayyouwerefromagain?" (*Snap*) "I justloveithere (*Snap*)…"

This goes on all the way to homeroom. Unfortunately, this is near the far end of the downstairs hall in the science wing. I try to smile and let Amelia prattle. I don't think she even notices when I don't respond. The secretary said she's on the student council, Ambassador for New Students. *Almost there,* I tell myself. Once I'm in my homeroom, I thank Amelia and wave. She stays and chats with my chemistry teacher.

I say hello and tell Ms. Sitwell I'll be back after I find my locker. She tells me she will have my textbook when I return. My locker turns out to be upstairs near the library. I remember the planner and drop it in the lost and found bin. I don't have my binder. It's on my bed at the trailer. So I pull out the notebook I use to write letters to Amber and head back down to homeroom. Ms. Sitwell delivers my chemistry book as promised, and I sign her log sheet.

"Where can I get a planner?"

"That's also me," she singsongs, digging around in her storage cabinet. "*Aha*, here ya go. Joel, is it?"

I nod and return to my seat to check my schedule. This school is on a block, so I only have four periods. Ms. Sitwell explains it's something new the school is trying this year. After homeroom, it's American history, English, chemistry with Ms. Sitwell, and lunch in the middle. My last class is math. I'm in a mix of algebra and geometry, since I flunked last year; I even took it over in summer school. It doesn't help that we switch schools all the time. I'm terrible at algebra. The letters make my head swim, and I can't figure out what's going on. Moving complicates the whole thing. Hope I'll survive the geometry part here so I can maybe pass.

All my grades started to plummet at Broad Run in the last few months. The crap with my mother's boyfriends and their need to assert themselves, coupled with the nightmares and the buildup to the trailer move, left me overwhelmed. When it comes time for homework, my mind's been blown apart with crap coming at me from all sides. I can't slow my thoughts down enough to handle each problem in the proper way. Likewise, I can't jumpstart my brain to keep up with the concepts. I know what I *should* do, but I can't follow through with anything.

Having run away, I don't have to worry anymore about my mother losing it in a major way over my grades. Normally, with me, she can count on them: up until now, they have been nothing less than honor roll material. But lately… let's just say my mother would come unhinged if she saw my grades, were she not distracted by so many other things.

Time to start fresh and show my mother I've turned a corner.

Everyone files into homeroom at the last second, and we begin the routine. There's a television channel for announcements; students deliver the report onscreen. I pay rapt attention to the monitor. This is my chance to make the most of this do-over. When we stand, I'm immediately up, hand over my heart and reciting the pledge with patriotism I didn't know I had. *Carpe Diem*, I recall from *Dead Poets Society: Seize the day.*

That is, until I'm called to the office through the classroom PA system. My patriotism fizzles. I shrivel and lose a few inches in the process.

I head down to the main office, derailed. I can't tell if I'm itching for another cigarette or if my stomach is trying to do backflips as I attempt to keep my legs from coagulating into a jellied puddle beneath me. Something has got to be seriously wrong.

I have no idea why I'm being called to the office, but the PA voice triggers a flash of the nice secretary. Only this time, her voice hardens, vicious along the edges and almost seething in its undertone, so only I pick up on it. Dread follows me like a shadow flung against the lockers. My palms begin to sweat. I'm caught in the office headlights, a deer waiting for impact.

When I step inside the door, the floor drops out from under me. My mouth opens, but only a wheeze comes out. I hold onto the handle so hard, I wonder how it's not crumpled within my grip. I force myself not to faint. My mouth opens and closes, accordion-like. I come to my senses and suck in air too quickly.

"Mom, I—"

21

FIRING SQUAD

The secretary motions me back to the principal's office through what could be a guillotine-shaped swinging door that divides the front from the back. My mother has me in the tractor beam of her eyes like tiny lasers that can shred me into oblivion. That would be better than standing before her right now. She rises, rigid, her eyes leveled right at me.

I'm doomed.

"You didn't have to come see me at school," I begin, somehow regaining the ability to speak, despite the firing squad standing in front of us.

"Oh, yes I did," she fires back.

Thinking it foolish to push my luck, I opt not to respond, which would further incriminate me. Instead, I snap to, a plumb line in her tensile grip. Time to man-up and take whatever punishment's coming to me. All things break under pressure. I just hope I won't spend eternity buried, *er*, grounded in the coffin of my room. I can picture myself wrapped in grave clothes—arms in rigor across my chest, a stoic look across frozen facial features. I need to come up with a plan.

"We've called this emergency meeting with the principal and the guidance counselor after the stunt you pulled. We're going to talk about *that* later, right when we go home." My mother fires this at me like shots from a semi-automatic weapon. I have no bullet-proof vest, so I take every shot—the words falling away, empty bullet casings clattering to the ground.

Somehow time is sluggish, and I witness everything in slow motion, which only intensifies the impact. Forget doomed: my mother means to wipe me out of existence. I'm attending my own funeral. How did this happen? The only person who knew where I was is Jonathan. It all begins to make sense. He told.

A tiny part of me is glad I was caught, because it means my mother, in her way, actually cares. Either that or she doesn't like to be crossed. I can't make out which one.

The other part of me, the one flooding my mind with multiple visions of how I will exact vengeance upon my brother, is preoccupied as I stand there. Jonathan is going to get his ass kicked. I keep clenching and unclenching my fists.

Mr. Hoffman indicates two chairs, and as I look around, I see two other staff members. *What is this all about?* Mr. Hoffman puts his hand out to welcome me, but I sit and pretend not to notice. He shakes hands with my mother and then introduces the other two adults.

"Mrs. Scrivener, this is Mr. Fleming, the assistant principal, and Ms. Moore from guidance." My eyes go wide when I see Corolla Lady standing before me in business casual. The last time I saw her, I was in an incriminating position on top of the dumpster, retrieving my backpack from the shed roof.

"Pleased to meet you," my mother says curtly.

Everyone takes their seats, and we begin. Now I'll find out what this is all about. I fumble with my planner as I dart a glance at the adults encircling. *This is a meeting about me.* My finger traces the logo on the front. A raven. They're staring in that way adults do when they think they care about your future. I curl my toes, gripping the floor through my shoes, surrounded by this murder of crows.

"Joel, you've been called here to discuss your recent..." Ms. Moore begins, pausing to select just the right word, "behaviors, such as your grades, as well as your decision to run away from home." *Is she going to say something about what I was doing out back, on top of the dumpster?*

My stomach wrenches. Suddenly, all eyes are on me, carefully studying how I react. Mr. Hoffman begins paging through what I can only presume is my academic file.

"We are not here to judge you, Joel. We want to help you take a look at the reasons you're failing your core classes. We believe you are in serious distress. This meeting is intended as an intervention."

"Well, I didn't ask for one."

I don't know these people, and I do not want to talk about my personal life. I can't even talk to my mother. *Why would I want to speak with total strangers?*

"Joel, you can do better. Let's try that again," Ms. Moore says.

I cross my arms and clench my jaw, grinding my teeth as I think of a response that won't get my carcass plucked clean.

"We move a lot, and it's hard on my grades." I don't want to talk about the other stuff, so I wait for the guidance counselor to continue. Apparently, she's running the show. Mr. Fleming scribbles some notes. My mother interrupts.

"Ms. Moore," my mother begins, "I called this meeting because I had no idea Joel was spiraling out of control. I thought everything was fine at school and at home. I don't know what to do anymore."

Ms. Moore smiles and reaches out to pat her hand. They sit right next to each other. *No way this ends well.*

"Mrs. Scrivener, we can help both you and Joel once we've had time for a formal assessment. We need to take a look at the whole picture as it pertains to your son. Then we'll come up with a plan together that will put Joel back on the right track."

Right. So, I'm the only one scudding like a kite before it suicides itself in a tree. Leave it to my mother to spin things her way. Mr. Hoffman pauses from what he is reading, looks up at me, then at my mother and Ms. Moore.

"Joel," the princiPAL says, "you do understand the seriousness of your situation, do you not?"

"Yes, sir," I say, giving the standard party answer.

"If you don't have a serious turnaround here at Sanderville High School, you'll be required to repeat the grade." My buddy (old PAL), Mr. Hoffman, breaks the news as gently as one detonates a bomb with the press of a button. Explosions go off in my head as I picture the horror that would be sharing classes with Jonathan and his entourage of popularity. I could never survive such a massacre.

My well-being cowers under my chair.

"For today, Joel," Mr. Hoffman continues, "you will attend all of your classes so you can meet your teachers, get your textbooks, and learn your schedule. However, tomorrow, you will be pulled from class to begin a formal assessment with Ms. Moore."

"Okay…"

My mother turns to me. "Joel, don't mumble. It's not polite. Sit up in your seat. Don't slouch. Answer Mr. Hoffman."

I visualize the semi-automatic again. No one else seems to notice my mother pointing a gun at me. She's got all her quips on speed-dial today. I straighten myself in my chair, look directly at Mr. Hoffman, and nod my understanding.

"Yes, sir. I understand, sir." I check with my mother to make sure I meet her approval. This is my attempt to diffuse the bomb that's about to implode in the princiPAL's tiny office. I smile, scrambling for any way out. I might as well face the firing squad. It can't be much worse than adults determining how to fix all my problems.

I have a hard time breathing. *Did all the air just get sucked out of the room?* I could swear Mr. Hoffman's hand moves ever so slightly. I remain in my seat, hoping I don't startle him into action.

If this were a real firing squad, at least they'd let me have a cigarette.

22

SCHOOL FIGHT

After school, Jonathan tackles me, in case I take off again. I might as well be a week-old balloon, trailing limply, trying to keep from touching the ground. The fight has gone out of me. I don't even want to try anymore.

Part of me thinks I was crazy to run away in the first place. Terrible things could have happened. Still, I'm not ready to forgive Jonathan for squealing, so I lay into him.

"What the fuck, Jon?" I say, shoving him so hard he almost falls on his ass. Guess anger's my second wind. "Don't do me any more favors, squealer. I should kick your ass right here, right now."

The anger builds, coupled with a compelling urgency to have a damn cigarette. I can't wait to get home and make for the woods. I don't want to be nice or fair to my jerk brother who couldn't keep his trap shut and has it coming. I catch a tremor in his eyes.

"Okay, okay, I guess I deserved that. You're right, you could kick my ass right now. Only, could you wait until we're home? Please?"

Jonathan stands slowly, adjusting his backpack. He holds his hands out, palms upward, and risks a glance back over his shoulder. A group of girls watches our interaction closely. I realize he must be up someone's skirt at Sanderville already. It might be a new record. Three suspects watch our every move. *Second day of school. Well played.* I just shake my head.

"Fair enough. I'll kick your ass on home turf."

Jonathan sighs, and then throws a huge grin at his onlookers. "Hasta la mañana, ladies." I taste vomit. While he waves at his adoring fans, I give Jonathan a serious punch on the shoulder and ponder a follow-through.

"*Ow*, Joel!" Jonathan looks at me in mock pain. Although he rubs his shoulder for good measure, I don't trust him. My take is he's working the sympathy vote with the girls, whose giggles betray the same thought. I could write this drivel.

Jonathan takes a few steps away from me, out of arm shot. I raise my fist and then relent. I'm being too soft, but I just don't have it in me. I start pacing. This wait is killing me. I need a friggin' cigarette. I look around to see if anyone else is lighting up. No such luck. I'm still pissed. I consider going back on my word to just finish it here with Jonathan. I hate it when I get like this.

"Dude," Jonathan says. "You have seriously got to calm yourself down." I must look half-crazed, the way Jonathan gawks, trying to placate, talk me down off the ledge. "I know you're mad. Just let me try and explain."

"Spit it out then."

"Okay. All right," he says, arm on my shoulder, walking me over to where we talked the day before. "I know I gave you my word I wouldn't say anything, but I couldn't lie. She saw right through me, Joel. I screwed up. She just caught me off-guard before I could tell her otherwise. Then she was furious. This weekend, you and Mom, I'm screwed."

"Damn it, Jon!" I say. "You fucked this all up."

"You've gone way downhill with the cussing, bruh."

"Go ahead and pest me. See what you get."

"You gotta chill. Say, 'what the hockey sticks' or 'get off my scribble.' Girls like a guy in control of his mouth." I don't respond to the double meaning or what he does with his tongue and fingers. I swear if I hear one more of his lectures, like he's trying to train me to be a player, I will beat the ever-loving shit out of him.

My glare sends him packing. *Good. Get the fuck away.* I'm not good company right now. At least I had a few days of freedom, "had" being the operative word.

I'll be on house arrest. As if my mother could try and keep me in that damn metal box. I'm ready to explode in flames. Instead, I pace and wait.

"Where the hell's the bus?" I say to no one in particular. Some of the others talk. I could care less. No one's walked in my shoes. They can think what they like.

Finally, the bus comes, and we pile on. No one balks when I push toward the front of the line. I could bite their heads off, the whole lot of them. I make for the back and sit down with a *harrumph*. Blocking the open seat with my backpack, I glare out the window. The bus isn't full, so no one dares sit near me.

When we get home, the trailer's empty, the car gone. Our mother's at work. So much for follow-through. I have no doubt it will come later. I make a beeline for the woods. Jonathan just stares at me, shrugs, and goes inside. If I were him, I wouldn't rock the boat.

I head into the woods; calmness radiates over me in waves. I breathe it in, pull out a cigarette and light up. I don't even pause before going onto a second one. I glance over my shoulder— expecting Jonathan to come looking for a fight—but he gives me space.

Maybe running away has changed me. As often as I can, I want to get away, to the woods or anywhere. That's a good thing. Like taking care of myself these past several days despite the challenges, also good. Other things have not been good, like cursing. Jonathan's right: it's gotten out of control. I don't like that about myself.

And smoking? I guess I could do worse things. For now, it helps me to try to calm the thoughts in my mind that have been bombarding me. More often than not, I just grab at strings far too elusive for me to reach. Then there's the untangling process. *If I could get these thoughts sorted out, what then?* Smoking is the least of my worries.

I decide to head back, hole up in my room and read. *Can I prepare for the onslaught I know will come when my mother gets home?* I'm not even going to fight it. Tomorrow, when I have to go to my "formal assessment," I'll at least fake it and play along. My gut warns me not to trust these adults. The way they would try to order every step I take to help me or, worse, rescue me. I don't agree with their version of salvation. God himself hasn't convinced me. *Who the hell are they to try and understudy God?*

Back in my room, I shove books on the floor and lie down. I don't even notice until I wake up that I needed a nap. When I sit up, I decide to clean out my backpack and set it back up for school. I pull out clothes, my food stash, and tear into everything I find, suddenly ravenous.

My mother comes into the trailer. I can't *not* hear her. We're on top of each other, so there's no getting away. I stiffen, brace for impact. I try to focus on reading, but I'm waiting for the guillotine blade to drop. I visualize my head rolling down the narrow hallway and into the living room. Maybe the cat'll play with it.

At least then I wouldn't have to pour out my soul to Corolla Lady. I read her as patronizing and full of her own agenda. She's got to have a reason not to address the dumpster climb. I can't trust someone like that, and I will not drop trou' for her, that's for damn sure. Then it hits me.

When my father left, I sort of lost it and had to be hospitalized for my own safety. This recent occurrence is familiar, like I'm relapsing, the way I freaked out and trashed my room when my father left us. Jonathan had tried to help calm me down until the ambulance came, but I went off on him, too. Just like today. I hope they don't think I've lost my mind. *Maybe I should cooperate.* My mother calls for me. Off I go. I tuck the cigarettes in my back pocket, just in case.

"Joel, what the hell were you thinking?"

Sledgehammer. Nice approach. Don't kid-glove me or anything. She can sling it. I'll give it right back.

"I don't know, Mother. I guess I was pissed when I saw your gambling stuff, so I bailed. If you're back with that, I'm not staying."

"Who the hell are you to tell me anything? You've got it backwards. I'm the parent. You're the child."

"More like the scapegoat. I'm out." And I'm out the door. I take satisfaction when it slams behind me. The door doesn't even have time to recover, flinging back open behind the force of my mother.

"Get back here right now, Joel Michael!" my mother pounds away. "I will not have you slamming doors." There's an awkward pause.

In the silence, I shout back, "Come and make me!" I keep walking. My mother stands her ground on the step of our trailer. Maybe she thinks I'll come back if she just waits.

"I mean it, Joel. Come back here this instant, or you'll regret it." I don't even look back. I wouldn't give her the satisfaction. I'm not thinking of running away, just going for a smoke. I can't breathe in that box. Thoughts keep circling back to when Dad bailed. *There had to be a reason, right?* What a nightmare. I head around the trailer park. As I near the end of the row, I notice Jonathan trailing me. *She sent the lackey.*

"Piss off," I say, not even looking at him. "I need space."

"Listen, Joel," he says, "enough's enough. You've put us through the ringer. You've gotta stop this. It's not all about you."

I whirl around. I can't believe my ears. "What part is about me? I can't even find myself in all this mess. That's why I left. I thought you'd understand, but instead you take her side."

"I'm on my own side, bruh. You think this is easy for me? You only care about your own needs."

Before I even realize what I'm doing, I swing my fist as hard as I can. He isn't expecting a fight. My fist shudders as it slams into his jaw, sliding off his cheek. I watch like a slide show as I complete the cross. Jonathan teeters, losing his balance. I turn and keep walking. Jonathan stays where he's at. Still, he might be stupid enough to attempt a counter attack.

I pull out a cigarette and light up. Watching the end, I catch Jonathan rubbing the side of his face as I inhale. *Did aliens take over my brother and mother while I was gone?* Maybe they joined the Trailer Park Colony without me. Now all I need to figure out is where they left that entrance ramp to the Mother Ship. I head to the woods. I doubt Jonathan knows what the hell to do.

Just me and the trees, as if we're having a private conversation; I breathe slowly under a watercolor-painting sky in warm tones. It's not just smoke I take in—it's heat, too, like a salamander. The warmth of it floods through me.

I can't believe what my mother said. She's not the responsible parent, wrapped up in her relationships, who put us in difficult situations, not from where I stand. Even though she works all the time, the bills aren't getting paid. It would be one thing if it was just about her salary; there's enough to pay the bills. Problem is, she's sneaking out and gambling.

She doesn't even tell the truth. She says she's working or running errands but actually goes to play bingo to try and win big. This is adult logic for you. Says she does this for our benefit. She's sacrificing her time to try and do us a favor. She's nothing but selfish. She goes because she wants to and because she likes the excitement.

The sun has almost set. I head back, dragging darkness in my wake. When I come in, my mother and Jonathan are watching TV. Walls are back up. I get a plate of Dollar Store hotdogs and freezer-burn fries before giving up and heading to my room. This is my mother's version of "food."

***

That night, the stairwell leads to a pit of snakes writhing all over themselves. I can't tell where one begins and another ends; it's just a mass of scaled, slithery bodies in constant motion. The snakes nearest me lift their heads and flick their tongues. Can they smell fear?

"...Not a word..."

I try to back away slowly, but they move in my direction. By the time I reach the stairs, they're already going up my legs. They wrap their bodies around and climb up the left and the right. I freeze as snake bodies root me to the ground.

"...Make a sound and you're dead..."

I can't move, and I can't look away, either. I don't want to think about where they're headed. Jaws snap shut in a chorus of fangs clamping down, biting into flesh. I watch in horrified fascination as they pile on top of each other, and I drown in waves of undulating serpent bodies.

23

RORSCHACH INKBLOTS

When I wake up, I'm cocooned in my blankets but alive. *Make a sound and you're dead* echoes inside my skull. It takes a few minutes of wriggling to loosen the bedclothes before I can break free of the shroud. I look for fang marks from the serpents and find none. Now that I'm back in the trailer, the nightmares have officially returned.

I get dressed and head to the kitchen. We have a few minutes, so I gulp down food before heading to the bus. The morning remains silent. I catch Jonathan looking a few times, but I can't tell if it's at me. I've got nothing to say to the suck-up. I'm used to being alone. Prefer it. I grab my backpack and leave. He arrives just before the bus pulls up.

I watch the route and make mental notes.

I get off the bus and head straight to the main office. I end up waiting so long, I think they've forgotten about me. When homeroom begins, I go up and ask. The secretary checks with someone in the next office. I learned next to nothing about Ms. Moore when my mother came in for the meeting yesterday. She was careful with her words. To her, I must be just the student who had the parent conference. I wait. More adults hold meetings about me. This is going to take all day.

Someone comes down the hall to shake my hand. I try to smile, but I'm not listening when she tells me her name. We head back behind the counter and down the hall to the guidance waiting area. She offers me a drink or a snack and indicates a seat. Ms. Moore will be right with me, she assures me.

I accept the bottled water and the pretzels. The walls have pictures of kittens and puppies. The snack and drink are more like a bribe than a caring gesture. *This is all wrong. I should just head to homeroom.* I'd need a pass. Maybe I could forge one, but my chemistry teacher might notice.

Ms. Moore walks briskly out from the back hallway where the offices are, a smile spread across her face. She's pretty hot for a lady who drives a Corolla. She must love her job. It's a gum commercial where everyone has smiles and extremely whitened teeth. I wonder if they glow in the dark. The only thing missing is the music.

"Why, good morning, Joel. I'm so glad to see you today. Won't you come back and have a little chat with me? You can bring your snacks along." Her voice oozes soothing tones.

What choice do I have? I follow her down the hall into the last room on the left. It's large with several places to sit. I stay in the doorway, unsure of where to go. To my left is a bookshelf, her desk and seats. Against the far wall is a couch and chairs with a coffee table. To my immediate right is a round table with chairs on both sides. Behind the table is a small kitchen area with a sink, refrigerator and countertop. I could stay here for a week if it weren't for the absence of a nearby bathroom. I think there's one down the hall. Every surface has short stacks of books, small plants with flowers, and jars filled with candles and funny-smelling woodchips. Like the puppies and kittens in the waiting area, the office artwork seems to be trying too hard. Ms. Moore fixes herself a cup of tea and offers me my choice of where we begin. One of many unmarked tests, I'm sure. I'm no dummy. I choose the couch.

"Let's have a seat, then. Make yourself comfortable, Joel. I'll be right with you." It almost sounds natural when she inserts my name at just the right spot in the sentence. I wonder if this is the intended goal—my comfort. It sounds too good to be true, and I've heard if it sounds too good to be true, it probably is. I have a seat. I sit on the end closest to the window, staring out longingly at the sports fields, and set my backpack down next to me with my arm around it.

"Would you like something warm to drink, Joel? I almost forgot my manners." Ms. Moore starts to laugh at how silly it would be to forget her manners.

"No, thanks." I shimmy down in my seat, slouching in a way that would prompt my mother to scold me. I wait for a reaction. She sits in the chair next to me, placing her tea on a coaster on the end table to her right.

"There now, nice and cozy, aren't we? Ready to begin?" I nod and try to smile. She makes no comment about my posture. I straighten up. Ms. Moore sips her tea, and then pulls out a pad of paper from a briefcase next to her chair. As she pulls out a pen, she smiles.

"Okay, then. Let's get to it, Joel. Before we begin with some questions, I want to explain the format so you understand how this works. I have several tests and evaluations for us to work through together. I'm going to need your cooperation to get accurate results. If the questions get to be too much or you need a break, a stretch, or if you need to use the restroom down the hall, just let me know. I expect this to take the majority of today. Don't worry, we can have lunch here, just you and me. How does that sound?" *Amazing how she delivers it like she's not reading it off a card.*

"Okay, I guess."

"Marvelous. Then, shall we begin? I'm going to ask you a question. You take your time, and when you're ready, tell me your answer."

I stare at the books on the coffee table in front of me. Some of the titles pop out at me. I wonder if they were selected with a secondary purpose.

"Do you know why you were having trouble at the other school before you moved to our district?"

I shrug my shoulders.

"Joel, I need to ask you to answer with words. Body language tells me some things about you, but I might misunderstand what you meant for me to understand. Try again?"

"I'm not sure."

"Fine." She scribbles down some notes, her pen scratching across the note pad in quick motions. I can't tell if she's writing in shorthand or cursive.

"What do you think precipitated or caused this to happen?"

"I don't know."

"Fine." More notes. Scribble. Scribble. I notice she smiles as she writes. This sets me on edge.

"How are things between you and your mother?"

"Normal, I guess."

"Great." More writing. More smiling. *What is she so happy about?*

"What about between you and your brother?" she asks, flipping through a file for her notes. "Jonathan, is it?"

"We're brothers. We act like brothers."

"Perfect." More writing, then she turns the page and keeps going. *What is she writing about?* I didn't think I gave her much of an answer. I can't help myself. I ask a question.

"Do you think I'm crazy or something?"

She stops writing and looks at me before responding. "Do you think I would call you crazy, Joel? I don't think that's the case at all. Try to relax."

Right, and I should have taken a nap yesterday while I stood before the adult firing squad. That makes perfect sense.

"Why don't we try something else? Let's go over to the table and look at some pictures." Ms. Moore stands up and brings her tea and notes along. She heads to the table near the door, offering me a seat on either side. I sit where I can still face the door. I wonder if I passed this unmarked test. Nothing slips by me. Ms. Moore pulls a stack of large white cards over in front of her seat. They are face down, and she straightens the pile.

"Joel, these are Rorschach Ink blots. There are ten. I will show them to you one at a time, and then ask you to tell me what you see. I'm going to ask to record your answers on this tape recorder, so I can hold up the inkblots for you. Is that all right with you?"

"I guess so."

She starts the recorder and holds up the first card. "What do you see here?"

"Two ducks back to back."

"That's fine. And this one?" She holds up the next one.

"A frog."

"Good. And this one?" She holds up another card.

"I don't know."

"That's all right. And this one?" She holds up the next picture. It looks like a dead body. No way am I telling her *that*.

"Road kill. A bat. Two birds facing each other. A snowflake. A butterfly. The center of an apple." I answer each one in turn. Ms. Moore stops the recorder, and then writes a half page of notes. I'm worn out. Not sure if I did that right.

"Can I have a break?"

"Of course you can, Joel. Help yourself to a snack, use the restroom if you need, or you can even lie down over there." She indicates the couch. It looks inviting, but I grab my backpack and head out of her office and down the hall to the bathroom. It's a private, one-person room. I go in and lock the door. I don't have to go. I just wanted to get out of there. When I flick on the lights, a flash of a candle floating through the darkness and the smell of cigars plays across my memories. A shiver goes up my back. My stomach jolts. I'm hungry and nauseous at the same time.

I stand in front of the mirror and have to grip the sides when I see how pale I've gone. *Who was in the dark holding a candle? And where was I in my memory?* I've got nothing. Instead, I run some water and wash my face. Doubt it will help, but it's something to do. I've got to try and hold out until lunch time. At least I don't have to go to the cafeteria. Then, I'll ask if we can continue tomorrow. Maybe she'll let me sleep for good behavior. I'd rather read than answer her questions.

When I head back down the hall, I'm hit with the smell of the office. Like vanilla or cookies. The way Hansel and Gretel might describe the witch's house. I try to shake the nerves away and take a deep breath before going back in. Ms. Moore is on the telephone at her desk. *Who's she talking to? Is it about me?*

"Oh, welcome back, Joel," she says when I knock and enter. "I was just checking my messages." *Am I supposed to buy that?*

I go and sit down in the chair in front of her desk. We sure are making the rounds today around her office. I've been on calmer roller coasters than this. Ms. Moore hangs up her phone and turns her attention to me.

"For the rest of this morning, I'm going to give you two written tests. Afterwards, we'll break for lunch. Does that sound fine?"

"Okay." I'm relieved there aren't more one-on-one questions, but I have no idea what to expect from the tests, either. Anything has got to be better than inkblots.

Ms. Moore invites me back over to the table, but this time I have a standardized test in a booklet format with bubbles to fill in. She lays three sharpened pencils down and smiles.

"These tests are not timed. You may take as long as you like. If you need a break, just let me know. I've got some algorithms to note from earlier. I'll be over there if you need me."

I can't figure out what this test is called, since the title's just a bunch of Roman numerals and numbers. I take my test, ignoring the sense of dread rising up, and hope my answers don't mean I'm crazy.

Everything is so calm and well-ordered around me. It's too perfect. There are alarms in my gut. My nerves are shot. I watch the clock more than I answer questions. They're all about my feelings and what I'm most likely to do in a situation.

If I come across an injured animal along the road, would I a) try to help it b) ignore it c) go get help or d) put it out of its misery.

I don't make it to the end of the test before our lunch arrives.

After lunch, I ask if I can finish on the couch. Ms. Moore gives me a clipboard, and I lean on the arm against a pillow and pull my legs up so I can rest the clipboard and write. Things get hazy after that. I startle when the bell rings, and I catch myself dozing between questions. Ms. Moore works quietly at her computer. She hardly glances over at me.

The couch calls to me, just like the one in the teacher's lounge, only this one is much more comfortable and modern. Somehow I finish the test, lean against the back of the couch, and I'm out moments later. When my hands brush across the surface of the couch, I'm suddenly back in the basement at Amber's, just before we were alone in the closet together. Amber's father comes out from the downstairs bathroom holding a candle on a small stand, tendrils of smoke curling up in wisps from the snuffed-out wick. He doesn't see me on the couch but goes up the stairs with purpose. Afternoon announcements pull me from my nap. *Was that another unspoken test?* It's the end of the day.

"I see you've had a little nap. I'll take your test, and then I'll see you tomorrow morning, Joel. Have a fantastic afternoon!"

I better leave before my lunch comes thundering back up and all over the nice area rug. I head to the door.

"Bye."

As I head out to the bus stop, I wonder what else she could possibly need to test me on. Will tomorrow delve into rare and extreme psychological analyses? I visualize a torture table, laid out with various surgical steel instruments, perhaps a blood-letting or leeches. I wouldn't put it past Ms. Moore to think outside the box a little.

I shudder and walk faster.

24

NIGHTMARE WEEK

That night and every night that week, I have nightmares. One ends where another begins, an endless series of bookends upended. The same stone staircase lures me into shadowy crypt corners. I cannot stop myself from going down. Terror is the song playing in my head when I wake or sleep and gurgles up in my throat like bile.

***

When I turn the corner, the stones become thick like mud. As I take tentative steps, searching for firmness, I sink into a sludgy, watery mess. I scramble to get back to the stairs but can't keep myself from submerging under the surface.

The stairs themselves become quicksand. Every movement makes it worse. Holding still, I watch myself sink, stuck either way. Hourglass sand runs hastily at the end; pulls me down until I'm submerged in darkness.

I try to hold my breath but wake with a gasping shudder that whispers I might not have made it a moment longer.

***

It started in fourth grade. I won the *I Have a Dream* Writing Contest in school. My poem was selected by the administration and the PTA. I read it in front of the entire student body at the Martin Luther King, Jr. assembly. It began with a quote by Dr. King, "Darkness cannot drive out darkness: only light can do that.

Hate cannot drive out hate: only love can do that," from his *Strength to Love* sermon.

From then on, writing became an extension of me. I carried a palm-sized notebook and a pencil. Words came to me the way planets orbit the sun. I drew in phrases, clusters of words, snippets of ideas, then laid them down on the page in neat lines of poetry or crafted them into paragraphs that later grew large enough to become a story.

I can't explain it. I just know when the time comes. I hide in my room, eat an obscene amount of junk food, and come out when the time has passed. My mother never complains, since it doesn't cost her more than paper and pencils, sometimes a notebook.

Writing is what drew me into reading. I read everything I can get my hands on. Once the well is full again, I write for hours.

Reading books and writing poems or stories are never enough. Sure, they distract from the daily crap but it's like I'm trying to climb out of quicksand—eventually I go under. Sometimes I want to.

Lately I've started rereading all of Amber's letters. They're the only thing that helps me calm down so I can go back to sleep. My favorite is about her Easter Sunrise Service on the beach. She described the way God paints sunrises and sunsets just for us to see how punch-you-in-the-gut breathtaking they are when we glimpse one at the shore, the edge of the world. I can picture her watching the sky, startled, as the immense sun rises from the water like a fiery bather, and later reading her Bible as the salty breeze rustles the pages. I wish I could find peace like that.

The other part of me is scared God would show up.

***

I turn the corner and am grabbed from behind by dark, muscular arms that envelop and force me down toward the center of the room where I am tied with rough ropes to a wooden post and then set on fire.

...He shoves me from behind. His weight presses me to the floor...

Searing flames leap at my feet. My heart beats in rapid thumps.

"...You had this coming. Make a sound and you're dead..."

I panic. In the heat of the flames, I can't breathe.

"...Make a sound and you're dead..."

I cough in spasms, my body wracked by blackened convulsions. It reminds me of an asthma attack. Eventually, I vomit. My mind races, in a thousand hysterical directions. I want to crawl out of my charred skin. Blisters rise with pain so excruciating they throb. Flames go up my legs and torso. The last thing I notice before I pass out—through flickering tongues of fire—are multiple pairs of eyes staring, encircling, yet far away and hidden in shadow.

"...Not a word..."

***

When I wake, the last tendrils of sleep cling to me like smoke curling and twining up the trailer walls. I can still smell the demon's fetid breath; it's cloying at my nostrils, making my lips curl from the press of nausea threatening below. I have the strongest urge to find matches and toss them at the kerosene tank until the whole place goes up in flames. Shudders from my nightmare wrack my entire body with convulsions.

***

This time, I'm still on the couch in Amber's basement, even though I'm also somehow in the closet, inches from kissing her on the lips. Amber's father stomps his way down the stairs, ratchets the door open so fast it might have bent the hinges, grabs me forcibly by the arm, and flings me like a ragdoll toward the stairs. Then, he shoves me from behind. His weight presses me suddenly to the floor.

I can hear and feel his seething words in my ear, "You had this coming. Make a sound, and you're dead." The next moment, he's hoisting me up, growling, "She's my daughter. You hear me? She's mine."

He drags me up the stairs and out the front door, out into the front yard, with its smell of cut grass and the harsh slices of light. The look on his face: a mixture of hatred and, oddly, of fear.

***

Over the past ten years since my parents divorced, we've gone back to visit my father's family for annual get-togethers and life events. We went back when my grandfather passed away. Another time, we were invited to my Uncle Brandon's wedding. He went to college down south and met Aunt Althea there. They shocked everyone when they announced their engagement. After their wedding, I thought it was cool we were finally diversified.

The best time we had on a visit was my grandmother's jubilee birthday, when she turned 75 and moved into the house she is in now. I might have been 12. Her party celebration went on for days. One night, I got restless and snuck out to meet up with Amber. I didn't think it could get any better, but it did.

We decided to head to the beach for a late-night walk and were lying on the sand with our heads touching when we saw our first shooting star. There was a meteor shower. Several shot rapidly across the dark sky-blanket and were gone while others shone bright, chugging their way in an arc we followed with our eyes. A few had tails like fiery comet wisps, eyes in the night sky.

I disrupted the silence with words. "Do you ever wonder where they all land?"

"Isn't something like 70 percent of the earth covered by ocean?"

"So you think they all land in the water?"

"Makes sense."

"Do fish live inside them? It baffles me to imagine them at the bottom of the ocean."

"That's so cool." She glanced up, her hands idling through hair tendrils. "If I were a fish, I'd want to live in a rock from space."

My thoughts wandered, imagining my hands running through Amber's hair, touching her fingertips…

"I think most meteors burn up when they enter the atmosphere. By the time they touch ground, it's all dust. But if I were a fish, I'd want to be transparent."

"Then I could see all your insides. *Eww!*"

When we turned to look at each other, we kissed before either of us thought too much about it. That one spark changed everything.

It violated our contract not to cross the line but made me hunger for more at the same time. If I think about it long enough, I can still feel her lips against mine. After a nightmare, I concentrate on a thought like that as I climb my way back up from dark places.

***

As I descend stairs, I'm overwhelmed by countless spiders that cover me before I can get away. I'm draped in webs before I realize, near the bottom, their tiny stabs pierce all over my body, sharp tears into my flesh.

I scream out, but they're everywhere. I can't see anymore. Their thousands of legs crawl over skin I wish was someone else's, then wrap me in sticky tendrils of webbing. I fall down the last few stairs, but they are busy and encase me in webs.

Oddly, they leave, in unspoken agreement, of one accord.

I can't move, not even a little, but I can hear them skitter away into the dark. Darkness surrounds. I gulp air in shallow gasps. The webs are so tight, they cut off circulation. Then I hear it. Something large and seething comes at me with legs moving in every direction, scraping across the stone floor.

I can hear it breathe right over me, and then I feel a terrible stabbing pain going in. My insides turn to liquid. Something pulls everything out of me until I'm an empty shell. As I drift away, I hear the smaller spiders return. Their incessant chatter pulses in my ears as they pour over every hollow inch of me.

***

My grandmother has a way of talking me into things. We were on an extended visit the summer after the meteor shower with Amber, and I let her talk me into Vacation Bible School at her church for a week. The only good thing about agreeing to VBS was that Amber was also attending my grandmother's church. Well, there were two good things. We did a lot of craft projects, and I almost forgot where I was.

One of the projects was a God's Eye. It's supposed to mean something like, "God is always watching over you," but things like that get under my skin. If I imagine someone standing in my room at night while I sleep, it terrifies me. We picked four colors of yarn and threaded them around Popsicle sticks. The teacher Mrs. Trimmer explained the meaning.

The Huichol are a people from Western Mexico, she said, and they make a God's Eye as a symbol to see what is unseen, to understand what has not been understood, and to know what is unknown. The four corners and the four colors illustrate the four basic elements: air, earth, fire and water.

The teacher shared how the God's Eye should be used.

"When a child is born, he first experiences God through his mother and his father. The way they treat the child is how the child sees God."

Any minute now, her head's gonna start to glow, I thought. I think God is just going to leave the way my father did, and if He does stay, He'll ruin my life the way my mother does. I doubt that's what the teacher meant, but I kept quiet, weaving my yarn.

I glanced over at Amber, who had finished hers and was making a second. We were supposed to hang them over our beds to remember that God loves us just like our parents. That didn't encourage me to want to become a Christian.

I shook my head at these thoughts. Amber leaned over to whisper, "Joel, she doesn't mean it the way you're taking it. Give her a chance."

"Guess I'll have to wait and see," I replied.

The teacher brought over a chair and had us take our God's Eyes with us as we formed a circle. I thought I was going to avoid *Kumbaya.* My throat tightened. I sat next to Amber. If we'd started to tear off the heads of chickens and drink their blood, that was where I was going to draw the line.

"I'd like to discuss something," Mrs. Trimmer began. "What do we do when our parents don't treat us the way God wants? Doesn't that send the wrong message? How many of you have parents who treat you less than perfectly?"

Everyone raised their hands, including Mrs. Trimmer.

"None of us have the perfect parents. That's the point of the God's Eye. Even if our parents aren't perfect, God is with us. He doesn't leave us, and He doesn't make mistakes."

"See what I mean?" Amber asked after the class let out. She put her arm around me and gave me a side hug. "Imagine what we'd think of God if that's all we had to go on."

I could imagine some pretty terrible things.

***

By the fourth night, I'm shivering when I get under the covers. It's not cold in my room. I try to stay awake as long as I can. I catch the glow from the full moon just beyond my window. Not a good sign...

This time, when I reach the bottom of the stairwell, I step into a darkness that surrounds and presses all the remaining light out of sight. It might be black ink or tar, this substance that pushes me like an oversized winter coat, forcing me supine against hard stones. I can't find the end.

The darkness is cold. My teeth chatter. I'm cold; I'm cold; I'm cold. I could be in the ground. I can't see anything at all. I lose sight of the stairs and am consumed by shadow and nothing else. I become absent, like I don't exist anymore. I am crushed beneath its girth, pulverized under this massive and pervasive force.

***

The first funeral I ever went to was my grandpa's. It was a time of firsts. The first time I touched a dead body and felt how cold and stiff and lifeless it was. The first time I tasted wine when no one was looking, and the one and only time I let anyone see me cry.

Jonathan sat in a corner and refused to go near. I couldn't help myself. I was pulled toward it, like Grandpa's coffin had its own gravity.

I stood in the quiet space between silence and grief, not sure I was doing it right. I could hear bits of whispered conversations, but they seemed far away. I couldn't move. Staring at my grandfather, I saw him lying there, the way he used to look when he slept through Sunday afternoons in his recliner. Peaceful. Only... something was missing. I couldn't figure out what.

I might have become a statue.

What pulled me out of the stillness was the person next to me. I don't know how long she stood there or what made her find and stand next to me. I noticed when her hand slipped silently up into mine, like it was meant to be there.

"Do you think he'll still exist after they put him in the ground?" I ask, not expecting an answer.

"If you keep all of the memories you share, he'll still exist," Amber answered, but maybe not just responding to me in particular.

Then the tears started, and I didn't care. I let them come. I remember thinking, *I don't want him to go down in the ground.*

***

The last night, I'm so worn out by the absence of sleep, I can't even fight to keep my eyes open. When I get home from school, I can barely get to the bed, and I'm out before I crawl all the way under my blankets. After closing my eyes, I have the sensation of falling, a downward pull…

I hesitate down the dark stone steps. Firelight flickers, bounces off the walls, the floor, the ceiling. Then, I hear something that doesn't belong. Water. It seems odd here, in darkness as quiet as a tomb, among the stony shadows. When I turn the corner, I know why right away.

A wall of water crashes down, wrenches me from where I stand into its terrible, unrelenting depths. I can't even catch a breath of air; I'm stunned by the suddenness as it sweeps me away down a passage. I can't tell where I am—only that I'm being pulled along—and I'm drowning.

My body slams against the walls on both sides, down the passageway, hurtling along under tremendous pressure. My chest burns, craving oxygen I cannot provide. I know I won't make it. Then I become entangled in some kind of net. The force of the water continues to rattle me. I'm crushed by the sheer weight of it but am unable to untangle myself, either. I fight to break free, wanting air, and knowing when I open my mouth, I'll drown.

***

All these nightmares and the memories they've brought to the surface have shaken loose other memories, previously hidden or purposely forgotten until now. Before my father left us for good, he planned our first big fishing trip to the lake, just the three of us, just the men. We had our fishing poles, we'd gathered worms, and we were planning to go that Saturday morning at dawn.

My father left in the middle of the week before. When we realized we couldn't go fishing, we were crushed all over again. First our father left, then he failed to make good on a promise. We moped for days.

My mother spoke with my grandmother. Grandma suggested we find someone else in our father's place. They had just hired Uncle Steven a month or two before, and he overheard their conversation coming in from the barn.

"I've got all the cows milked, Mrs. Scrivener. You want me to pour some milk in the chicken feed? Or wait 'til the next time, then?"

"That'll be fine, Steven. You can bring in the eggs and milk awhile."

"Yes, ma'am."

When he turned to leave, Jonathan and I clomped in with our poles.

"We're never gonna use these. I don't want mine anymore," I said, handing mine to my mother.

"Now, Joel—" she began.

"Mine neither!" Jonathan said, stomping away and throwing his pole down; it clattered to the ground.

Uncle Steven turned and picked up Jonathan's pole. "I don't know much about boys, Mrs. Scrivener, but I know an awful lot about fishing. I could take 'em if'n you want."

The next morning, we got up early and headed to the lake in his two-tone blue pickup, just the three of us and the worms. Uncle Steven saved that day and many more. Without him, I guess I would have gone on hating the bastard.

25

RELOCATION PROGRAM

At the end of school the next day, I get called down to the guidance office for another parent/counselor death-row-execution session. My vote is for lethal injection. If I'm going, I might as well get to pick the format where I go to sleep and never wake up. It's perfect and ironic all at the same time.

My mother is meeting with Ms. Moore in her office. I picture them chatting in the comfy seating area, sipping tea and nibbling scones. I sit in the waiting area and smile at the secretary: I'm a dead man walking. Now would be the perfect time for my X-ray-vision mutant ability to kick in. Doesn't a traumatic event precipitate the onset of the mutant gene? I should read more comics.

Instead, I read a book for English. These kids spend all their time trying to get a neighbor to come outside of his house. It takes place in the south during the Great Depression. I know because our history class is covering the same time period, and we are doing a massive WWII unit next. Our teachers organize projects that can overlap in both classes.

At least the book is decent. I'm reading chapter ten where the father, who's a lawyer, has a secret talent. Kind of like a mutant ability. It turns out he's an expert shot with a gun. Only he doesn't like to use his ability unless he has to. He thinks it's an unfair advantage. I haven't figured out if I have a talent or not. Maybe writing. I think Jonathan's talent is screwing as many girls as possible, skittering around venereal disease.

The phone rings at the secretary's desk. I look up.

"Ms. Moore and your mother will see you now. Do you remember where her office is?"

I nod and gather my things. "Right this way," she says, pointing down the hallway where my mother and Ms. Moore *prep the syringes* collaborate. I hope they won't hurt me. I find myself meandering slowly down the hall *c'mon, see through the wall, see through the wall. Eh-nee year.* I'm not a fan of needles. Or death *it's so final.*

My mother is the first to look up when I enter. I cross the room and take a seat catty-corner from where I first sat the other day. Ms. Moore sips from a steaming mug. *Oh, to be the edge of that mug just below her lips…*

"Joel, we were just talking about you," Ms. Moore says. *I knew it.* Conspiracy theories flash through my mind. "Why don't you have a seat, and we can discuss your test results together?" I sit. Ms. Moore offers me refreshments. *Gotta love guidance. You'll never leave hungry or thirsty.*

"The reason I discussed your results with your mother first is out of concern *fear for my job* for your well-being, Joel." *Oh, right, I must have forgotten.*

"Listen, Joel," my mother says in her super-mother tone. "We are very concerned *think you're a pain in the ass* about your transfer grades and with some of the behaviors you've exhibited as of late. Not the least of which is your running away, stealing money from my purse, fighting with your brother and smoking." She pulls out an empty cigarette pack. *Shit.* I must have thrown it away somewhere she could find.

"Joel," Ms. Moore continues, as if it were rehearsed, "your mother is very concerned *if we say it enough times you'll have to believe us* about you. She is. She just shared with me information about your past, when your father left, how that was a very difficult time for you. These patterns of yours are very similar in structure to what happened in your childhood. We are concerned *convinced you'll be a serial killer* you could relapse."

There. They've said it. *I'm crazy.* Now that we've gotten that out in the open, flapping in the breeze like a cold piece of fried chicken, I think it's time to leave. I stand and pull on my backpack.

"So, that's what you think this is about? A relapse?" My anger swells like hot scraps of metal behind my eyes. "You just try to put the spin on things to take the heat off your gambling problem." I let that fester and turn to leave. "I think we're done here," I say as I head to the door.

"Joel," says Ms. Moore, "we don't leave in the middle of a conversation *monologue*. I need you to come hear *the rest of* what we have to say. I promise to give you a chance to respond, okay?"

I stop, lean my head against the door frame, and then turn toward Ms. Moore.

"I told her about the nightmares, too, Joel. We need to deal with this and make a plan for you that doesn't end with your face on the side of a milk carton." My mother must be going for an award. I ignore her.

Instead, I will myself to turn and walk back to the chair. I slink down in the seat and am overwhelmed with exhaustion. *What are they driving at?* They talk around what the actual plan for me is, like they want me to warm up to the idea. This can't be good. I know what happens when you put a lobster in a pot and turn the heat on.

"Yes. About the nightmares, Joel, are you still having them?" Ms. Moore asks.

"I've had a few off and on."

"How about recently?"

"Uh, yeah, I guess so."

"You guess so, or you know, Joel? Which is it?" my mother interjects.

"It's okay, Joel. We're just trying to help *ourselves feel better about what we're about to do.*"

I'm not sure what to say. *I can see the elephant in the room.* This is a smokescreen to the real agenda. I want to know what this is about.

"So, what's going to happen to me?"

"Joel," says Ms. Moore, "your test results reveal some… concerning *alarming* trends. I've gone over the algorithms and checked them against the written test results. You're in a crisis. Whatever these nightmares are about, you need to face what causes them. That's why they've come back."

Okay, I'm listening. If she knows how to help me get rid of the nightmares, I should hear her out; although, I'm more interested in the pattern of the carpet beneath the coffee table. Lobster. Pot. Screams ensue.

"I called your grandmother and your aunt and uncle. Between the three of them, you're going to go and stay out there for a while. At least until the end of the school year. I can't be home enough for you with my work schedule, and I think heading back where you grew up, where you were when your father was still around, might help you through this *I've had enough of you.*"

Sounds good, but still fishy. *Where's the butter?*

"Joel," says Ms. Moore, "I'm going to speak with the counseling department of the school district there and make sure you will have a place to go when you need to talk about anything *the mandatory counseling sessions will continue.*"

"Okay, thanks *for not jabbing me with that needle.*" I don't know what else to say.

If my mother sends me back to the shore, I'll get to see Amber again. Since she's only interested in investing in her relationships nearby, moving back to the shore is my only shot at rebuilding things with Amber. As far as I can remember, I get along with my grandmother and my aunt and uncle, so staying at either place will be an improvement. It's been so long since I've been there, though, even for a visit, that I can't recall what they think of me.

I only went to elementary school there, so I don't know anything about the high school. I'm not opposed to being sent away from here. The trailer is awful, and these nightmares are awful. I wonder if a change of scenery would help. I was just starting to get used to this new school, though. And Jonathan will be pissed at me for leaving again. But this time it isn't my idea. Besides, he's still testy since I punched him in the face. The distance might help smooth it over.

Lost in thought, I barely hear my mother and Ms. Moore plan away the rest of my life. *Did I sign a contract without realizing?* I feel hot, like I've been sitting in boiling water too long.

Since my mother came to meet with Ms. Moore, she drives me home. The buses have already left for the day, so my mother spends the drive telling me all the details of the travel arrangements. Jonathan rode the bus and will get home before we do.

My mother can only afford a one-way bus ticket. She'll take me to the station, and my Uncle Brandon'll pick me up when I arrive. They'll decide the best plan for housing me. From what my mother has said, they're discussing these plans right now. I'll bring the transfer papers with me and complete my school year at Ticonderoga High, near my grandmother's house.

My mother's been working on the details all week. I must have missed that part. I was a little preoccupied by my lack of sleep and the nightmares. I can't remember most of the week. I must have looked like a walking zombie (minus the flesh-eating part).

"So, how many days until I head to Uncle Brandon's?"

"When we get home, you need to pack all your things and be ready to go. I've got to get you to the bus station before I go to work. Jonathan or I will return your books and things to Sanderville."

"Wait, I leave tomorrow? Tomorrow morning?"

"First thing."

26

ONE-WAY TICKET

When I get to the trailer, I head straight to my room to pack. Most of my clothes are still in the bag I packed at the townhouse; I guess I haven't unpacked. Since I don't own much, it's an easy process. I condense what I have into a few bags. To make sure I don't take old library or school books with me, I start with my backpack.

I wish I had an iPod. I'd be grateful for an MP3. I don't own a CD player or any CDs. I don't own any books. All the ones I have are checked out of a library. What would I have if it weren't for library books? I don't know what I'll do with nothing to read or music to listen to. I wonder if I could guilt my mother.

When I go to ask, she's on the telephone. I sit and wait. It takes me a few minutes to figure out who she's talking to: my grandmother, my father's mother, or my Uncle Brandon and Aunt Althea. They are my father's brother and his wife. She could be talking to either.

When she talks to other adults, she sounds different. The way students flip a switch in class. When they're in the hall or if they think the teacher can't hear, they cuss, discuss anything sex-related, and sound as different as my mother does on the phone. Of course, she could just be being nice, since my father's family is willing to take me. I hope to stay for the summer. I don't want to be here, slow-cooking in a metal box.

They talk about the way I reacted when my father left. He joined the military. He got placed on a solitary assignment. My mother told him, if he left, they would get a divorce. Eventually, they did. I didn't handle it well. We lived in a house with a split-level staircase.

I hid in the storage cabinet under the stairs. A few times, my mother found me there after I'd pulled my blankets and pillow down during the night.

Then I started playing with matches.

Once, I took a box into the downstairs bathroom, lit them and watched them burn down; I blew them out before they singed my fingers and tossed them in the waste can. I remember locking the door absentmindedly behind me, not realizing the matches would catch the trash can on fire. By the time smoke poured out beneath the bathroom door—flooding the house in a white haze—it was too late.

The house was on fire.

Part of me had wanted to do it, I don't know why. I couldn't stop. My hands wouldn't listen to the alarms going off in my brain. I needed a way out. I wanted to burn everything down to the ground, and when I walked through, all that remained—gray drab ash flapping and fluttering like wings—I'd find a way to begin again.

I changed my mind, but then I couldn't get the bathroom door back open after I'd locked it shut by accident, and I freaked. Until then, fire had been soothing, a way to calm down. I ran to the neighbor's house to get help. Luckily it was just a smoke fire. The neighbor managed to pry the door open before the fire department arrived. The plastic can had melted in on itself, and the fire had smoked up the wall. I got in a heap of trouble.

My mother came unglued, or so I've heard. It got spotty after that. I remember stomach pains so terrible I couldn't get any relief, no matter what I did. Finally, I lay on the carpet, and the counter-pressure helped ease the pain a little. A few weeks later, I fell asleep sitting upright in a chair.

When I woke, I screamed so loud, everyone came to see what was wrong. I didn't understand why everyone ran into the room. I never heard the scream. It didn't register.

My mother drove me to the hospital, and after a battery of tests, I was admitted for observation. I was put on a liquid diet and had to drink this terrible stuff—mineral oil. It was supposed to help with the pains that doubled me over, that I felt down to my bones. The doctors told me I had growing pains. My gut told me this wasn't the whole truth. I couldn't figure out what they weren't telling me. *Why would they lie?* But what the truth was or is, I never found out.

Finally, my mother gets off the phone.

"I won't have any books to read on the bus. I don't even have music. Any suggestions?"

"Joel, it's too late to go out and get anything. I can see if there's anything at the bus station. Maybe there will be a cute girl. You two could have a conversation."

"Okay, Mother. Whatever."

"You never know."

"Well, I'm packed," I say, ignoring her prodding. "Good night."

In bed, I find myself retreating to thoughts of Amber. I wonder if she got my letter. *Will she think I'm still a runaway when I get there?* I hope our newfound proximity will help matters. If I try, will she let me kiss her more than just a peck? What if that ruins the friendship we've maintained? Would I rather have one attempted kiss or keep the relationship safe?

An image tiptoes through my mind. When we were little, Amber had freckles splayed across her nose and cheeks like a map I'd love to trace with my fingers or lips. Does she still have them? Or did they fade over time? She asked me to write a story. I should work on that while I'm on the bus. For now, my mind fixates on the deliciousness of her freckles.

27

TONGUE IN GROOVE

My mind has lingered over that kiss for so long—how my finger traced the side of her cheek before turning toward those cherry lips; the way the last two pieces of a puzzle fit exquisitely together. Sometimes with an audible sigh. Others, in that inaudible way tongue-and-groove pieces click together.

That's why I know we were meant for more. It was there on the beach and in the darkness of the closet, tangible between us. But a kiss is just the first step. Every one that follows has been almost effortless for us.

As I sit on this never-ending bus ride, I know I'm past the point of no return. I can't go back. I've got to take a chance, or I'll regret not trying. I might lose everything, even our friendship, but I'm willing to face that if it happens. I don't think it will.

Grasshoppers make daring leaps inside my chest. My hands tremble. I get out paper. I've got to try.

Maybe I'm crazy for running headlong at it, not knowing the outcome. After all, puzzle pieces can wear out over time. That's not the point. The point is to go for it, because clarity comes in a moment, the same as certainty comes and goes. It *can* go. I know that. But what remains is worth the time it took to find how each piece fit together in the first place.

That's how love is born.

***

Dear Amber,

Writing can be such a lonely experience. As I write, I am alone with just myself and my thoughts, although mostly I think of you. And me. And us. It's funny because I'm sitting on a crowded bus, headed back to you.

We could be together. The way I imagine it to be. But that would be the future. When I write, it might be the present—in that moment—captured in words on the page. When I finally get to share it with you, time will have moved on, and it's just my past, our past, or my imagined future I'll share with you.

It's not here. It won't be when you read it. That's not why I wanted to share it with you. Sure, writing can be a safe place from which to explore something from all sides, analyze it, pin it to the page. But I've decided to do something else.

It's a radical decision, so bear with me. I'm going to stop writing. I'm going to keep myself in the present (as your father suggested and even you suggested in your last letter), not the past or an imagined future. A present I hope to share with you in the now. Will you join me, as my girlfriend?
Joel

THE GRIEF OF THE RETURN

From the journal of Joel Scrivener

Far away I hear the wind pressing nearer,
the corners of the house begin to buckle in, ashamed.
I climb inside the dusky words of a book unclaimed
for all the dim years past, becoming clearer.
On those dark pages no one writes what is missing
and I cannot wait for this grief to make sense.
The beaten child hunches over, tangled in the fence;
at length, his shadow distended by dark waters, fishing.

The windows have eyes facing ever inward,
staring down shadows at all these dark places.
Panes shudder, rattling in their frame cages
at the lost things: a boy I unearth from pinewood.
Unlidded, my eyes clamp shut, against murky depths
laid open, his stare long saddened by rejection.
The death I gave him refusing the question,
whose guilt I now bear like an old hermit, unkempt.

Underneath, floorboards groan, creak with the great weight
I gather around my body. A storm approaches, raging
along the horizon, tossing seagulls inland, waging
unwieldy fielded currents, worms strung on hooks like bait.
The boy brings bruises back into the house, deep wounds
surfaced by winds and new rain. He climbs into my lap
and holds me quietly for long moments, like a clap
of thunder rumbling up from darkened and muddy ground.

The light switches refuse to stay turned down.
They throw light all over the house, pressing darkness
down into the cellar like an uneasy calmness
numbing our bodies to sleep, or else be found,

knowing what we have become: the wizened hermit
and the boy undone, by a life lost in stasis,
the way we allow shame to create the basis
for the storm to rise, lifting the shadow into respite.

PART III

TICONDEROGA HIGH SCHOOL

Home of the Oceanside Sharks

28

BACK HOME AGAIN

I don't know how I made it through eight hours on a bus with a loud woman who didn't stop talking the entire trip to Oceanside, especially without a way to block her screeching, nasal voice. My ears are still ringing.

I spend most of the ride thinking about all the stupid things I've done. I need to buck up without a dad as my wingman. I'm tired of running. Whether I like it or not, this bus has brought me back where home used to be, where everything began, including the nightmares. This is the place where my dad left us; in the space he left behind, I intend to take a stand and stop running, despite his example.

It's time I get serious and quit trying every fool-headed idea I think up. I'm mad for dangling dangerously close to the edge of failing out of tenth grade, for running away, for smoking, even for excessive cursing. I peeked at my transfer paperwork during the endless bus ride and saw my current grades, partway through the third marking period. It's clear. If I don't do something to change, I'll be stuck like this forever.

The realization is sobering.

If I want a chance with Amber, I'd better become someone she wants to spend time with. It's bad enough I'm poor and grew up a loser. She's a knockout and smart and has a cell phone and maybe a car. I've got nothing. If I want to get her attention, it's got to be for more than just running away and flushing my grades down the toilet. It may be too late to turn things around, though. *What was I thinking with that letter and phone call?*

Before I realize it, we pull into the bus station. As I come off the bus, my Uncle Brandon is waiting there, ready to help carry luggage. I don't have much, just everything I own.

Uncle Brandon has aged since I saw him last. He's my father's younger brother. It's weird being sent to stay with my father's family because I haven't seen or heard from my dad since he left. Uncle Brandon may be older now, but he's always been nice to my brother and me.

I pull my bags out of the storage bay, and he grabs most of them, leaving me a crate and my backpack. I follow him to his truck where I place the crate at my feet and the backpack in my lap. I feel like I owe him for helping me. I don't like to owe anyone anything. I'm not some indentured servant. Being indebted to family is the worst.

"The ride out okay?" he asks, interrupting my thoughts.

"It was all right. Just a lady talking the whole time."

"Well, enjoy the peace and quiet at your grandma's house. We decided that was the best place. She's the closest to the high school, and you can help her around the house."

I nod then spend the rest of the ride staring out the window, watching for places I might remember. Some things look familiar, like the Circus Drive-In and the tourists. Amber told me in a letter one of my favorite burger joints burned down and they're not rebuilding it. I loved their loaded chili fries. It's going to take some time to get used to the changes. But I do recognize that we aren't very far from somewhere I'd like to go.

"Uncle Brandon, can we drive along the beach? It's been forever since I've seen the ocean." He gives me the look, the one only those who live here understand. Sometimes it calls to you and you have to go—take in the smell of the salty air, watch the tide tumble toward the shore, soak into the sand beneath your toes, hear the waves and shorebirds echo back and forth in a private conversation. It's like a reset button for the soul.

We turn left down a side street and, after a few turns, bear left slowly along the boardwalk. There's a breeze, and we roll the windows down despite the spring chill. I hear the metallic creak of bicycle wheels spinning, see dogs with lolling tongues dragging their people behind them, and notice couples strolling at a pace to match their conversation. Farther down, children laugh or scream as they slide, climb, and swing at playgrounds built next to the boardwalk. Other kids mill around stores or eat at tables out in front of restaurants and coffee shops.

I take slow deep breaths and watch waves crash as we head north. I see a few people climb on the breakers, looking for shells. *What the hell am I thinking?* This is a punishment, but I'm having trouble remembering why. I've gotten so used to waking in a cold sweat; I can't believe this is deserved. I'm afraid if I pinch myself, I might wake up and be back in my mother's trailer where the nightmares torment me. Maybe no one will notice and I can stay through spring and even for the summer.

My stomach growls so loud, I look out the window so my uncle doesn't see how red my face goes. I catch a glimpse in the side mirror.

"Bus food doesn't stick, does it?" Uncle Brandon asks.

I try to laugh. "I guess not."

"We've still got time. How about you and me grab a bite?"

"Okay."

"I assume this won't wreck your dinner if we grab something to hold you over. I think your grandmother is making her world-famous lasagna to welcome you."

That last words lodge in my throat. I have to swallow before I choke. *Don't they realize I'm here because I've screwed up?*

We park in front of a street-side shop. Uncle Brandon buys a couple of hot dogs, an order of cheese fries, and two Cokes.

"You want chili on the dogs?" he asks me.

"Sure," I say.

"Make that two chili dogs," he tells the cashier. We eat like two men sneaking an in-between meal, wolfing down our food in only a few minutes, sitting at a table along the sidewalk. The food is hot and fresh and reminds me of years ago, when safe was still a word I used.

"Thanks," I say, my cheek stuffed full of hot dog. "This hit the spot."

"No problem, my man." I guess he and my father are related after all. They can't help but be corny. My throat is tight again. I hate that I'm thinking about him right now. It must be the familiar sights stirring up long-forgotten memories.

"Uncle Brandon, can I ask you something?"

"Sure, anything."

"How'd you turn out so normal?"

He looks at me for several moments before responding. "How do you mean?"

"Well, you are part of this family, right? It can get pretty crazy…"

Uncle Brandon laughs. "C'mon, let's not keep your grandmother waiting." We head back to his truck and drift into the comfort of silence.

The last time I was here for longer than a visit, my father left my brother and me standing in the doorway in our pajamas, sobbing, pleading for him to stay, not to go, not to leave us. *Daddy, you can't just go!* I'd thought, if I screamed loud and long enough, he'd listen, come to his senses.

What was it that made him leave?

I'd clenched my jaw as his car door slammed, and then he drove away without looking back even once. Now, tears prick my eyes, but I let anger force them down. I've never said that word since: *Daddy.*

29

GRANDMA'S HOUSE

We pull up to a house that looks like it shrank in the dryer. Suddenly I'm the Jolly Green Giant. I have to duck when I go inside.

One thing that hasn't changed is the smell. Right off, I catch Grandma's signature dish. It brings me back, like I never left—the sauce and the gooey cheese and layers upon layers of buttery noodles, under a cloud of humiliation over tucking tail and leaving. *I'm not going to think about that now.*

My aunt is here with her three kids and my grandmother. I hear Althea's laughter when I walk in. I don't remember all their kids' names. Some were born after we left. The oldest is Emily. We used to play in the backyard. I wonder if they live in the same place. This isn't the same house Grandma had when Grandpa was still alive. They had a farm. She kept it a few years after he passed but moved here just after the neighbor boy died and Uncle Steven disappeared.

My aunt watches me fidget. She brings me over, reintroduces me to Emily, their older son Cody and youngest son Christopher. Seeing them makes me feel old.

I have a seat next to Grandma after giving her a hug and telling her the lasagna smells insane. I smirk at the tablecloth: I think the same one has been on this table for more than a decade. It has a plastic coating on top and cotton batting beneath. It's the same sunshine yellow I have etched on my memory, along with her Tupperware containers and canning jars in the pantry.

I would bet a million dollars they're all still there. I want to go see if I'm right, but I can't wait to eat, even though we snuck food on the way. I share a glance with Uncle Brandon, and he kicks into host mode, offering to cut and serve. Grandma asks us to bow our heads as we say grace. Some things never change.

Sometimes I don't want them to.

Everything tastes as good as, if not better than, I remember. I eat a second helping before my belly bulges, distended under the strain. I'm going to hurt later, but it's so worth it. I moan, rub my belly and push away from the table.

"That was ah-may-zing, Grandma."

"You're quite welcome, Joel."

"No one cooks like Mom," Uncle Brandon says before realizing he just put his foot in his mouth. The "*Ow!*" presumably in response to Aunt Althea's foot firmly reminding my uncle's shin how he blew it. We laugh. Uncle Brandon shoos Grandma and Althea to relax in the living room while the rest of us clear and put away.

I take the opportunity to peek in the pantry. *Just as I remember it.* The copper molds are hung around the top of the wall a few inches away from the ceiling. So many things I thought were lost to my childhood; only now do they come flooding to the forefront.

Grandma puts me in the front bedroom. I set my things on the floor by the dresser and change to shorts and a T-shirt then say goodnight to the family and head to the bathroom to brush teeth. Everything here is too quiet and peaceful. *Calm before the storm.*

I'll start at Ticonderoga High in the morning, so Grandma says goodnight, and I'm on my own. I ask if I can borrow a few books, and she shows me where she keeps them in the study, the room behind mine.

"Of course, there's a Bible on your nightstand, but you can choose from these ones if you like," she says before heading back to her bedroom. "Good night, Joel."

I pull several that look interesting. I'm so relieved to be in a normal-sized room.

I wait for the punch line or the camera crew to bust in and laugh along with the live studio audience. This was all a prank. I've actually been punked.

Nothing happens.

I'm weary from travel but not tired enough to sleep, so I pick up a book. Before long, though, my head bobs and jolts me awake as it tips forward, so I give up and go to sleep in my comfortable, non-trailer-park bed. It's a full size with a bed frame and box spring. I can't remember the last time I was in a bed this big that I didn't have to share with Jonathan. I stretch out and drift off.

***

In the morning, Grandma fixes breakfast while I stumble for the bathroom. There is an alarm clock here, so I get up on time. The shower is wonderful, and I don't remember waking even once during the night. Not even a hint of a nightmare.

Grandma's shower has amazing water pressure. I think I'm in too long or had it on too hot, because I'm a red sausage when I come out. Steam covers the bathroom mirror and pours from the walls like summer sweat. I tuck a towel at my waist and head to the bedroom.

"Breakfast is ready."

"Thanks, Grandma. I'll be right there."

The urge to pinch myself overwhelms. I must resist. After I'm dressed, I head to breakfast where Grandma sits drinking coffee and juice while reading the paper. Her pills and vitamins are in a small cup next to her. Old people and their routine habits fascinate me.

I'm reminded of several times I spent in the kitchen with Grandma, working on cookies or making a treat. I think of the peanut butter and confectioner's sugar balls we would roll out on wax paper. For breakfast, Grandma made eggs and toast with strips of bacon. I wash this down with orange juice, and we head out the door.

"I'll drive you in for your first day, but watch the route. It's very easy to get there. You can walk home on your own."

She's right. We drive two blocks up the street to the right and then turn left. One block up and we hang another right along a main road that's a divided highway. This part sparks a memory I can't place.

"Why is this road familiar?" I ask.

"It's the same one our farm is on, just outside of town."

After three or four blocks, we turn left into the parking lot. I can still picture the way the farm was surrounded by a grazing field up by the road and a barn and chicken coop further back, behind the main house. The field beyond was mostly corn; the outhouse I remembered was at the back field. I wonder if it looks the same, now that there are new owners.

Grandma heads for a handicapped spot near the entrance. Ticonderoga High School is a modern brick building with two floors and lots of windows. A large walking area in front of the school leads to the flag poles and the drop-off circle. There's a long narrow roof over the walkway, the kind you might find in a bus station terminal. It reminds me of various stations on the trip out here.

Grandma gets out the manila envelope with my records while I grab my backpack and the lunch she made. We head in under the front portico, where we have to be buzzed inside.

I guess Sanderville was behind the times. No chance I could break in here overnight. I see security cameras and scanners by the doors. Lucky for me Grandma's cooking and comfortable bed slays school food and the teacher's lounge couch any day of the week. I think I'll stick to Grandma's house.

Once I hand in my papers, Grandma takes over and I take a seat. There's a question about my schedule. The secretaries take my paperwork and head over to guidance. Since I brought failing grades from Broad Run High School and wasn't at Sanderville long enough to turn things around, this is my last shot to pass tenth grade.

By the time the paperwork is complete and Grandma heads home, it's partway through first period before someone walks me to class. *Amber is here.* This is her freshman year. *Her house isn't far.* I've got to find her before the end of the day. My mind whirls and flutters. She knows me better than anyone else.

Starting over at another high school—the fifth one so far—is hard enough without doing it alone, especially with Amber this close. I'm nauseous and excited, even giddy when I go into the class. The teacher looks at me a bit funny when I reply to her, "Welcome to American history" with too much exuberance.

"Thanks," comes out of my mouth before I can stop it. More like a squawk than anything. Giggles erupt from the back of the class. I take my fire-engine-red ears and cheeks to a seat near the windows. Mrs. Dixon brings me my textbook. When we open to chapter 17, I try to lose myself in the Salem witch trials.

I focus on taking notes. Most everyone at least feigns doing some semblance of work. Another chance has been put in my lap, and I want to take it this time. Sure, I could blame it on the nightmares, my crummy home life or my single-parent family. But at some point, I have to own up.

It's nice being around more functional family. My mother and Jonathan are too self-absorbed and busy with their own demise. Just being around them pulled me into a morbid tailspin, like a toilet endlessly flushing.

Here, I can breathe the ocean air, recharge on the beach and spend time with my grandmother. If I do it right, she might let me stay. *What am I missing back at the trailer park?* Sanderville is nothing like Oceanside. I could get used to this.

My next class is English, and I ask for directions on my way out. It's upstairs, about midway down the front wing. According to the schedule, my teacher's name is Mr. Castell. All the teachers stand in the doorway between classes; must be some kind of protocol.

"I'm Joel Scrivener, your new student."

"Hi, Joel. Mr. Castell. Nice to meet you. My first failing student of the year." He glances over his shoulder at the students entering class. "And not because they don't try, but I do not tolerate failure here. You got me?"

"Loud and clear."

That went well. Right off the block and I stumble in the race. English is usually my best subject. All I brought with me was a failing grade. I'll have to show him what I can do.

The class is about a week or two into a play about the Salem witch trials. *What's with all the teachers who like to do their teaching units across core classes?* Maybe chemistry class will be about testing each other to see if we're a witch or a—*what's the word?* Warlock. Math will cover the effects of witchcraft on the New England economy. I can't wait.

Since this is a play, Mr. Castell wants us to read it aloud in class, each of us assigned a part. I have the whole first act to get caught up. I'll be assigned a part tomorrow. For now, I get to listen. The hardest part is the strange way they talk, almost too proper. I could be in church or something. The girls in the play lie to the town like they're in league with the devil. *They were just trying to get the boys to like them.*

Next up is chemistry, and Mrs. Woerther has us doing a lab on different kinds of plastics. I think we make a bouncy ball, but mine is lumpy and bounces funny. Right before lunch, I have geometry with Mr. Reidinger. He has the personality of a calculator. I may need a private tutor to understand what everything means.

I stand inside the doorway, not sure if I'm in the lunch line, and scope out seating. Instead of the usual long tables, this cafeteria has a sea of round tables with six or eight chairs apiece, a slice of pizza for each seat. I choose a table with about half the seats occupied.

It takes me a few minutes to get lost in my brown bag and thoughts before it hits me that I haven't seen Amber. *Maybe she's at a different lunch.* No sooner am I struck by the thought than I look to the right, and she walks out of the lunch line and heads to a table near the other end of the cafeteria. I haven't seen a picture of her in a while, but I'm certain it's her. Time slows. I may hear actual music. A waltz. She's stunning, and I've forgotten to breathe. She walks with a friend, and they laugh together, but all I see is her smile and those eyes…

I take a huge bite of my sandwich. I must have shoved a third of it in with one large chomp. As I look up, I see her frozen at her table, poised to sit, her hands still on the tray she's just put down. She stares right at me.

"Joel? Is that you?" she asks in such a loud voice the majority of the cafeteria goes stone silent. She leaves her tray and waltzes over. All eyes are on me, the new kid.

I don't remember standing up.

When she pulls me into an embrace, it's like she isn't thinking about it. My hand slides to the small of her back and, *bam*, we're back in that moment we discovered together in closet darkness, the place where we knew...

"What are you doing here?" she asks and then pushes me away. "I thought you ran away from home." Everyone listens for my answer. Fortunately, they can't hear what I'm thinking. I'm stuck on the answer to her first question.

Dying of embarrassment.

30

REUNION

"Amber. *Uh*, I can explain," I say, fumbling and backing away with a mouthful of sandwich. I can't help myself; I'm hopelessly distracted by her dark, slim skirt and front-button top. Green is hot on a girl with red hair.

She pauses, taking an almost imperceptible breath. I would have missed it had I not mirrored the same breath, the same sighed exhale. I know what I'm thinking—the earth just tilted, and I lean into it, facing her—and I'm pretty sure I know what she's thinking. But when I step closer and my hands reach out to pull her closer, I catch myself.

Something in her demeanor shifts, and I watch in alarm as she buries the thought that just flashed across the curves of her face. I've seen that look before, and I have zero desire to go back there. Too bad that doesn't stop her from crossing her arms while I chew and swallow the half-masticated bite. It's painful all the way down. *Where did everything go?* It started off so well and then… While I feel the lump sliding down my throat, I try to think of something to say. By the look on her face, I can tell this is the wrong time to bring up the stuff I remembered about her father from the basement. "So, I tried to write a story for you on the bus trip out here. Maybe I can go over what I finished with you later?"

I've officially shelved the letter until further notice.

Amber purses her lips. If she wasn't irritated, that would look damn sexy.

"Joel. I got your letter. I read it. Why...?" For a moment, she's overcome, eyes shimmering. Then she shifts back and harpoons me with those eyes, searching. "What's happened to you?"

"I don't know. A lot's changed."

This would be so much better if we were on the beach right now, instead of in the cafeteria.

"Are you going to be okay?"

"I think so. I'm staying with my grandmother."

"But what happened? Why'd you run away?"

"Well, I did run away, until I got caught. Then I had to see a shrink."

"Do you really think running away was the best choice?"

"Maybe. I couldn't stay there any longer. You know how awful the shelter was the last time."

"You've transferred here? Why? What is this about a shrink?"

"I got shipped back here to stay with my grandmother and finish out the year, since I'm failing most of my classes. That was decided after the psych eval." Everything I say sounds awkward. My mind whirls, a plane with one wing and no engines. This is total crash and burn. Her eyes flick across me, up and down and, *oh, God, how I want her to keep looking.*

I don't know if I can keep my hands away from tugging her close, and I'm not sure I want to, either. Standing here, I can smell the bloom of her perfume, the air ripe with jasmine that draws me in. I inhale, afraid she'll be gone again too soon.

I can't tell why she hasn't responded yet. "Amber? What's going on? You look like you've seen a ghost." She startles, her eyes suddenly wide and piercing. *What if I remind her of her stalker?* Sadness creeps across her face, and my senses go numb.

"I... underestimated you. You've completely changed, and not entirely for the better. There's something unsaid. You were supposed to be——" She pauses, collecting herself before continuing. "I thought I knew you better, but I guess not. You're like most other boys who've crossed my path. Broken. Look, I've gotta go. I'll see you around." She turns and walks back to her table. Her steps clip hard against the ground. I can't tell if her voice cracked at the end. My body refuses to move.

Her words buzz around my head, and I go down in flames. *Did I hear her right?* That was not the verve I wanted. Now I'm here, and she doesn't want anything to do with me. *Did I read that right?* I think I may have scared her somehow. *How can I fix this?* She's hurt, and didn't let me explain.

My mind goes blank. I'm a writer, and I can't formulate a single coherent thought, a phrase that would explain things better with Amber. Silence is probably better.

I finish the sandwich, but my appetite's gone. I shove the rest in my backpack. Reviewing what she said doesn't make it any better. Maybe I should lie down in front of a bus.

***

After the fallout with Amber, I slog through the rest of the day. My last class is study hall, but instead of attending, I have to report to guidance for one of those required counseling sessions. I forgot to tell Mr. Castell, so I go to his class and ask for a pass. After school, I have mandatory tutoring at the Writing Center.

"Actually, I have your pass right here. They sent it to me this morning. Guess I missed it during class. My bad." *Adults should not use our phrases.* Mr. Castell lands at the top of my dork list.

"I don't know how long I'll have these appointments instead of study hall."

"I'll check with the counselor and find out. Thank you, Joel. If your appointment runs the whole period, I'll see you tomorrow."

I head down to the office and ask for guidance. One of the secretaries takes me over past the front counter and down a hall. She points to a glassed-in door with windows instead of a wall. "See the sign for gui-dance? It's right there. You have a good rest of the da-ay." I think she's had one too many Diet Co-okes.

I go in, present my appointment slip, then take a seat. The appointment is with Mr. Faber. Just like Ms. Moore, he's a school psychologist. I wonder if they have a secret network, sharing stories of their students, like who's the craziest kid they know. I can picture their emails and phone calls to each other. They might even attend conferences about us. I imagine Ms. Moore calling Mr. Faber...

"Hi, Mark. It's Madeline. I've got a doozy for you. Joel Scrivener. He's completely delusional. I think he might be the next big serial killer. Think you can handle him?"

I'm sure they laughed about my file, all the way to the espresso machine.

I think she overnighted my information so Mr. Faber could see what kind of psychopath he got. When he appears, he scans the file for my name.

"Joel. Welcome. Do come on back. Ms. Moore told me a lot about you. I'm glad to meet you in person."

He offers me a limp handshake and ushers me back to his office. I sure hope this is only for a week and not the rest of the school year.

Mr. Faber's office is not as cushy as Ms. Moore's. There's a table and chairs by the windows, two armchairs and a few very sparse decorations. The walls have motivational posters with people climbing mountains or running marathons.

"Joel, I've looked over your file and the results of your recent evaluation administered by Ms. Moore at your previous school. Part of the reason you were sent here was because I attended the same graduate school as Ms. Moore. When your mother mentioned to her you had family in Oceanside, she contacted me to see what my caseload was like and whether I could add you or not."

I start to freak out, hearing how this is all connected. *Are all the adults planning to ruin my life?* I'm stuck with Mr. Faber. *How's he gonna help me?*

I only half-listen to him blather on about how everyone is concerned for my well-being, how they want to help me face my problems with my parents' divorce, and how those problems have manifested lately with my running away and fighting with my brother. All behaviors that cry out for help, and Mr. Faber wants to help me by responding to my request. *Same shit, different day*. I almost miss what he says next.

"Joel, we have contacted your father and asked him to come in for a meeting next week. Your grandmother has his contact information, and I understand you're staying with her right now?"

I knew I was coming out to Oceanside to stay with my father's family, but I had no idea I might see him again, especially after the way he left. I'm not sure I want to see him, either.

"I don't want anything to do with him. Why would you call him? You didn't even ask me. Why does every adult think they know what I need better than me? I'm not coming to that meeting. Call him back and cancel."

As I stand, I grab my backpack and turn to head for the door. Mr. Faber puts his hand on my shoulder.

"Joel, I can certainly—" he begins.

"Get off me! *Stop touching me!*" I explode, turning back to face him. I grab his creepy limp hand and fling it down off my shoulder then bolt for the door. Tears well up, and I have to stifle them, pressing them back down with the surge of anger that's flooding my insides.

Why would I want to talk to my father after all these years? I don't even know where to begin. Even if I could put my thoughts into words, I wouldn't have anything nice to say.

What an asshole.

31

CLEANING OUT THE GARAGE

I skip tutoring and blaze a trail to Grandma's house. I can't believe I fell right into this setup. I'm pissed my mother sent me back here, under the guise of her work schedule. I guess she thought I wouldn't come if I knew they'd planned to drag my father back around. The lies are stacking up and marinating in a pan of betrayal.

I double over and wait for the wave to pass.

Maybe they're just trying to do their job. Still, they shouldn't talk behind my back as if they know what's best. They don't have any right to mess with my life or force me to do what I don't want to do.

All I care about is not failing tenth grade. Well, that and fixing things with Amber. I don't want to have to go through either of these again. No one owned up to contacting my father. They could have asked first and found out what I wanted before they scheduled this meeting next week. I should have seen it coming.

I can't think about this shit right now—it was years ago. My mother said she told him I ended up in the hospital when he ran off, but he must not have cared. He never called or wrote or visited. Years later, I heard about their divorce. I was in middle school, and my mother mentioned it like she was asking me to pass the salt.

"The divorce papers were finalized last week. It's over between your father and me. Pretty good casserole, huh?" she said one night during dinner. There. *Ka-boom.* Divorce. She was so cold and detached, like it didn't even matter.

"What?" was all I could manage. My throat clamped whatever I was eating, then I had to bolt. I lost everything in the toilet back at the townhouse. That was before she started dating all those different men, before everything went to hell.

When I reach Grandma's house, my eyes are wild and bleary. If I don't find something to do with my hands, I'm going to go ballistic, maybe lose control. I hope she has a chore.

Taking a deep breath, I try to calm myself, blowing the air out. The driveway runs along the side of the house, and the garage is separate. The garage door is open. All bets say she's in the backyard gardening.

"Grandma, I'm back."

"Oh, hi. I didn't see you there. Just weeding a bit."

"Do you need any help?"

"Oh, no, dear. I've already got a helper. Maybe you know her?"

Amber comes out of the garage, carrying garden gloves and gardening tools.

"What are you doing here?" I ask, dumbfounded.

"Helping your grandma weed the garden. What does it look like?"

I'm trying to complete the equation in my brain that explains why Amber is here, helping my grandmother, but there are too many missing variables. Before I've thought it through, I ask, "No. Why are you here?" Anger roils in my stomach on a low boil. Amber's face shifts from pleasant to something that makes me burp stomach acid.

"Joel, your grandma invited me. Who do you think has been helping her the last several years?"

"Uh…"

She smiles and passes gloves to my grandmother. My mind scrambles to catch up. I guess it makes sense. Amber has known my grandmother since my grandfather's funeral, years ago. I just never— she never mentioned she was doing this. Why would she—unless she'd been angling to gather intel on me from my grandmother?

"So you two don't need any help?"

"No, dear. We've got this under control. Weeding gives my hands something to do, if you know what I mean." I do a double take. I'd better get busy, or I'm liable to give Amber a puke show.

"What about the garage? Do you need anything done there?"

"Well, I hadn't thought much of it, but I have a stack of boxes along the far wall that need to be gone through. I'd like to donate to Goodwill. Most of it's your grandfather's things, maybe some from your father and uncle. See what you can do."

I never realized how similar we are. Grandma gives me a look before returning to her weeding. The garage boxes at least give me something to keep busy, and who wouldn't want to know more about their family? Besides, with Amber here, the urge to duck and cover is screaming in my ears.

As I enter the garage, I estimate there are about a dozen boxes stacked along the side wall. I pull a trash bag from a nearby shelf and open the first box. Inside I find stacks of old comics: *Strange Tales* and others I've never heard of. *Who collected these?* They could be my father's or grandfather's. I see stories of vampires, werewolves, and swamp monsters.

I'm not sure Goodwill would want these, but maybe Grandma could find a collector who will. I make stacks on the ground and keep going. The next box has bundled letters. They're pretty old. I can't picture my father, grandfather or uncle as writers.

I find clothes in the next four boxes. These appear to be my grandfather's and still smell like him. When the scent of his pipe tobacco hits me, I'm reminded of the farm and his routine in the early daylight hours: feeding the few cows, the dozen or so chickens, and the rooster, the horse, and the pigs. I remember seeing him up and out, tending the animals, whenever I was up early.

The farm wasn't very big, but it was big enough. I think that's why they hired Uncle Steven, as we called him, to help manage the chores and the fields. Going fishing was a bonus. My grandfather let his pride get the best of him: he liked to think he could continue working up to his dying day. The truth was he needed the help.

When my father left, my mother asked Uncle Steven to help with watching us so she could go to work. I would have been bored if it weren't for him. At least he could take us fishing. That continued until I ended up in the hospital. We left not long after I got out. Sometimes, I catch myself thinking how much I miss Uncle Steven. I guess he stayed and helped Grandma with the farm. Maybe I should ask.

I step out of the garage to check if Grandma is still weeding, and I don't see her anywhere. Amber's nowhere to be found, either. I figure they must have gone in the house.

I go back to sorting boxes. The next two yield books. I scan titles to see if there are any I might want. There are books on farming and planting, animal husbandry, and a *Farmer's Almanac*. I pull out a book called *Walden* and flip through. Tucked between two pages, I find a handwritten letter. It's from my father to my mother.

> *Carrie,*
> *I've been assigned to an isolated post. While I'm there, you can stay in base housing with the boys. I'll make sure there's money in our account. I know this is a shock. I hope we can work through things. We just need some time. Time to get your affairs in order. Maybe the distance will help.*
> *Brian*

I can't believe it. *Is this real?* Did my father leave because he was sent away? If that's true, then he didn't just leave us. There has to be more. *Why didn't he tell us once he arrived at his post?* Maybe he did…

My thoughts swirl like the tremors shooting down my back.

Why didn't he fight it? He could have stayed. They still divorced a few years later. A bomb implodes in my mind. Roads and buildings collapse as I try to reconcile what I just read with what I know, or thought I knew. *Something isn't right. I bet it has to do with my mother.* I don't think she told either of us the whole truth. *Why the hell was I sent out here on a ruse, to have this impromptu meet up with my father?* Maybe I should go through with it.

How else do I figure out what's missing?

32

UNEXPECTED ANSWERS

Grandma calls me in for dinner. Amber has gone, and the rest of the night is a different rude awakening: all my recent slacking off has caught up with me. I'm buried in homework for chemistry, multiple readings in history and English, classwork for gym, and a project entirely in Spanish I can't even begin to get my head around. I may never trudge through all of these. Why did I have to transfer at the end of the marking period?

I'll have to tackle the garage tomorrow. School is the most pressing thing, if I ever hope to get back with Amber. *Who am I kidding? I was never with Amber.* In my mind doesn't count. Besides, I've got to figure out what doesn't add up with my dad's letter.

***

I don't remember falling asleep. I'm out of bed and groggily stumbling to find a glass of water when I sense his presence. Without warning, I'm slammed against the wall, wedged hard against the flat surface, his body squelching mine. My voice wheezes out, exhaling as he presses more air from my lungs. No way am I letting this go down without a fight.

"Shh. Shh. You're okay. It will be okay. Shh…"

All I can hear is his breathing, a ringing in my ears, while I'm choked by the stench of sulfur. My throat clenches.

"It feels better if'n you don't fight it, Joel. Lean into it. I'll learn you to love it."

Leading with my shoulders, I pivot with a jerk left and right, briefly breaking his hold for much needed air. I can't see anything in the dim shadows and absorbing darkness. I'm surprised by the gurgle crawling up my throat, and I'm screaming before I can make sense of what's happening. My elbows fail to find their target. Not enough to break free, anyway.

"Get off me!"

Panic joins the unspoken message firing in my brain: get away!

His massive arms pin and then bind me, immobile. I can't feel my wrists. Scrambling, I fight to break his grip. He shoves me so hard, I can't pull in air or get my hands to form fists.

He rips open the back of my shirt, and then I feel enormous hands gripping the waist of my pants. I'm lifted up off the ground until the seam finally gives way, and then I'm falling. My hands slip free and my fists and elbows swing with all the pent-up force I can muster, until I feel the wall giving way. A vague numbness wafts over me as I punch, kick and wrestle to get away.

"Better... nngh... when you fight it, Joel."

"Bastard."

I don't waste my energy on more words; I'd rather cling to silence.

If I could, I would crawl right out of my skin, leaving this bag of bones and organs, like my ripped clothing, in a heap at my feet.

I wish I couldn't feel the rhythmic jabs as they cut through each remaining inch of my body.

He doesn't stop, and neither will my fists.

***

In the morning, my arms feel tight, bound from the struggle of fighting to break free from his grasp. I can see the bandages wrapped around my hands and wrists, but my mind can't compute where they came from. Instead, I try to shake it off, but it lingers despite my best efforts to focus elsewhere—anywhere else. To forget how real that dream felt... a living nightmare.

I am determined to ignore the ache that throbs just below the surface and move on.

All through school, I'm antsy. Several classes add homework to the current heap. Mr. Castell pulls me aside at the end of English to give me more bad news. He eyes me strangely before proceeding.

"Joel, I need you to complete a portfolio assignment for me, to help pull your grade out of the failure zone. Since your transfer grade is so low, you need an extra-credit assignment to bring it up, or you'll still fail for the year no matter what your final quarter grade is. I have no other choice. Read all the poems in this packet the class completed before you came and write analyses of all 20, or write a collection of your own original poems using the poetic devices referred to in the packet. If you write your own poems, I will accept 12. Otherwise, I can't pass you for the year."

After Mr. Castell nails the lid on the coffin of my homework load, I skip out on my appointment with Mr. Faber and head to the library instead. The buzz in the hallway has to do with someone's attempted suicide. I can't deal with that right now. Once I'm safe in the library, I vaguely register someone passing out flyers for an upcoming regional poetry slam. I need air, but it's like I'm already underground, buried beneath these assignments.

I did find a few interesting books at my grandmother's house, but pretty slim pickings. I defer to my usual haunt and scrounge up a handful in short order. I don't remember taking one of those flyers. I tuck it in one of the books.

I catch a flash of red hair in the Writing Center. *Amber*. She's talking with her friend, the one who wears her hair up in scarves.

"Joel? What happened to you?" both girls echo in unison. They're staring downward. At what I can't tell.

"Nothing. I'm just drowning in homework. Listen. Do me a favor and don't come over to my grandmother's house. I'll take care of—"

She interrupts. "Joel, you can't just boss people around. I made a commitment to help her until the end of the year. You can take over after that, but I'm finishing what I started."

Amber's friend is looking at me funny. *What is everyone staring at?* Time to bail.

I blow off mandatory tutoring and head to Grandma's house. Might as well go three for three. I don't even go through the house, just straight up the driveway and into the garage. I promise myself I'll finish at least one project after dinner.

Most of the remaining boxes are an assortment of outdated clothing, books and one interesting box of war memorabilia. Too bad we don't cover the World Wars, or I could score extra credit for bringing in artifacts. Even after I sort through every book and look for other hints about my father's departure, I find nothing.

I box up everything by categories and report to my grandmother.

"I finished sorting all the boxes, Grandma. We can go to Goodwill now, if you like."

"Oh, have you now?" Old people humor. *Heh, heh.* I get it. She stares at me a good long time, her eyes tearing up for some reason. She reaches out to me tenderly before pulling away.

That makes me think a minute.

"You're not done with that project, Joel. Sorry to say. Now that you started, you're going to have to finish the whole thing. I still have a storage shed over at the farm house. Mrs. Porter owns it now, ever since I moved here. I'll have to get you the key, but it's all in there. Oh, and I think there's still some things in the attic. Maybe you can climb up and get them down for me?"

"Okay, Grandma. I guess I can keep going. Is there a lot more?"

"Not too much. But enough, I reckon."

"Well, what are we waiting for? Let's go."

"Let me get that key, and I think I have a bicycle you can use to ride back when you're done. It's not far. That way, I can finish dinner. You'll be on your own, I'm afraid."

"That's fine. I don't need any distractions to sidetrack me."

"That reminds me. I haven't seen Amber yet. Was she at school?"

"*Uh*, yeah. I saw her in the library. She looked pretty busy. Maybe we should get going."

"Such a nice young girl. Not like the rest of them, right?"

"Sure, Grandma. Sure."

We head in the opposite direction from the high school, out to the main road and then left. After a few miles, we're out of city limits into farmland. I remember the barn-shaped mailbox at the end of the dirt and gravel driveway. Split-rail fences line either side.

Edith and Horace Porter have been friends of the family for all the years I can remember growing up. Mr. Porter and my grandfather worked in the fields when the crops came in. Now it's just Mrs. Porter, and only the chickens to tend. She likes her eggs fresh. Grandma points out how it's all different since the last time we were here. The driveway hasn't changed, though. It's bumpy in all the places I remember, but Grandma is an expert at avoiding the potholes.

We turn in between the house and the barn, and I pull out the bike from the back. Grandma starts to back out then rolls down her window.

"Here's the key. Shed's around the side of the barn. Even though she's away, the house should be unlocked. We never locked it ourselves. The steps to the attic are at the end of the hallway, near the bedrooms. I'll see you back at the house."

Being here again brings back memories of Jonathan and me. We used to climb around in the barn loft, feed carrots to the horse, milk the cow with Grandpa, and chase the chickens around the yard, hearing their offended clucks amidst our laughter. At nightfall, we caught fireflies in canning jars and watched their tails light like the pulse of a lighthouse. We'd sit on the porch and listen to Grandpa tell stories, sipping sweet tea with sprigs of mint.

Sometimes, the coastal storms sent all the seagulls inland. We chased them around, squawking and flapping our arms, and then fell in the grass, exhausted but happy. When Uncle Steven was here, he took us fishing at the lake almost every day. I forgot there were times I felt more than alive. Those times were long ago.

The summer my father left... or got stationed far away. Wish I knew. I remember gathering night crawlers after sunset for bait. My brain floods with so many fond memories, yet I'm struck by another thought forming at the back of my mind.

The thought drives toward me from far off like a Mack Truck. It's too far to know what it is for sure. My senses pick up on it, though, and I'm uneasy. *No doubt it's nothing.* I can't push it out of my mind, though. Not completely.

I wish I knew what went on between my parents just before I saw my father load his bags and drive away. *Did they have a fight?* I don't remember raised voices or the electricity in the air when parents silently rage within range of children.

The boxes aren't going to sort themselves. I head to the shed and tug the padlock open. There are 15, maybe 20 boxes. Okay, so this isn't going to be too difficult.

When I open the first box, it's a jumble of papers, records, letters, information about the military; I realize this belongs to my father. A thought jumps in my head. *Does Grandma know? Is she setting me up here? Why would she purposely give me a project that has me sorting my father's things? In fact, why are his things here? Is this where they ended up? Why hasn't he come back?* Digging faster, I scan for something that might start to make sense.

I can't trust my mother to tell the truth. Maybe I can find something here. When my hand reaches the bottom of the box, my heart takes a nose dive beneath my feet. If it were anywhere, it would be here. *Where is it? What is this leading me to?*

Going through several other boxes, I find clothes—his "civvies." At least that's what I think he called them. I can't remember the last time I saw my father out of uniform. How odd I only realize this now. He was in the military forever. The next two boxes yield more clothes, then books, some old model cars and a box of dusty trophies. I don't remember my father winning anything, or even talking about winning. Maybe they're from his childhood. I don't know.

I gnaw on my lip. *Why does it stop here?* I've got to pick up this trail and see where it leads. *The attic!* I head for the house and leave the rest where it's at. I'll take care of it before I bike back.

The side door goes into a mud room and through to the living room. To the right, the kitchen is flooded with light coming through a bank of windows. To the left, the living room sits dark and empty. I see furniture, but not what I remember.

The Porters have their things here now. It seems strange somehow. As I look around the room, I mentally replace the furniture around me with what I remember used to be here: the couches, chairs, lamps, even the rocking chair off to the right and lace doilies on every table top—everything in its former place. Looking back at the kitchen, I recall the plastic-covered chairs my grandparents had and the metal legs of the kitchenette set. Grandma had a bench where she would sit and snap the ends of beans as she worked on supper, staring out the back. I haven't thought of any of this in over ten years, maybe…

***

I remember I sat in the rocking chair, but when I move to go sit in it, I realize it's no longer there. *Weird.* I keep seeing things the way they were in my mind's eye. In my memory, I had come to sit in the living room since it was cooler there. I sat in the dark and rocked in the chair for a long time.

Outside, I heard Uncle Steven mowing the yard. I could see him as he passed the back door—which was open; just the screen, keeping flies out. It was so hot, he had his shirt off and even so, he sweated terribly when he came in, the screen door slapping the frame. I remember the grains of dust—shaken from the screen door—falling down all around him as he stood in the doorway, wiping at sweat with the shirt in his hands.

"I'll be out in a bit. Gonna take me a shower and change."

I kept rocking. The front and back doors were open, giving me a nice cross-breeze to rock in. I watched some birds twitter away in the branches in the front yard. I don't know what they were doing, but watching them calmed me. I started to relax.

After a while, I got up and walked into the kitchen to look out the windows. I could see the chickens going in and out of their coop and the cat skulking around near the barn door. No one else was here, but I can't remember why. Just then, Uncle Steven called from further down the back hall. I guess he was already out of the shower and changing in one of the rooms.

"C'mere once-et, would ya?"

"Do you need something?" I hollered back.

"Just c'mere a sec."

I walked down the hallway. There was no way to tell where he was.

"Where are you? Which room?" I asked.

"In here." To my right. Just ahead. I turned to the right in the doorway, and the world tilted on its side and fell down around me in slow motion. Standing before me in the middle of the room was Uncle Steven—naked—his clothes cast off in a heap on the floor and his towel on the bed. I was frozen. Terrified. *What the hell?* Nothing made sense. The walls bent and started to go funny. Somehow, he reached way too far across the room and pulled me toward him.

"C'mere, I said!"

His arm gripped the back of my head and forced me down toward him. I cried out in pain as his hand wrenched at my hair. Right away, I gagged and started coughing. I was crying, coughing, gagging.

I didn't know what to do.

I put my hands up and tried to push at his waist to get him to let me go. I tried to scream with him thrusting in my mouth, but I only managed a gargling sound. The smell of sulfur burned my eyes. I was stunned by the warm liquid and the way he cried out and pulled away as I grimaced.

My hands fell to the floor as I reeled and spit out the gummy fluid. I looked up at him—angry, horrified, shocked, numb; tears made jagged cuts across my face.

"Why did you pee in my mouth?"

When I realized he didn't have a hold on me anymore, I scrambled up, wiped my mouth against my sleeve and ran. The room still swirled, and I had to put my hands out to find the walls. I can't remember how I got back down the hallway or out the front door. I just remember I threw it open and leapt down the steps with my heart beating fast and loud, and I thought it might rip right out of my chest, like the birds shooting out from tree branches.

Then I ran and didn't stop and didn't register anything other than running as fast as I could. *Get away. Get away. Now! Don't stop! He could be coming after you!*

Running through the cornfield, I watched as stalks beat against my face. I broke through row after row. I didn't want him to see me.

Maybe he could hear me, but I had to hide. I had to get away. I had to keep running.

I retched at the back fence that edged a horse pasture and riding trails. Ducking through the slats, I ran in the tall grass. Now that I was in the next field, I risked looking back once to see if he pursued me.

Pausing long enough to hear if there were footsteps bearing down on me, I exhaled when none came. Still, I couldn't be sure, so I turned and kept running. Under a copse of trees back by the riding trails, I stopped and caught my breath.

I was shaky, dizzy, and light-headed from the exertion. All of that was far away, happening to someone else. I couldn't feel anything anymore but the mechanical rise and fall of my lungs. Pinpricks across my face revealed tiny cuts from the cornfield. In the cool of the shade, I lay—chest heaving—sucking in air, letting it out, sucking in air again, like bellows.

But I couldn't get his taste out of my mouth.

WAKING

From the journal of Joel Scrivener

I realize I've been sleeping.
I bolt up, breathe like bellows.
In that breath my lungs
rattle, weigh me down to the floor.

It's all right. I kneel beneath the table,
knuckled, aware of heat and tears
my breath emerges. Perhaps my bones
turn to wood. In these moments

I knock against glass and rupture.
What do I see when I fear my reflection?
It is difficult to feel others, outside. I am ashamed
of tears. I will not speak the words swelled against

my skull. I break glass. I gather
my words or blink them back. I share
these surges with others, inside. Do you hear me?
Don't realize my eyes have opened.

33

A WORLD APART

I jolt up and look around, frantic, like he'll be on me any second. Then I sit up from the discarded-carcass position I'd assumed under the tree—half underground—wondering where this all came from, why did this have to happen to me? I hadn't simply run in my memory. I ran for real just now. I've been running for so long. Now what am I supposed to do?

No one's going to believe me. No one knows. This happened so long ago, what good would it do to bring it up now? Everyone's mad at me for flunking out this year. They'll just think I'm trying to get out of my responsibility. I must have made it up. I hallucinated.

I pinch my thigh. *Ow.* Nope, real.

I get up and jog, running in place. I make a few small circles, still running. I turn to the right, to the left. I don't even know where the hell I am. It must be late.

What is wrong with me? I'm dirty; I disgust myself. Now I'm a stain I can't scrub out. I stop, but sweat pours right through my shirt and sticks to my back. My senses go haywire. I must have short-circuited back there. Now, I malfunction.

I thought this was all about my father leaving. That's just the tip of the iceberg. What I've uncovered below the surface… I'm not sure I believe it myself. I've got to get back and see what time it is. I need to make it look like I've done enough of the work to head back to the house.

Grandma said it might take a few days to sort it all, so I can finish another day, when I'm not living my nightmares. I'll keep this quiet and try to figure it out. I won't tell anyone. I can't understand it myself.

Is this real? Did it really happen all those years ago? The whole family trusted Uncle Steven to watch us while Grandma had Grandpa at therapy and my mother had to work. She could have lived on base housing and used Dad's money, like he offered.

I head back to the farmhouse. I think I'm going in the right direction. These horse trails look familiar behind the farm, past the horse paddock. It looks late, so I jog.

Movement of any kind is better. Maybe I'm not completely numb. The breeze is good and helps to dry my shirt. Boy, do I need a shower. I still have to bike all the way back. And I've got a lot to think through.

Past the trails, I come to the horse pasture then the cornfield. I wasn't too far from recognizable things. This riding trail is how I used to reach the neighbor's farm, the one with the outhouse and the barn where the boy died.

I wonder if Uncle Steven was responsible. *Did it happen before or after me?* I slow down. *What if the boy died because I didn't stop Uncle Steven? What if it was my fault?* I'm doubled over before I realize my stomach is heaving. Dizzy, I cut through the split-rail fence and head right down the middle of cornstalk rows.

As I start toward the house, I'm agitated. *What else could I find?* I shudder from imagined scenarios. The house is empty, and I look around the living room for a clock. Nothing. In the kitchen, I see the stove has an old-fashioned clock, but the hands aren't moving; the sun hasn't set yet, so I'm pretty sure it's not 11:37am or pm.

It's a good thing Mrs. Porter is visiting family, but it feels strange, creeping around her house.

I sigh and head toward the hallway. My stomach flops and flips like someone who can't get comfortable in their bed. I guess this is my bed now, but I refuse to lie down again. Maybe one of the bedrooms has a clock that works. I need to get this over and done with. My skin twitches from the proximity, being near the place he forced me to give him head.

Maybe that's not what it's really called... I know it wasn't sex. What he did was hurtful, abusive. I didn't want that, and I tried to fight it.

I run to the bathroom and dry heave, trying to catch my breath when the waves pass. I turn the water on and rinse my face then cup my hand and suck in water to rinse my mouth. I remember the terrible taste. That was ten years ago. *Why must I remember? How does he still have this hold over me?* I want to pummel the shit out of something, only I don't have his face handy. I consider the barn. Maybe a hay bale or a burlap sack would suffice. A place to get this rage out of me—like a volcano erupting; purge myself of what he did.

Down to my toes, all the way to the top of my head, I scream loud and guttural, fuming with gurgling anger as my head pounds and my ears ring.

I scream until I'm spent.

I want to kill him. I hate him so much, I want to kill the bastard. I don't care. He should feel the way I do; he should be made to suffer. Then I'd be just like him. *How did I let this happen? What did I do to make him think I wanted that?* I sure as hell didn't ask for it. I wasn't even aware until—*gah!* I've got to get out of here.

I force myself to take deep, slow breaths in through my nose and blow out slow breaths through my mouth until I start to calm myself down. My hands scramble to find a wall to hold myself upright.

Bike to Grandma's house. Get the hell out of this dark cellar of horrors and shadows. I don't believe I can ever think well of the times I spent here. Not after this, not now.

There are two more rooms down the hall, one on both sides, and then the pull-down for the attic stairs. I find a clock in the bedroom on the left, where Mrs. Porter must sleep. It's digital so I think it's right. It's been almost two hours. I should at least check out what's in the attic to help cover my time.

To the right is the room where Jonathan and I slept. It's an office now, but I remember the bunk beds. Uncle Steven stayed in the guest room, back when the floor went out from under me...

***

The room is dark when I wake up, and his silhouette blankets the doorway. I freeze in the bed, hoping he will go away and not make me do anything else. I don't know what time it is. Jonathan is asleep below me. He still has side railings on his lower bunk. I make my eyes close almost all the way but look through my eyelashes at his dark form, outlined by the light in the hallway. *What is he doing? Please, just go away!*

He doesn't.

I scrunch my eyes and hold my breath. *I'm sleeping. I'm asleep. Don't wake me. Don't touch me.* He's near me, leaning in, since there's no side railing on the upper bunk. He pulls my covers back and then pulls down my pajamas. The next thing I know, his mouth, his tongue and saliva are on me. *He's doing it to me!* I concentrate on breathing, in and out, slow like I'm asleep. I can feel my toes cringing against the sheets, curling to get away. *If I'm asleep, he can't make me do any more, right? Breathe. Just breathe until it's over.*

Lie still, in my own coffin.

I don't know how long it takes. When he leaves, he doesn't even pull up my pajama pants or put the covers back. I hear him make terrible breathing noises. I turn my face into the pillow and muffle his sounds. The hall lights turn off. I hear him go back to his bed. He's in the next room, and I'm trapped. His spit is still on me. *Dirty. I'm dirty. Just like him. Why did he do that? I don't understand.*

I pull up my pants and burrow under the blanket, an angry crab, as far from light as I can get. I shove my body against the wall and tremble. My body convulses. I can't stop shaking. I bite my pillow to keep from screaming and swallow back the cry threatening to wreck me.

***

Where was my mother? Why wasn't she there? Why didn't she protect me from what Uncle Steven did? Is any of this real?

How many more times did it happen?

But she was there. With *him*. Right after my father left. Maybe that's why...

I don't have the luxury to lose my mind again. I slap myself hard. Twice. I can't come unglued like I did the first time. I have to get done and out of here, pretend this is all a bad dream, get to Grandma's, take a long shower, and go to bed. Maybe then I'll be able to wake up and it'll have gone away.

I pull the stair ladder down and flip the switch for the attic light. I climb up. When I reach the top, I peer in and see a few boxes sitting on a flat board that rests on the rafters. To the right and left are nothing but beams and rafters and insulation. Behind me are more boxes and, against a support beam, the fishing poles Uncle Steven showed us how to use at the lake. I thought there would be an orange Adventurer tackle box. I guess not. But the poles are there.

So that was real, too.

I have trouble telling which things are real and which are not. If I haven't lost my mind by now, I'm not sure how to keep myself from slipping off the edge, tumbling into the fathomless depths below. *I can't do this anymore.* I head back down.

I turn off all the lights, collapse the attic stairs and close the shed. Odd sounds and images play like a movie on the inside of my eyelids.

I've got to get back before Grandma notices I've been gone too long.

I jump on the bike and wobble-wheel my way down the bumpy driveway. I thunk in a few potholes and startle, like I'm on autopilot, as I make my way toward the level road. I'm clammy and shell-shocked; the blood might as well be drained out of me.

I pinch the cartilage between my nostrils with my fingernail and then slap my cheeks again for good measure. Still, I drift off in my mind, the way I used to when Uncle Steven came in to do more. I couldn't stop him; he was too strong and tall to fight off.

And the way he got off on the struggle. *Ugh!* So I found a different way to go absent from what he did. He took what he wanted then left me in a crumpled heap. I would climb in a boat in my mind and push as far away from shore as I could paddle. I watched him from the middle of the lake. I saw my body thrash or struggle and then go limp beneath him, watched as he pinned my arms down and slammed himself inside, over and over, until he cried out with a kind of broken, awful joy.

It hurt worse than any spanking, even the kind where one of my mother's loser boyfriends would break a wooden spoon or a switch on my bare ass. I felt it in the hollow of my pelvis.

A tearing, stabbing, bleeding, pointed pain.

I let it happen. I did nothing to stop it. How can I live with myself, knowing that? No one will do anything for me once they find out. Who even knows where he is by now? No doubt using another child somewhere. Is that my fault, too?

If I tell someone, won't I just go to jail? How sick is that? All those years are gone now. I should have reported it to someone who could have stopped him from hurting anyone else after me, but I didn't. Instead, I kept it to myself. *Maybe I deserve jail.*

I pedal and focus on getting to Grandma's so I can shower and sleep for a week. I'm relieved when I see the sidewalk and the city streets. I pass the sign to Oceanside and keep going. *Just a few more blocks.*

When I get in, my grandmother meets me at the door. A look of alarm flashes across her face when she sees me. She stares hard. Behind her, in the hallway, I see the hole, deep gouges from fists where smooth drywall once was. Where my fists fought hard against... him.

It takes a moment for my mind to make sense of what I'm seeing. *That was real?*

I hear myself gasp. "Grandma, I—" My throat seizes. Words fall away. She reaches out to hug me or keep me from falling down.

"Joel? Are you okay? You look deader'n Lazarus coming out of the tomb."

"I thought I dreamed that. I'm so sorry..."

She grips me tighter, pulling me in. I feel hot tears soaking into the shoulder of her blouse. "*Shh, shh.* It's okay, Joel. It's just a wall. It can be fixed."

"But I—" When I look up, I see words in a frame hung over the center of the hole. They read:

Refrain from anger and turn from wrath; do not fret—it leads only to evil. For those who are evil will be destroyed, but those who hope in the Lord will inherit the land.
—Psalm 37:8, 9

"Why don't you go get yourself cleaned up? You look terrible."

I don't even know where to begin. That's when I notice the bandages wrapped snugly around both my wrists again. They've been there all along, since the nightmare last night. It feels like it's been a week since then. *How did I miss that?* Grandma must've been there, too. She knows. And she took care of me afterward. *Was I sleepwalking?* "I'm really tired from the sorting and the bike ride. I need a shower. Then we can talk, okay?"

"You don't have to hurry or even finish, Joel. Take your time, if that's what you want." I smile weakly. Then I grab clothes from my room and head to the bathroom. I turn on the water, strip down, and unwrap the bandages. I can see my eyes go wide in the mirror as I hold up bruised and bloodied arms in front of me. My wrists are covered in torn, jagged skin, already scabbing over. I turn and step under the flow until I'm numb from the heat. I crank it all the way up.

After a while, it's almost cool, and I laugh at nothing in particular. Before I know it, I laugh and laugh. I can't stop myself, and I don't care. I shake my head wildly back and forth, the water spattering on the wall and shower door, and I don't know if I'll ever feel normal again.

THE FALL OF MAN

From the journal of Joel Scrivener

An empty room
    of an old farm house,
        down the hall began
            to turn in on itself.

A clogged drain,
    desperate to break free,
        a chugging spiral downward.
            A dance, really; darkened, elongated

movement.

His naked haste
    to call the boy here—
        there were words, certainly,
            but lost in screaming silence

of the reeling moment,
    rag doll thrown on the ground.
        Taking it in, the boy sputters and
            coughs, like on a cigarette toked too early.

He wants to vomit;
    instead, he gags and spits
        phlegm, fluid, mucus on the floor.
            The boy staggers, lurches, darts

from the room, the isolated farm house,
    the surrounding fields. Bright sun stabs
        into his eyes, what he has seen, tasted,

felt.

The screen door slaps
    the doorframe, shuddering.
        Humid haze presses the clouds down;
            he feels a shortness of breath, then, nothing,

numbness, a swallowing of the pill—a serpent's bitter fruit.

34

CLIMBING THE MOUNTAIN

When I come out of the bathroom, fluttering bandages trail behind me. Grandma's in the living room with the TV on, doing a crossword. Steam curls up from her tea. She gestures toward a cup to the left of the couch. I don't deserve any such kindness after what I've done.

"Can you help me with these?"

Her fingers start to work, placing and carefully wrapping my forearms, but not without turning them over, checking them with her glasses perched on her nose, and glancing up at me with tender eyes. My throat tightens.

"Must have been one heck of a fight," she prods.

"Do we have to talk about it? I'll just finish them myself." I start to leave, surprised by the harshness in my tone.

"No, not if you don't want to." She places her hands on the sides of each arm, tugging me back. "I know you're strong enough to fight it on your own, but you don't have to. It was your screams that pulled me from the bed last night."

"Grandma…" I can't put it into words. They're all jammed in my throat.

"Well, if you'd rather not talk, let's at least get some food in you." She heads to the kitchen, bringing her tea along. I follow, dragging the silence behind me.

This stuck place I'm in is too familiar, like the final box unpacked after a move; sometimes it's not ready to be unpacked, or we're not ready to face everything that's inside, so it sits there until we have to face it, one way or another.

I don't eat much at dinner, mumble something about not feeling well, and head to bed. Grandma lets me be. Not sure if I'm awake or asleep anymore.

I'm still raw from the farmhouse. Hollowed out. Gutted.

Somehow I get in bed and attempt sleep. After I spend what seems like hours changing positions, I accept it. Comfortable no longer applies. I'm too hot, I'm freezing cold; I quake under the covers and fling them off. All I have on are boxers and these bandages, but I'm still sweaty.

When I do get spots of sleep, my dreams are a montage of encounters. I cry out, but no one comes to help. This time I'm on my own. I should be used to that by now, but I'm not. Uncle Steven keeps using and discarding parts of me, and when he's done, the part of me that remains is beaten down like waves of an inky black sea, pounding the shore without end. When I wake, I'm relieved it's over, but my eyes are bleary and sore. I wipe tears away.

The last image lingers when I find myself awake: a large, heavy crow perched on my chest, its claws gripping for purchase on my torso. Not like a massage; like I'm being devoured. His talons tear into my flesh, voracious. Beady eyes follow me as he tilts his head into a question mark before pecking his beak into my mouth; I choke and cough until I discover I'm not being devoured by a crow from the inside out… It was just a dream.

I have the sensation of his weight upon me, pressing me down.

I'm worse off than when I went to sleep. Only the clock tells me it's time to get up and get ready for school. At this point I'm just going through the motions, so I fling my legs over the side of the bed and sit up. I'm not motivated to get up or get ready.

I can't sit here moping. I've got to face it. This has gone on long enough. If all I do is walk around in a stoic haze, he's won. I've got to find a way to muster up a fight, but all I want to do is lie down and sleep without the threat of nightmares. Somehow, I've got to put this away on some shelf in my mind, and pretend I never opened Pandora's Box.

That's what I tell myself, anyway.

I get dressed, grab my backpack and try for breakfast. My grandmother is a great cook, much better than my mother, yet I can't eat. I grab a piece of fruit and force myself to drink some juice. I accept the toast my grandmother insists I take.

"I hope I didn't push too hard, asking for your help with the project." She steers around the rest of what's unsaid. Still, I know she knows something is going on, and she's not going to let me avoid it forever. For now, I'll leave it where it's at.

"Thank you, Grandma. I'll catch up with you after school."

Since I'm not ready to talk, I head out to school. The weather is pleasant and nice, and I sense the beach calling. As I walk, I'm reminded of one of Amber's letters about when she was reading on the beach. I've got to get back there soon.

Thank goodness she wasn't around when all this happened.

I look at the bandages and remember: *wait. She saw them.* In the Writing Center. So did her friend who was with her. I guess maybe they were what she was asking me about then; I thought she was asking about the way I looked, weighed down by all my assignments. What if she sees me today and asks what they're for? I've got to come up with something. Even if she knows I'm lying. I've heard people talking in the hallway about a suicide. *Did they mean me? Is that why no one said anything about the bandages?*

I'm in my Spanish class, working on a food chapter, when I realize something else. *No one knows.* No one has noticed how awful I look today or that I didn't get any sleep. No one says a word about the bandages. I get a few strange looks but nothing else. I could keep going through this routine of school and work, of sleeping and getting up again, and no one would care.

Everyone is busy with their own stuff. They have their own worries to think about, their plans and hopes and dreams. What I've got are haunting memories that plague my waking and sleep. And even though I trudge through it all, no one around me could care less.

I know this happened. *What's the word?* Molested. While I would like to pretend it didn't or argue with myself into thinking it must have been my imagination, I know in my gut that it is as true as I am here, and I don't care what the names of fruits and vegetables are in Spanish.

I follow along, I listen and write things on the worksheets that we complete in groups, but my thoughts are elsewhere. *How did I get here? How did I waste this much of my life, running and hiding from this monster, too scared and too afraid to face it like a man?*

What does a man even do with this?

I remember hiding in the closet beneath the stairs, but I thought it was because my father had left. *Did I block it out? What was I hiding from?* I've wasted so much of this year, and if I give up, all I will do is let him defeat me again. I can't let that happen. I was too little to fight him back then. Now I'm big enough, I could take a stand. But what good would that do?

Then there's the question of talking to someone, seeing if the police can arrest him, and whether I should press charges. *Can I still do that?* I don't know. I don't want my family to know. I know that. I don't want anyone close to know. Especially Amber. *How can I continue to face all the questions that slam around the inside of my head?*

I can't tell if my counselor suspects something. *Will he ask the questions that will lead him to the truth, or stir up a confession from me?* Ms. Moore never figured it out, though, so maybe he won't either. I can't expect much from a counselor who sounds like everything he says came out of a brochure. *What else happened between Uncle Steven and me? Have I even remembered everything? Or is there more freak show that needs to work its way to the surface?*

I shudder.

The bell rings, and I head to chemistry and, after that, geometry. Today we're working in pairs. I sigh but try to follow the steps. Mostly, I rely upon the smart girls who make this look so easy. The one with hair down to the middle of her back is Osita Quiñones. She's from Puerto Rico. Fake it until you make it, right? Osita and I are partners.

A few times, I catch her staring at the bandages around my wrists. She attempts to form the words to ask, but she never says a word.

I've heard whispers that sound like "suicide" from groups around me. Maybe that's why no one dares to ask.

Flashes of memories come hurtling to the surface of my mind. One is from around the time that my father left. I was walking barefoot in the house and stepped on a nail without realizing until it had gone clear through, from the sole of my foot to the top. I howled and screamed, tears streaming down the sides of my face. My mother removed it and made me soak my foot in Epsom salts for a week.

Maybe I should get to the Writing Center and actually attend the mandatory tutoring I've been skipping the last few days. If I don't, I'll probably fail the upcoming geometry test. It's posted on the homework board at the front of the class. Not to mention, I'd like to get Mr. Castell off my case about it. I'm not sure I'm ready to face Amber. At least doing something will help keep my mind off these other memories.

I've opened the floodgates, and now the memories won't stop rising to the surface.

I'm struck by the sudden recollection of the taste of mineral oil. Every time I drank it, after waking up screaming from the "growing pains," I nearly gagged. I had to add lemon juice just to get it down. It was awful. The doctor said my colon was swollen. Now that I think of it, I realize it was probably not related to growing pains or from waking up, screaming as I sat upright in the living room chair. I suspect both are related to what Uncle Steven did.

I think Uncle Steven planted the nail. He used to do lots of strange things. He would beat my brother and me with his belt, whether we'd cleaned our room or not. He'd line us up against the wall and pace back and forth like a panther in a cage, slapping the belt across his left palm over and over again. I stood trembling against the wall, my hands instinctively hovering over my backside. I remember glancing at Jonathan, who was covering his ears.

"You two are gone git it," he said, pointing at his belt. "This here bowling ball and spikes needs to teach you boys a lesson!"

He shoves me from behind. His weight presses me to the floor.

"…You had this coming. Make a sound and you're dead…"

"…Not a word…"

"…Make a sound and you're dead…"

It was Uncle Steven. *Not* my father. And not Amber's father, either. Vertigo sends me reeling. I have to catch myself and take a deep breath. Exhaling slowly, I try to remain calm. I know I should be finishing up my geometry worksheet like the other pairs, but I can't force these thoughts from my mind. *There was a reason no one told me the truth about why I had to take the mineral oil.*

I don't know the word for it, but I know how it felt, and I know I started having accidents in my underwear from it. The first few times, I was terrified to find dried blood there, too. I was afraid to show anyone. The mineral oil was supposed to help.

But if the doctors knew, wouldn't that mean my mother knew as well? Did she know more and never told me? I'm knocked out by a wave of tingles and anger so sharp it could cut through this mountain rising up in my memories: everything I've held back or left unsaid between me and my mother. The mountain crumbles, burying me beneath its great weight. The overwhelming feeling toward my mother nearly doubles me over in my seat. I clench my jaw so tight, I think my teeth might shatter or meld together and never open again.

My mother knew the whole time and did nothing.

Osita looks at me funny, reaching her hand out toward me.

"Joel? Joel, are you okay? Joel?"

ASHAMED

From the journal of Joel Scrivener

Stand in
the dim room
sun goes down
on the child
who tries
to sleep before
his silhouette
slices forward
devours
like locusts
a boy
forbidden fruit
forced across
his lips
stained
with touches
he could
not refuse
until the day
came into
all darkened
places where
the boy
tried to wipe
away what
the man
left behind
or took
with him
leaving a trail
of glittering
empty skins
trembling

35

I HATE COUNSELORS

Next up, I have my appointment with Mr. Faber. Somewhere far off I hear remnants of an echo, like someone calling my name over and over. It's happening again. Soon, everyone at Oceanside will know. I might as well be dragged away in a straitjacket.

When the bell rings, I climb out from beneath the rubble of the mountain, dust myself off and trudge off to guidance. *What the hell is wrong with me that my own mother would do that and hand me over to him?* I check in with the guidance secretary.

"Mr. Faber will be right with you," she says pleasantly, as if the world weren't full of mothers who lie and betray their sons. Bearing the weight of an entire mountain has done nothing to abate my anger. I may never forgive her. My molars grind against each other as I clench and unclench my jaw. *I never want to speak to her again.* It's not enough.

And what do I do about spacing out in geometry class? Will they figure it out? Someone besides Osita had to see what happened. *Will they start whispering about me as I walk by?* It's like Broad Run all over again.

When I'm called back to Mr. Faber's office, I walk with brutal, echoing steps along the short hallway. I enter, cross to the sitting area, and flop in the empty chair, catty-corner from Mr. Faber's.

"Joel, welcome."

I nod, look down.

"Rough day?"

"You could say that."

"Anything you want to talk about?" I watch his eyes glance down toward my bandages.

I shake my head.

"Well, the last time we spoke, you were upset about the idea of meeting with your father. I can understand your reluctance to open up old wounds, so I have cancelled those plans permanently."

I turn and look up at Mr. Faber.

"I was wrong to set up a meeting without getting your permission first, Joel. I am sorry. I hope you will forgive my ineptitude."

"I don't answer things I don't understand."

Mr. Faber laughs. "It means I was not being a good counselor. I got ahead of myself. I was wrong."

"Oh."

After a pause, he says, "Joel, can I ask you another question?" *Here it goes*.

"I guess."

"Would you tell me why you think you're here to see me, beside the fact that it is a condition of passing the tenth grade?"

My insides cringe. *Do I look stupid enough to fall for this?*

I wonder how long I'll have to keep coming to these appointments. Probably until Mr. Faber thinks he's made some kind of progress. I'd rather be at the beach, climbing out on the breakers or searching for shells beneath the dock. Anything's better than this. Better give him an answer or the appointment will never end.

"Well, to help me, I guess. Figure out some things I'm having trouble with." *Did I just read that from a cue card?*

"I certainly hope you find these visits helpful. Of course I would like to help you with some of the things listed in your file. But it's more than that, Joel."

I nod, unsure of the punch line. My mind has moved on to the boardwalk, running barefoot down the dunes that pull at me the way the moon draws the tide.

"Joel," Mr. Faber begins again, "am I correct in assuming the behaviors of most adults often leave you... baffled?"

"Yeah." I try to sound unsure of my answer, but inside I'm screaming so loudly, I imagine the blood rushing to my face, making my veins pop out.

"Do you know any adults you can trust?"

Nope, none whatsoever.

"My grandma and my Uncle Brandon."

"When you think of the word 'trust,' what do you mean?" *He must know what a loaded question this is.* I give him the party answer.

"They're not trying to get something out of me or hurt me."

"Have there been adults who have hurt you?" Heat on my face warms my cheeks to some shade of red. I must be part chameleon. "You don't have to tell me who. Just yes or no is fine."

"Then, yes."

"I take it you haven't figured out whether you trust me enough to share more about that?"

I nod. My eyebrows go up. *Duh!*

"Fair enough." Mr. Faber looks around like he's just remembered something. "Are you hungry, Joel?"

I shrug. He doesn't even realize how similar that is to a con Uncle Steven used to pull, directly followed by a beating. And then…

He looks at me funny. "Excuse me for a moment." As he flips through my file, I pick at my cuticles. I'd rather be down by the water on the beach with the waves washing over my toes, pulling my feet down in the sand.

"Would it make you feel better to know the snacks are in sealed packaging? Or are you just not hungry?" *Nice try.*

"No, it's just—" I don't know how to put my thoughts into words. *Guess I'd better explain.* "Someone said that, and then they hurt me."

"I see. We can pass on the snacks. They're not important. I'm not here to hurt you, Joel."

"Okay." *What are you here to do to me? I mean,* for *me.*

"I spoke with Ms. Moore, and we have a few short tests to complete your full evaluation. You can sit here or over at the table. I'll take them when you're done."

I stay where I'm at and fill out the forms. I'm tempted to blow off the test but continue answering questions. At least here, the people who are taking care of me actually do their job. Starting over won't remain an option if I screw up again. Mr. Faber interrupts.

"I know our time is about up for the day. Listen, the Writing Center contacted me. They told me you were a no-show for the last two days. I need to hear back from them that you're attending those tutoring sessions. I'll see you tomorrow." He starts to write some notes in his files on me. I must have done something right.

"All right, I'll go today. I need the help, anyway."

"Good. Glad to hear it."

36

WRITER'S CRAMP

When I get to the Writing Center, it's not too full; maybe six students working with tutors. *Who else is here because they have to be?*

I sit at a vacant table and wait for the next available tutor. Meanwhile, I pull out my math homework and English writing portfolio. Screw math; I work on a poem. My mind is all over the map, but I can sense the seed of an idea forming. I try using the cluster method Mr. Castell suggested. I write down words, draw ovals around them, and use connecting lines to link them without focusing on the connections.

"Why are you here?" I hear from a familiar voice. Turning around, I see the connection. *Amber.* I asked her the same thing in my grandmother's back yard.

"I have to be here. It's mandatory. What about you?"

"Oh, I'm a volunteer. It's for an internship I want to get into next year. I do this and the Poetry Club. I'm trying for an Ivy League school, and that process starts now."

I saw her talking with her friend the other day, but I had no idea she worked here. The more I get to know about Amber Walker, the more I know she's beyond my reach. If she's going off to an Ivy League college, she's looking for a doctor or lawyer type. My biggest aspirations are to write and get published. Maybe read at a poetry slam. I have as much of a chance to impress her as I do of identifying a new mathematical theorem or identifying something smaller than a quark. I'd better ask for help with chemistry while I'm at it.

"I need help with geometry and chemistry. I have a test soon."

"Joel, did something happen to you? Are you okay?"

"What, my bandages? Nah, it's nothing. Just fightin' the bad guys. I'll be okay."

"Is it bad?" She looks me dead in the eye.

"Honestly? Sometimes, it is. It really is. But I'm fine now. Really."

"You take care of yourself, Joel." She leans over and gives me a hug, whispering, "We all have things we keep to ourselves. I'm praying for you."

"Uh, thanks." I don't know how else to respond.

"There are several tutors here. I'll see who's up next on the rotation." She turns to leave, checks her cell phone, and excuses herself, saying, "I'll be right back."

After a few minutes, while I'm working on the poem again, wondering if words on a page might get her attention—I look around—hopeful. *Is Amber a tutor? Would she seriously help me?* Amber is one of the few people in the world who knows me, with all of my family troubles and ups and downs over the years; if there's anyone I want to talk to right now, it's her. Although I'm not ready to say anything about Uncle Steven—I may never be. Which reminds me: I never asked her what happened with her stalker. Everything's been so messed up, I haven't had time to ask.

A question startles me from my thoughts.

"Are you Joel? Amber said you needed help with math." I nod. The girl is attractive; she's the one who was with Amber the other day. She has thick, glossy hair pulled back in a flowered silk scarf, medium skin, and smoky eyes. She's rockin' the nose ring, too.

"Is, *uh*, Amber coming back?" I keep thinking about the hug and what she said. *Maybe…*

"Oh, I don't think so. Her boyfriend just came to pick her up. You're that guy with the… bandages." A flash of recognition washes across her face.

I look down at my wrists, even though I know they're there. I can feel my skin itching beneath. I look back up. She glances nervously away. *What did she say?*

"I can't believe she's already dating a senior. It's only her freshman year. My name's Padma." She sits down, setting a leather bag on the floor next to her.

"I see." I try to hide the disappointment in my voice.

"I think I can help you with… geometry, was it? Anything else?"

"Well, besides this poetry portfolio I have to write to pass English, I could use some help with chemistry." I can't help myself. I keep looking around for Amber, like she'll come back if I will her to do so.

"Not many boys I know write poetry." Padma rakes her hair across the back of her neck into a silky twirl between her fingers and holds it over her left shoulder. *Now I remember: I've seen her do the same thing in the cafeteria, like she's trying to keep her hair out of her lunch.* Only, here, it's because she's concentrating on something. That and she was the one passing out flyers for the regional poetry slam the other day. I wonder if she's involved.

After an awkward pause I say, "Maybe we should get to work," and Padma shifts from introductions to reviewing my geometry terms for the test. Only, I can't concentrate. Well, I can concentrate, but not on what I'm supposed to.

Instead, I think sine refers to the heart shapes Amber and I might draw in the air, the letters we write to each other, and how those could be more like love notes. I imagine opening scented envelopes from Amber, addressed in her perfect cursive with hearts over all the "I's" and arrows over all the "T's". When I think of tangent, I picture us leaving the Writing Center and heading down to the beach to hold hands along the boardwalk. Cosine makes me think of buying a car together, dating, going exclusive. For a guy who's got no chance now that Amber's spoken for—with a senior, no less—I don't know where any of this comes from and why it comes so suddenly, but I'm in no shape to do anything about it. I need to heal first.

"—Are you even listening to me?" Padma is asking as she plays with her hair scarf.

I nod, a shock of embarrassment spreading across my face.

"I mean about these terms. Just remember SOHCAHTOA, and you'll be fine." I think she rolls her eyes, maybe tucking a smirk behind her ear. *What is that supposed to mean? Does she know something about Amber and me?* I'm confused. Instead of saying anything about her body language, I work on getting through the sample problems for each side of the right triangle I'm studying. We finish with the Pythagorean Theorem. I think I'm ready.

"Is there something wrong?" she asks.

"No. Why do you ask?"

"You seem awfully distracted since Amber left. Do you like her or something?"

"Uh, not exactly."

"I see. You mentioned a poetry portfolio. Well, if you think you've got poems worth sharing in front of a crowd, we practice weekly, on Thursdays." Which reminds me...

"Can I still sign up for the poetry slam?"

"Actually, all the slots are full, I'm afraid. Maybe next year." *Damn.*

She looks around and then leans over, whispering next to my ear. "You should probably know her boyfriend's about to ask her to senior prom. If you were planning on making a move, you might've just missed your chance." Padma stands and excuses herself. "Good luck on the test." I couldn't have heard her right. *I'm too late.*

My insides suddenly slam down to the bottom of my toes with nothing left to hold them up anymore. They cramp up from the strain. I'm dashed among the rocks by an unforgiving ocean, finally reaching the shore of reality. I cover my head with my arms, wishing the table beneath me was a hole I could bury my head in or an ocean that could drown me and finish off the job.

ABOVE THE WELL

From the journal of Joel Scrivener, included in a letter to Amber Walker
John 5:4

Most days I wander thick fields,
watching sharp movements of the pine.
I cross the fence through waist-deep grass,
keep pace under boughs still wet with rain.
When the storm hits cold stones below
my feet smell like wind stirring the water.

What pinches the switch of my soul?
Such marks feed heat like hot scraps
of desperation raging the storm.

The branch comes crashing down, tangles itself
in the fence. My hands hurry to build an earthen ladder
from the remains, wrestle God against the open spaces,
throw down language from a new Babel.

A dry thirst pulls up from the well an ocean,
a puzzle with missing pieces, and questions
we've never been brave enough to regret.

The earth grips cracks near the well
in deep rock where mud salves my eyes;
I climb an inner rope to sight,
yet here I am clinging to the earth.

What do I hope for in the depth of the well?
Sometimes the ocean stands from its stone valley,
stretches, curves up over breakers where I now
crouch, watching seaweed curl, spread out like needles
around a fire. Here, small crabs, angry and clambering
stomp back beneath the rocks away from light and eyes.

37

STORM FRONT

Over the next few weeks, I buckle down and focus on completing my daily schedule. I can't block out every whispered comment at school, but it helps to be doing something. I've lived more than half my life without the full knowledge of Uncle Steven, and I'm determined to live the rest of it without letting him overtake my thoughts, haunt my dreams, or keep me under his hold.

Some days are easier than others.

After finishing the sorting job at the Porter's house, including the attic and the shed, I load what I've sorted from my grandmother's garage into her car. Then Grandma takes me over to the farmhouse to get the remainder, and we bring it to Goodwill. I'm glad to be done with this chore. It's a weight lifted to be moving on. I hope the next one isn't as traumatic.

One day, in English class, Mr. Castell calls me up to his desk while the class works on our study guide for the play.

"Joel, I want to talk to you about your writing. I know you've been working on the poetry portfolio, and you've turned in a few poems for me to check your progress."

"Yeah, I'm not sure poetry is my thing. I can't think of some of the rhymes."

"That's just it. Maybe the reason you're struggling is because you're trying to make it something it's not. If your poetry is structured in free verse, don't try to nail it down into the form of end rhyme."

"So, I don't have to make it rhyme?"

"No, you don't, and I want you to write it the way it comes out. Just let it happen. Free verse has its own structure, too. Use the other poetry devices from the packet to give it form and function. Rhyming doesn't make it poetry."

"Okay, I'll give it a try."

"Let me see how it turns out when you're not trying to butcher it. And maybe you should join the poetry slam that's coming up."

"I already talked to Padma. She said all the slots were filled for this year's team."

"Well, you're in luck, because there's a slot open from what I've just heard. There's been a last minute cancellation."

"I'll ask about the opening at tutoring."

As I stand, I feel my gut plummet. I don't know if I'll ever make it as a writer. I can't even impress my English teacher. *Does he have any idea how long it took for me to come up with some of those poems?* Now I have to start all over. I spend the whole afternoon in the Writing Center, trying to hammer out one poem without forcing the rhyme. At least I kept my initial outlines and cluster webs, so I don't have to start from the beginning.

Padma confirms there has indeed been an opening. After looking at my poems, she encourages me to come to practice. I'm not sure; I need to clear my head.

After school, I take the bike and head to the shore, away from my grandmother's house. Even though it's cloudy and somewhat windy, I am determined to get to the ocean. Not many others are out. I see some other bikers, a man run-walking his dog on a leash next to him, and a woman walking in what looks like a winter coat. *Did she not get the memo it's spring?* I find it funny how the locals act when the temperature is slightly off from perfect beach weather.

I prefer it like this, overcast with the ocean churning away on the edge of a storm. There's a tangible charge to the air; the hair on my arm stands up on end. Out at sea, I spot a ship cutting through the green frothy waters. After parking my bike, I head down from the boardwalk, peel off my shoes and socks, and drop them in a spot at the top of the hill. Then I head down to the edge, where the waves collapse into the sand, each a fervent, tiny death of its own.

I can feel something coming.

It reminds me of the sensation of drowning. As I walk along the shore, watching the tide come in, I notice the beach stretches as far as I can see in either direction. Behind me, the boardwalk is deserted. Before me, the huge ocean crashes, reminding me how small and insignificant I am. Above me, the clouds press together and darken, reflecting the water, seething and tumbling below. This is nothing like Amber's letter, when she read her Bible at the beach and found God, unless He's pissed at me.

Along the horizon, I watch the ship moving slowly in front of me. I hear a crackle before the first of several lightning bolts flash and rip across the sky. The clouds open, and a heavy torrent of rain slams like needles into me, the water and the sand all around. No matter what I do, I'll be soaked, so instead I stretch out my arms and surrender.

***

Once, when Uncle Steven was watching Jonathan and me, he was angry and yelling at me for something. I can't remember why. We were in our grandparents' living room. The television might have been on. I just remember him grabbing me by the hair and dragging me down the hallway. My brother screamed and covered his head with a pillow. I watched him cower on the couch as I was dragged toward the bathroom.

Uncle Steven shoved the curtain aside and turned on the shower full blast. As I pleaded for him to stop, to *please let me go, I'm sorry, I'm sorry, I won't do it again, just let me go,* he gripped me by the hair and held me under the water until I was drenched through my clothes.

Next, he took me to the bedroom and bent me over the edge of the bed to give me a beating, or so I thought. He yanked my pants and underwear down as I sobbed into the blankets. I was beyond the thought that words could help me at this point. I stiffened, waiting for the first spank, but instead I felt his hand, wet from something, rubbing between my legs and up my backside. Then I knew.

He entered, tearing into me. It felt like the largest bowel movement I could ever have, and each thrust tore a little more. My face was shoved into the blankets, but I could hear him huffing and wheezing behind me, finding a rhythm, a strange urgency to his haste. When it was over, I lay there, pants around my ankles, my clothes heavy from water, and I wondered if the rawness—the burning pain—would ever go away.

***

Now, standing at the ocean, I face every drop with arms raised, fists and jaw clenched, and a scream rises up from somewhere deep and painful, shattering me to the bone. I realize I'm crying, but I don't care. This kind of rawness took a long time to surface, the storm itself drawing it out of the ocean depths. I scream again and again, until I can't hear myself over the pounding in my ears.

Eventually, the rain subsides and slows, calming me. I sit on the hill, up far enough to stay out of the rising tide. I look for the boat and realize it's gone from sight. I am alone on the beach, with black thoughts and painful memories.

Strangely enough, I'm better after being soaked, hollowed out by screams, and sobbing until the rain has washed away any lingering tears. I wipe my face, but it doesn't matter. The rain hasn't stopped completely. I stand and walk.

My grandmother must wonder where I'm at. I stop at a bench on the boardwalk, put my shoes back on, then walk my bike toward Grandma's house.

Does any of this make sense? I can't tell which end is up or if I'm moving in the right direction. Words swirl in my mind, churn like the sea. I feel an urgency to capture this, share it, to release what has been pent up for too long. This is not meant for me to carry alone. *I've got to tell someone. But who? How? Where do I even begin?*

When I get home, Grandma scolds me for getting caught in the storm, but she's glad I'm okay. She sends me to the shower and heats water for tea. We sit in the living room when I'm clean and dry, sipping together.

In my gut tumbles a surge of energy, as if I drew in the charge of each lightning bolt while I screamed beneath the storm. I feel it wriggle around, a powerful force rising like a tide inside of me. I know what I have to do—I need to write; sort it out on paper before I lose my mind.

"How's the tea, dear? Warm enough?"

"It's wonderful, Grandma. Thanks."

We sit together and listen to classical music. Afterwards, I stay up half the night writing poem after poem, like a dam has burst and the words tumble out from a well I never knew was there before. My hands shake with their own electricity as I write, sometimes faster than I can keep up with.

I stay up and write until every word has found its way to the page, and then I realize I know how to take back what he stole from me.

WHERE THE MIND FINDS THE HIDDEN

From the journal of Joel Scrivener

Along the shore
beside the sea,
I step from rock to rock,

the cold and spray
fog rolling in.
Seaweed peels

off the dock,
glazed figurines
sinking to their graves.

The sand is burdened,
my clothes are drenched by
the great gray fog snail of the ocean.

Out on the sand surrounded
by the pathway of shorebirds,
the houses are weathered, brittle,

dun-colored children
clustered in the wet sand.
What instinct harbors a migration?

We each hinder the step our souls take
trudging through this hidden dance
when the tide is out, and the sand

glistens with its own inner light.
I wait there, torrential and damp,
for the waves.

38

SHIFTING TIDE

A few weeks later, I try calling my brother when I know my mother isn't home. It takes a few tries, but Jonathan finally answers. When I hear his voice, I'm struck by a pang of homesickness. *What would make me want to go back to that dingy trailer/coffin?*

"How's it going, flying solo with Mom and all?"

"I'm all right. I can handle myself. At least until recently."

"What happened?

"One of the girls I was seeing at Sanderville started talking. To her cousin. Her cousin is Elise Stone from Broad Run."

After a pregnant pause, I say *"Uh-oh."*

"Yeah. *Uh-oh* is right. They started comparing notes and figured out my game. Now everyone's on to me. I got shut down by a girl."

"That's rough. So now what are you up to?"

"Nothing. Literally, nuh-thing." I have to stifle a guffaw.

"How so?"

"The girl from Sanderville told her mom, and she called our mom, so I'm grounded for all eternity, pretty much."

"That sucks, man."

"Yeah, well. It was fun while it lasted."

I want to tell him something, but I'm not ready to share what Uncle Steven did. He should know I found stuff out about our father. I wonder what he remembers; he was pretty young. I decide to broach the subject.

"Uh, Jonathan. I found out something about Dad. Did you know he left because he was sent on an isolated tour in the military?

Mom said he just left us, but I have a letter he wrote that says different."

"I thought he didn't want anything to do with us. It was so long ago. I don't remember much. Did I tell you Dad's called a few times? Outta nowhere. And he's planning to visit soon."

"No, you didn't. He almost came here, too, but I stopped him."

"That's harsh. Sure you don't want to see him? It might help you remember stuff from back then."

"Speaking of, I found the fishing poles. The ones Dad bought for us to go fishing before he up and left. Remember that farm with the windmill? There was a park where we went with a lake."

"How'd you find those?"

"I'm helping Grandma with a few projects. Trying to pass tenth grade, otherwise I have to repeat it. So, I'm going hard and helping where I can."

"I bet you're a helper. How's that girl you wrote all those letters to?"

"Amber? She's here. She helps Grandma, so I see her sometimes, but she's got a boyfriend already. I think he's a senior. Trust me, she's not interested."

"Tough break."

"I have other things to take care of anyway. If I want a chance with her, I've got to get myself together. Right now, she's moved on. Listen, I've gotta go. I'll talk to you soon."

After I get off the phone, I ask Grandma if I can ride down to the beach. I seem to be going there a lot lately. It's a good distance for a bike ride, and it gives me time. I don't even have to pay attention to where I'm going anymore. I could get there blindfolded.

The weather is always nice, and the boardwalk traffic has started to pick up. The beach isn't too crowded, at least not with all the tourists. Not yet. Locals call them "bennys." It stands for where most of them come from, but it's not always a nice term. In fact, some people use it like a swear word. That's another thing I'm working on. I'm trying to clean up my language and speak without cursing. *Will Amber even notice if I do?*

Occasionally, I let one fly, but I've curbed it way back from what it used to be.

I've been talking more with Mr. Faber. I swear he's brainwashing me with his brochure-ese. I haven't told him what I found at the farmhouse, but I think I'm ready. Writing it down helped me get control. Now it's just words on a page, something I created. Maybe if I share it, others can get something out of it.

I ride along the boardwalk and stop to watch someone flying a kite. There's enough wind; not sure if the shape of it is the problem. After a few minutes of struggling, the kite is airborne, and I catch myself smiling as it swoops and swirls through the air. I might even be happy. *How did that happen?* I keep going then turn back a few streets before the end of the boardwalk and start to head home.

I start humming a tune I overhear from a convertible I pass; it's one of those catchy, summery tunes that's just good and wholesome. Positive message. I could use more of that, so I hum along. I need to let music back into my life. I've gone through a long, dry desert with no sound, just the wind whipping like the inside of a shell.

That's when I hear someone calling my name. I stop and turn around. Stepping out from a nearby vehicle is Elias Stone wearing a tie-dye tank top over khaki shorts. "Joel! It *is* you."

"In the flesh." My mind is reeling, wondering what made our paths cross here, of all places. Elias signals the person driving to wait a minute and points at a vacant parking spot along the boardwalk. I step off my bike and flip the kickstand.

"Who would've thought we'd see each other again at the beach?"

"I know, right?" *That is pretty weird... now that he mentions it.*

"I stopped by your grandmother's house looking for you. She said you'd be down here along the boardwalk. I guess she was right."

"Why'd you come all the way out here?"

"Oh, I'm going to an event nearby. Maybe you've heard of it? The annual Pride Celebration." He nods his head toward the driver. "My friend invited me, and Jonathan said you were staying out here with your grandmother, so I looked you up."

"Does that mean you've come out?"

"What do you think?"

"I guess so."

"The question is, what are you going to do about it?" He steps toward me.

"Elias, I haven't…"

"You haven't, or you won't?" He sounds upset.

"I don't know. I haven't figured that out yet."

"Tell me you never felt anything between us."

"That's not the point."

"Why not? Be who you are, man. Not who they tell you to be."

"Is that what you said to Jonathan? How'd he take it?"

By Elias's sudden laughing spurt, I'd venture it didn't go as planned. "I guess he'll have to get used to it."

"Good for you," I reply.

"Why do you say that?" The way he's looking at me, I can tell he knows with certainty.

"Because you know who you are."

"And…?"

"I wish I knew myself like that, but I don't. Not yet, anyway. I'm still trying to figure things out." Elias may have known about my nightmares through the YouTube videos, but not what caused them.

"Look me up when you do."

"All right. Enjoy your celebration."

"I will. Good to see you, man. I'm glad I found you." He embraces me, and I hug him back. He looks me in the eyes, and I stare back, caught momentarily by all the thoughts we've left unsaid. *I wish I knew how I felt.* When he's driven off, I climb back on my bike and spend some time lost in thought.

It's dark by the time I return home. Grandma shakes her head at me before saying goodnight.

I've started having normal dreams again. The best thing so far about writing, other than getting that stuff out of my head, is the nightmares are gone. I haven't had one in at least two or three weeks. I think they're finally going away.

Then I realize I'm going to make it through this. I'm not a victim anymore.

39

CHAIN REACTION

My portfolio is due today. I have it set out on the desk Grandma let me move into the bedroom. I have a few minutes, so I read through to see if it's as terrible as I remember. Instead, I'm startled. *Did someone else write these?* I may have pulled it off. Hopefully it helps me pass tenth grade. That's on Mr. Castell now.

Maybe if I change the order, it will read better. Twenty minutes later, I'm still fiddling with papers. Better put it together and let it go. It's time to move on. I head for the shower. *Is it too late to ask Grandma to bake something?* I'm not above bribery.

Grandma's well into the morning paper when I come to breakfast.

"Good morning, Grandma."

"Good morning. Sleep well?"

"Yep. My portfolio's done, and I'm coming into the home stretch. I might even pass tenth grade if I'm lucky."

"It will take more than luck to do that, but I trust you'll do fine. You're not the same boy who came here a month ago. I've noticed changes. Have you?"

That stops me for a minute. *How long has Grandma been watching me?* Maybe Jonathan came by his sleuth skills more honestly than I realized. Grandma seems cut from the same cloth. I'd better watch myself before I give too much away.

"When do I get to read your portfolio?"

"After Mr. Castell grades it," I say, grabbing food and heading for the door. "I'd better get going or I'll be late. Have a good day, Grandma."

"You too, Joel."

When I get to school, I head right for Mr. Castell's room. I want to get it over with, turn it in before anything happens. I've worked too hard for it to get crumpled, lost, or messed up. Mr. Castell is surprised to see me before class.

"Hello, Joel. Is this what I think it is?"

"My portfolio. Finished. Glad it's over, I think."

"Not entirely sure?"

"Until you grade it, no. See you in class," I say, heading to homeroom. Now that it's in, I try to stop thinking about it, but I'm easily distracted in American history class. I'm not alone.

All the students can talk about is the Underclassman Formal. When Mrs. Dixon writes due dates for an upcoming assignment on the dry erase board or gives us PowerPoint notes on the Smart Board or finishes up with group work for us to complete, whispers crisscross behind her. Notes are passed, stealthily. The class pretends to listen, but they continue to talk about who's going with whom, what they're wearing, and whether they're going to go in on a limo together. *Can't they wait until their actual prom to blow money like that?*

I'd groan out loud, but there would be no point. Not everyone is going, so I'm not entirely alone. I try to concentrate on the Great Depression, Rockefeller's reaction to the Wall Street crash, and Roosevelt's "Fear Itself" first inaugural address, but instead I just become greatly depressed.

Should I try to get a date to the dance? I wouldn't even know who to ask. The only person I want to ask hates me, and I'm sure her perfect senior boyfriend has already asked her to his prom. *Why would she slum with me at the Underclassman Formal over senior prom?* I can hardly wait for tutoring, where I'm sure I'll have to hear all about it in great detail. Padma will spill if Amber's not there to share the deets. *Maybe I should skip today.* I haven't missed in weeks. Now that my portfolio is in, maybe I can ask to be let out of the Writing Center for good behavior.

***

A week ago, on my way into the library, I nearly walked right into Amber's Sasquatch. He has six inches easy on me, dark wavy hair, and clearly pwns a regular workout routine. The dude is built. Either the ground around me became quicksand or I shrank in his presence.

I ducked back around the corner before I saw Amber run up and jump up on her tiptoes to give him an enormous hug. I watched as they kissed. My stomach plummeted.

"Darren! How'd you get off work? Wait, let me get my things and you can tell me everything."

I don't know why I keep trying to repair things with Amber. I've got no chance to surpass this guy. He'd squish me between his fingers.

When I jetted from my corner spot to slip past the happy couple and into the library, my weakling Joel body beaned off Darren's muscled brick wall.

"Hey, watch it, dude."

"Sorry, *uh*, my bad."

I scraped myself off my knees and grabbed my bag off the floor where I'd stumbled, and then I bolted for the back, silently wishing a wormhole would open up and swallow me.

No such luck.

"That's the one you were so heartbroken over?" He starts to laugh.

"Darren!"

"No, seriously. I can't believe you were ever into that guy."

My eyes go wide. I can see Amber glancing my way.

"I told you not to bring that up." He's pleased with himself. Amber crosses her arms, looking right at me.

"Is that really true? What he said? I thought you said you'd never— So why did you—?"

Her eyes shimmer. "Joel, I—"

"This doesn't make sense..." *Why won't she come out with it and end it already?*

Her voice hardens. "And neither do you. You can't even find your voice long enough to spit out one coherent sentence."

"I do. I did." My mind crunches data, scrambling for a solid example. "All the things I've written..."

"That's not enough. I'm not one of your characters you can control. You can't pin me down on the page with your words. I'm here. Be here. Now."

I'm held in the grip of silence. I might as well have no mouth.

"When it comes down to it, you shut down and say nothing. I'm done with guys like that."

"That's my girl," he says to her, and then to me, "I like 'em feisty."

"Let's go. Enough's been said." As she walks away, Darren's arm presses gently in the small of her back, she tilts her head to the side and says, "And unsaid," leaving me alone in my silence.

***

In English, Mr. Castell calls me over as soon as I walk in the room. I'm instantly nervous and hope it's not bad news. I brace for impact.

"Joel, I read through your portfolio during first period. I was amazed at the quality of your writing."

Mr. Castell makes such a large pause, I'm waiting for the "but" to negate everything he's just said.

"Due to the content, I had to make a few phone calls. One to Mr. Faber, who needs to meet with you right now. And one to a professor of mine from university. He's the head of the English department, and with your permission, he is willing to accept poems from your portfolio as a late entry in this year's Secondary School Poetry Prize contest. I hope you don't mind my sharing your work. My professor was quite impressed. I faxed him a preview."

"You did what?" I'm not sure whether to be proud or angry. Some of the poems are personal. I don't know if I want to enter a poetry contest. This could stir things up worse than they were at Broad Run.

Mr. Castell does not expect me to be upset. He looks surprised. "Nothing has been finalized, Joel. If you'd rather not have your work considered, I'll ask my professor to withdraw your entry. I don't think you understand how big this opportunity is, however. The contest is run through Princeton University."

I am mute.

He hands me a pass to go see Mr. Faber, but my feet have become cinderblocks, and I can't walk or move or talk. If Mr. Castell thought the poems were good enough to share with his university professor, I think I'll pass English. Ironically, I'm at a loss for words. All I manage to do is open and close my mouth a few times.

Finally, I take a deep breath and blurt out, "What does this mean?"

"Well, Joel, I think it means you've turned a corner, and it doesn't hurt to make an impression with an Ivy League school like Princeton while you're still an underclassman in high school. Congratulations."

"Thanks."

I head to guidance. My head is spinning. *Princeton University?* I haven't even started thinking about college yet. This is insane, even for me. As I replay the conversation in my mind, I recall something Mr. Castell said about having to make calls. *What did he mean? Why would he have to call Mr. Faber about my portfolio?* Maybe it has to do with me passing for the year. I head back to his office when the receptionist tells me Mr. Faber's ready to see me.

"I hear you've had some good news, Joel."

"I don't know the details, but I guess it's good. Why did Mr. Castell have to call you? Is it about me passing for the year?"

"*Uh*, not exactly, Joel. Why don't you have a seat? I need to explain something. It's pretty important."

I don't like where this is headed. I grab a pillow.

"Am I in trouble?" I venture.

"No, you're not in any trouble, Joel."

"Then what is it?" I try to calm myself, but I can feel the anger ratcheting up inside, fueling a flood of words. "You're all the same. You're not there for me when I need you, just when you want to help. All you do is make decisions without asking. You're just like him. All of you are just like him!"

"Joel, you need to know schools are mandated to report within 24 hours of suspected abuse. Mr. Castell had to report it after reading your portfolio, for your safety. If not, he could lose his job."

"He did *what?* Wait, you're reporting me? Am I going to prison? What kind of messed up—? *He* did that stuff! *It wasn't me!*" I'm up and backing toward the door.

Every part of me screams *run*, but what holds me there is that Mr. Faber would just call the police. This is bad enough; I don't need the police chasing me down. And to think I told myself I was ready to share this with someone. Instead, those I should be able to trust have betrayed me, just like my mother, and hurt me just like Uncle Steven. *Is there any adult who doesn't use children the way everyone uses me?*

"Joel, you're not going to prison. We're reporting this to protect you. You were the victim, not the perpetrator. Try and calm down." He motions toward my seat.

He says he's not sending me to jail, but how do I know for sure? I need to figure this out. None of it makes sense. I'm starving and tired, and I start yawning out of nowhere. Mr. Faber watches closely.

"That's better, Joel. I can see you have a hard time trusting adults, myself included. Given what has happened, I'm not surprised."

Now he's starting to be clearer. Maybe he isn't out to get me.

"How old were you? Five, six?"

"It was right after my father got transferred. I was six. We were supposed to go fishing, but then he left." I focus on breathing, but I keep yawning instead.

"And you're 16 now?"

"Almost 17 My birthday's in the summer." I grab the pillow again, just in case.

"I see. I'll have to research the statute of limitations in this case. It might be too late to consider prosecution. This was your uncle, you said?"

"*No!* He's not related. He worked on my grandmother's farm. The only person who could watch us was 'Uncle' Steven. It was just a title. I think his real name is Steven Jacobs."

"Is he somewhere nearby?"

"I don't know. He took off after I ended up in the hospital. I was having growing pains and woke up screaming. I forgot about that. I never realized those happened at the same time."

"It's actually more common than you think. Forgetting is a way to survive, until you can deal with what happened safely."

That actually makes sense.

"Mr. Castell told me you wrote about your experiences in your poetry. I haven't read it yet, but if it's okay with you, I'd like to see your portfolio. Do you think you're ready to talk?"

"Well, since I turned in my portfolio, I thought you might find out. I planned to talk to you today. Just not like this."

"It's amazing how far you've come. Not everyone survives. Many give up, some are institutionalized or, worse, take their own lives. The fact that you were able to write about it and speak up for yourself is incredible to me. You should be proud of yourself."

"Wait, what did you say before about a statute?"

"The statute of limitations protects the rights of the accused. If the victim does not file charges in a timely manner, time runs out, and you cannot file afterwards."

"Is there a set rule about that?"

"It can vary from state to state. I believe ours is ten years. I will have to check."

"But, it's already been longer than that! Now what am I supposed to do? I just realized what happened. You said it yourself—I had to forget to survive. Are you saying I can't go after him or press charges for what he did to me?" I grip the pillow tighter.

"I'm not sure, Joel. We can check with the police or file an appeal with the judge. Perhaps your case can change the current precedent. But let's not get ahead of ourselves. First we should discuss what happened. Let's start from the beginning."

I tell Mr. Faber about the nightmares, how they returned and led me here. I explain what happened when I ran away and how my mother shipped me back home. I talk about the sorting project. I explain how I finished the garage and how I ended up at the farmhouse to finish with the shed and the attic.

I tell him how I had a vivid memory of the first time Steven Jacobs abused me and what he'd made me do.

"The term is fellatio, but what you've described is still sodomy."

"What's that?"

"Well, sodomy covers anal or oral intercourse. However, that implies consent."

"But I didn't."

"Right. You should know that the perpetrator can commit forcible sodomy by making you do things against your will. I'm guessing he intimidated you somehow?" I nod. "And in your case, because you were younger than 13, it would be ruled as aggravated sexual battery, due to the severity and the number of occurrences."

By the end, I'm exhausted. I'm also starving, but I'm not sure I could eat. Mr. Faber asks the secretary to arrange for us to have lunch in his office. Meanwhile, I get a drink of water.

"I didn't know this was so... complicated."

"It can be. Each case is unique. But there are also commonalities. Mr. Jacobs followed the pattern of a perpetrator. He used his age and size, as well as frequent threats, to physically harm you and your brother, to intimidate. He took full advantage of the situation with your father leaving, your mother working and your grandmother caring for your ailing grandfather. You were completely isolated, and he could do whatever he wanted in that scenario. When he thought he might get caught, he ran. Very typical behavior for his kind."

We stop for lunch. I talk about the things I've been working on to make changes in my life. I'm still helping my grandmother complete jobs around the house; I go for bike rides and am working hard to pass this school year. I talk about trying to curb my swearing and how writing helps. I've also started going to practice for the poetry slam.

"It makes perfect sense to turn the assignment you already had to complete into the motivation to reclaim your childhood. You've got a strong testimony, Joel. One that needs to be shared."

I try to picture myself at the regional poetry slam. It's only a few weeks away.

Mr. Faber asks if he can go through some tougher questions. I tell him if what we've already covered isn't tough enough, we might as well go onto the next round.

"I want you to know I'm not asking these questions because I believe they are true, I simply need to ask them. It's just protocol."

"Okay. Go ahead."

"Did you do anything to encourage Mr. Jacobs to pursue sexual encounters with you?"

"No. Sometimes I didn't say anything, but I was afraid he would do more."

"That's fine. We can talk further, if you like. For now, I'll try to get through these questions."

"What's next?"

"Did you ever do any of the things Mr. Jacobs did to you with anyone else?"

I doubt Elias even counts. Besides, what we had felt good, not like anything Steven did. "No. If Mr. Jacobs hadn't done what he did, I'd still be a virgin." *Technically*.

Now it's time for me to ask a question. I'm nervous about the answer. Should I even ask?

"Mr. Faber. If I enjoyed any of it, does that make me gay?"

"Joel, childhood sexual abuse has nothing to do with sexual identity. It has nothing to do with sex. Regardless of any erection or ejaculation from you, that still doesn't imply consent, no matter what he said to you. What he did is something completely different. Sex isn't about power. You determine your sexual identity based on who you are attracted to, but survivors of CSA need to go through therapy to ensure they clearly understand their sexual orientation apart from their abuse."

"Okay."

"You've also survived childhood sexual assault. What Mr. Jacobs forced you to do does not make you homosexual." *I don't know what I am. Bisexual?*

"Does that mean I can ask someone out?"

"Sure, when you're ready. Just take it nice and easy. Intimacy can trigger flashbacks and cause confusion. If you get serious, you'll have to let them know, so they can be sensitive to what you're going through. It won't be easy for either of you, but you can have a normal life. It's just going to take a lot of work."

No way am I telling Amber about this. Not that I have much left to even keep us as friends. Knowing this, she'd drop me for sure.

"This just keeps getting bigger and bigger."

"Unfortunately, that's very true. But you're already well on your way to recovery. Have you told anyone else? What about family? Do you have a plan for how to tell them?"

"No, I didn't tell anyone. Are you kidding? I hadn't even thought about that. I don't think I'm ready."

"Tell you what, let's take the rest of this week, and we'll work on a plan together before you tell your family."

I don't answer what I'm really thinking. Instead, I nod my head.

WORMS IN THE SUMMER GRASS

From the journal of Joel Scrivener

It isn't that far into June when the heat stings soft
Spring away, and my family migrates to the sticky lake
to cool ourselves beneath the shade of a beach-umbrella.
Rusted fishhooks and burnt grills surround the lake

like ants around a rotting tree. The sky floats across
the water, as I rub my hands on wet grass,
dripping sweat and bugs. Silence unnerves me.
He brings us here, like a family affixed, but

the worms and I know differently.

He rocks on water-logged sneakers near lake weeds
where the mosquitoes hover and snails are born.
I concentrate on threading a dying worm and imagine it's him.
The ground around makes a sucking sound

like a dry drain. I sip from an empty can praying
he slips into the water. He sits away from us,
over where the boy from Rochester Farm choked
and died a few years back. I never knew that boy.

At some point his presence wakes me.

He hovers over the bed; I notice my sheets peeled back
towards the wall. Encumbered by his weight, I await the end,
clenching my eyes as his hand holds onto the mattress.
My line jerks and I reel in a throw-back. I wait until nightfall,

when we will travel back to the house,
and I will scrub ground worms from beneath
my fingernails—and he will come into the bathroom
to pee with me, the worm burdened around a rusted hook.

40

FAMILY REUNION

When I get home, I hear voices in the back of the house. Grandma told me Uncle Brandon and Aunt Althea were coming for dinner, but they're early. I expect to see them as I walk back toward the sounds, since their SUV's parked out front.

Turning the corner, I'm not expecting the person who is actually speaking.

"I've been stateside for a while now. Didn't think the time was right to come back just yet—" And then I see him. He turns and looks right at me, midsentence. Dad.

Sounds so much like his brother, Uncle Brandon; he's taller, though, and in uniform. I knew the voice was different, but I'd told myself it had to be Uncle Brandon. Then it hits me.

"Who said you could come? No one wants you here. I told Mr. Faber not to let you come."

"I'm sorry to hear that, Joel."

I know there are reasons he left that I haven't gotten my head around yet, but it's like the initial hurt needs to lash out before I can process the rest.

As an afterthought, he adds, "I shouldn't have come."

"You're much better at leaving."

My grandmother jumps in. "Joel."

"He's right. Let him be," Uncle Brandon replies.

"You've every right to be pissed. I never explained why I left. Distance made it easy for me to get lost in silence. What good has that done? The truth is I never found the words to explain it myself. How was I supposed to tell any of you?" He's on the verge of tears. *Some soldier he turned out to be.*

"You could have tried."

After a pause: "Yes." He stops short of saying any more.

"None of this would have happened if you'd stayed." *None of them have any idea what I mean by that.*

Memories of every argument I ever imagined between us volley around my head. I scrunch my eyes. "Look, we don't have to do this. It's fine. I need to lie down. Headache."

***

When I wake, it's time for dinner, and my father hasn't left. Neither has the headache. Our conversation remains safe until my father looks over and asks, "So, are you staying here for the summer?"

"Well, I'd like to, but I guess I have to ask Mom first. Uncle Brandon, do you think I could stay?" I notice my dad flinch.

"I don't see the harm. Let's ask your mother and see what she says." He takes me to the office to make the call. My dad doesn't seem to know how to fit in here. I'm glad to leave him in the other room.

"Carrie, hi, it's Brandon." He pauses. "We were talking over dinner about summer plans. What do you think about Joel staying here until the end of summer?" He pauses again. "Fine. Well, he's here. You can ask him yourself," he says, handing me the phone.

"Mother."

Either she's oblivious or she doesn't miss a beat. "How are you doing out there?"

"I got caught up with my classes, I'm going to tutoring, and I turned in my English portfolio today. My teacher thought it was so good, he wants me to enter it in a contest."

"Sounds promising."

"I think I'm going to do it."

"All right. You want to stay there for the summer? Be my guest. My only condition is you've got to pass this year and get good grades.

If you do that, you can stay. Otherwise, I put you back on the bus, and you're out here with me. No beach for you. Hear me?"

"I hear you."

"All right then. You can put your uncle back on the phone." I pass the phone back without even saying goodbye. I don't even realize until I'm out of the room. I head back to the table to clear, but dinner is already cleaned up. I join the others in the living room. When Uncle Brandon comes out, I turn to see how the rest of the call went.

"She said you could stay as long as your grades were good. Think you can make it?"

"I know I can. By the way, I've been entered into a poetry contest run by Princeton University."

I hear gasps and amazement.

"My teacher liked what I wrote, and he went there. He told me he called one of his professors and asked if I could submit late. After he faxed over some of my portfolio, they gave me permission to enter. I have a few days to decide. I didn't even know I could write."

"Are you serious?" my dad asks. "Didn't you know that's what our family is known for? Scrivener means writer."

I'm just beginning to ponder the meaning of my family's namesake, when two police cars pull up in front of Grandma's house. The sirens turn on just as they arrive with a *boo-whoop boo-whoop*, red and blue lights flashing through the front window curtains, the glass in the front door, the picture frames and light fixtures, the television. I hear radio discussions over walkie-talkies but can't make out what's being said. I'm frozen in red-blue-red-blue lights. The doorbell rings. My dad answers.

"Good evening, officers. May we help you?"

"We need to speak with Joel Scrivener. Is he here?"

"He's right here. Please, come in."

And then I know why they're here. They need me to give a statement about Steven Jacobs. This is how my family is going to learn what happened all those years ago.

So much for making a plan with Mr. Faber before breaking the news.

41

911

The police officers come in and sit at the dining room table. Grandma goes to brew a pot of coffee and find something else to offer. Uncle Brandon, my dad and I all take a seat. Aunt Althea gathers the children and takes them home for bed. We settle into a quiet uneasiness, although mine is warranted—I know what's about to be discussed.

This is all wrong. I thought Mr. Faber was going to give me a week to plan and prepare. There goes another adult over to the I-can't-trust-them team. *Wait.* It was Mr. Castell who filed the report; Mr. Faber's hanging on by a thread.

Still, once it's out there, I can't take it back or make it go away. I have a hard enough time just dealing with my anger, even on a daily basis. I've found a routine, and it doesn't include everyone knowing each intimate detail.

There is one male and one female cop in full uniform. They could be Aunt Althea's brother and sister. I notice a kindness in their eyes I often see in hers. I think I can trust them. More importantly, my gut tells me I can. I hope what I see is because they know and they're on my side. The only other time I've seen a cop is when my mother got pulled over for a speeding ticket. She tried to get out of it, but the cop was all business. He had a huge moustache; she got the ticket anyway.

The male officer begins, looking at his police report. The female officer pulls out a pen and notepad.

"Joel, I'm Officer Carter, and this is Officer Newborn. We've come to take your statement regarding a report we received today about Steven Jacobs. Are you aware of the matter we are referring to?" His voice is steady, straightforward, but has a timbre and a resonance that calms me.

Even so, I don't respond. Instead I stare straight ahead, eyes fixed on the table. My grandmother brings in coffee, cups, cream and sugar, and pie. I eye the pie longingly. *Guess I'll have to wait until the interrogation is over. I hope there'll be some left.*

"We received the report from Mr. Castell, since he was the mandated reporter in this incident. Did you know this would be reported?" Officer Carter continues.

I cross my arms. Officer Newborn glances with meaning at Officer Carter. She writes down a few notes. Officer Carter looks hard at me, and then something about his countenance softens.

"All right, Joel. I understand this might make you feel uncomfortable. You can either discuss it here, or we can take you down to the station. Your choice."

I glance at Uncle Brandon. He returns my gaze.

"Joel, do you know what's going on here?"

I fix my eyes on the table. *No way do I want to talk to anyone about this. I'm not ready. They can arrest me for all I care.* I imagine my skin turning to stone like a basilisk.

"Joel, you need to tell these officers anything you know." When I don't respond, my dad sighs and turns to Officer Carter. "What's this all about? Has Joel done something wrong?"

I start to panic. I need to think. I wish I could talk to Mr. Faber.

"Sir, we appreciate your concern. However, this matter concerns Joel. He did not do anything wrong. Mr. Jacobs is the accused," says Officer Carter.

"What are the charges?" Uncle Brandon asks.

"Sodomy." *All I need is for this to get out and spread around the school.* I know how the students at Broad Run received my nightmares. *How would Oceanside handle this?*

"What? Are you serious? How did this happen?" Grandma asks.

"Steven Jacobs is charged with molesting Joel approximately ten years ago."

"I can't believe it," my dad says, his voice wavering. After a breath, he steadies himself. "This is my fault. That's what you meant before, 'None of this would have happened...'" *So he* was *listening*. His voice trails off like he's about to lose it.

I swallow hard.

"That's terrible, Joel!" Uncle Brandon finishes. Everyone seems upset. Now I feel bad. *How strange: I'm thinking about this like it happened to someone else, and they're the ones who are upset.*

"Joel, are you ready to make a statement? We need you to tell us everything you remember. Do you think you can handle that?" continues Officer Newborn.

I already had a practice run at school today with Mr. Faber. "I don't have anything to say. If you have to arrest me, go ahead."

"That won't be necessary, Joel. Now will it?"

"Joel. If any of this is true, you need to speak up. Don't make these officers cuff you and take you downtown. What's gotten into you?" Uncle Brandon places his hands on Grandma's shoulders to console her. I've never seen her like this.

"We don't need to use handcuffs. I'm sure Joel will behave himself while we travel to the station. Isn't that right, Joel?"

What am I going to do, run away? I nod at Officer Carter.

"Who will accompany Joel?" Officer Newborn asks.

Grandma and Uncle Brandon look at each other. My dad went out the back door, the sound of the screen door only now registering in my mind. Flight seems to be his go-to response.

"I'll go with him," Uncle Brandon answers, then to me he asks, "Do you want me to see if they'll let me drive you to the station?"

I shake my head no.

We head for the door and load into the squad car. Uncle Brandon sits up front with Officer Carter. Officer Newborn sits in the back with me. There's a metal grate dividing the front from the back. With a blip from the speakers, Officer Carter picks up the radio intercom.

"This is car 4219. Officers Carter and Newborn. We are en route to the station with a minor, Joel Scrivener, for questioning. He is accompanied by his uncle, Brandon Scrivener."

When we get to the station, Officer Newborn lets me out. We are escorted into the red-brick building then turn down a series of hallways before heading into a room with a table and chairs. The walls are blank. The only thing I see is a mirror on the wall behind us. I wonder if it's a two-way. My stomach flips as I sit. *Maybe I should have just talked while we were back at the house.*

Officer Newborn pulls out a tape recorder. "Do you mind if we record your statement, Joel?"

I shrug and wipe my hands on my pants.

"If you want to know what happened, why not start with my dad. He's the one who left us." I clench my teeth as anger burbles up like the heat on my neck and face.

"Joel, do you even know why he left?" Uncle Brandon interjects. "Your mother cheated on him."

"What? Are you serious?" Then I remember the letter. I must be blind to have missed the most important phrase that comes flooding back: *get your affairs in order.* How did I miss that? *Because I've been wrapped up in myself and my stuff, that's why.*

"Yes, and you seriously need to stop with the stubborn act and answer these questions. We'll stay as long as you need. It's time to face it," Uncle Brandon adds.

I've been running so long, I don't know what it's like to stand and look fear in the face. But I think I'm ready to get it over with.

"Recording your statement is the best way to ensure we keep an accurate account. This is what we will use to arrest and prosecute Steven Jacobs. It's important that you only tell what actually happened and you state it as simply and directly as you can," Officer Newborn says.

Officer Newborn begins recording, then continues.

"Statement taken from Joel Scrivener, a 16-year-old Caucasian male." Officer Newborn lists today's date, my birth date, and identification number before proceeding.

I feel foolish for refusing to talk. Eventually, I've got to face this, or it will never go away. If I have any hope of resuming a normal life, I'd better get this done.

I start at the beginning and recall the first time it happened in the farmhouse and then describe each subsequent time I remember. Since the first one, I've recalled at least a dozen different scenarios—either things he made me do to him or he did to me.

I watch my uncle's face go pale and ashen, horrified by each occurrence as I describe them. *It seems terrible to put my family through this.*

I'm tired all the way down to my bones. Hit by a tsunami of exhaustion, I'm pressed under its sheer weight. I manage to get through the entire statement, and then the officers finish up with a few clarifying questions.

"Joel, according to your statement, you have described repeated encounters with Steven Jacobs that transpired over a six-month period, totaling a dozen different instances of sodomy and aggravated sexual assault. Is this correct?" Officer Carter asks.

"Yes, it is." I stare hard at the plain table in front of me, watching the tape spin inside the recorder. The spindle goes around and around. I hear Uncle Brandon exhale as I watch him clench his fists.

"Do you know if Steven Jacobs is still in this area?" Officer Newborn asks.

"I don't know. He disappeared when a neighbor's son was found dead. They said he choked or something. I don't know what happened to him."

"We will investigate that. Thank you, Joel. You did a great job. We'll take it from here. Once we file the police report, our commanding officer will issue a warrant, and we'll begin a search to bring him in," Officer Carter says.

"Can we get a restraining order to protect Joel in the meantime?"

"Certainly, sir. We'll get right on that," Officer Newborn replies, making a note of it.

I'm hollow and numb, an empty shell kicked beneath the table. Uncle Brandon comes over and puts his arms around me but removes them when I jolt reflexively.

"I didn't mean to jump."

"It's understandable, Joel. You've been through a lot," Uncle Brandon replies.

Officer Newborn stops as she passes me at the door and crouches beside me.

"It's going to be okay, Joel. We'll get him and hold him accountable for what he did to you." She looks directly at me. I'm overwhelmed a complete stranger would care in the slightest.

I've reached the tipping point; tears flow unchecked down my cheeks.

"Why didn't I say something? Maybe I could have stopped that boy from being hurt. I hope he didn't do it to anyone else."

"Joel, you aren't responsible for something a grown man chose to do to you or anyone else. That's on him. You don't have to beat yourself up. It's enough that you've survived."

"If anyone could have done something, it should have been my mother."

"I guess we'd better call her, too," Uncle Brandon suggests.

"Could you make the call?" I ask. "I'm not up for going through it all a third time today. I'm pretty tired."

Uncle Brandon agrees. I don't even want to know how she will react. I'm too tired to think straight.

The officers lead us back through the hallway maze, and we head out to the parking lot. When we get back home, my grandmother meets us at the door.

Grandma looks at Uncle Brandon to see how it went. He nods.

"Joel, that's a brave thing you just did. You make me proud."

I don't know how to respond. After a huge yawn, I ask, "May I go to bed? I'm wiped out."

Uncle Brandon thanks the officers and shuts the door. "I'll let your mom know what happened." I head to my room and collapse into bed. Kicking my shoes and socks off, I crawl between the sheets and dive into the ocean of sleep that has been demanding my immediate attention.

***

My alarm does not go off.

I forgot to set it. My grandmother has to come in and wake me. I grab a quick shower, get dressed in under five minutes and give my grandmother a kiss before heading off to school, carrying breakfast with me out the door. I don't see my dad anywhere. *Good.*

I'm determined to go on with my life. First on my list of ignoring the large rhinoceros in the room is to select the poems from my portfolio that I will submit to Princeton for the Secondary School Poetry Prize contest. Fortunately for me, everyone is focused on the Underclassman Formal. I go quietly through all of my classes. My poetry club teammate Osita tells me she is going with Marques Bellamy, that guy with long braids down to his shoulders. No one else ventures to talk to me, so I busy myself with work or a book.

I am left alone.

A week passes. I go to school, I go to class, and I meet with Mr. Faber. I don't have to go to the Writing Center anymore, so I stop. When I went to get some new books from the library, I found Amber sobbing in the Writing Center. She was too preoccupied to notice me, so I kept going. I think something bad happened at prom, but it's none of my business. Right now, I'm just trying to live and be normal, whatever that is.

One day after school, I head to the library to research a paper for English class. We're writing a persuasive essay on someone famous who has influenced us in the past year. I'm researching M. C. Escher, the tessellation artist. I've been studying his artwork, the *Metamorphosis* series, and how he transforms one object into another. I'd like to figure that out myself.

I pull out a few books and sit at a computer to type up my notes. Hopefully, this will save me a step later, when I write the actual essay. I don't even notice someone standing behind me, studying the pages I have open, until she speaks.

"Wow. Where'd you find this?" Amber asks, taking a seat at the computer next to me.

"I learned about it in art class. Tessellations."

"Is that what they're called?"

"Yeah."

Amber doesn't respond. She picks up the book and looks closely.

"*Hm.* Nothing but crickets."

"What?"

"You seem quiet, lost in thought."

"Yeah, that. I've been distracted lately. My parents separated, and my boyfriend turned out to be a jerk."

"I never thought I'd hear that word in connection with your parents. Wow. And I thought you and your boyfriend were serious."

"Yeah. It didn't turn out that way."

"Really?"

"He stood me up."

"What? That's terrible."

"Yeah. It kinda was terrible…"

We've come right up to the edge of the truth, the secrets we've long-guarded clicking against the back of our teeth. I know she's not telling me everything. She probably knows I'm keeping things to myself, too. We won't go any farther until we can trust each other. Most times, we shrink back, doubting our intuition to guide us and keep us safe. Instead of recoiling, we should go with our gut.

"Sure you don't need me to go pound him?" I whisper.

"No," she says, laughing. "He'd probably pound you, no offense."

"None taken. I'm not that buff. My grandma could probably take me if she wanted to."

"I see."

"In fact, *you* could probably take me out. I thought you were mad, so I've steered clear of the Writing Center."

"I was mad. Not at you in particular, not anymore, just… boys in general."

"I didn't want to be caught on the receiving end, so I laid low."

"Well, I don't hate all guys anymore, just most."

"Where does that put me?"

"I'll let you know."

The heart is a strange, unknowable beast at times, a kind of monster all its own.

"Well, I've gotta get to work." Amber heads into the Writing Center.

I return to my research. Once I'm done, I try to start a new poem. I haven't written in a few days. Writer's block. I stare at blank paper until the lines blur on the page. Thankfully, this didn't happen before I finished my portfolio.

Mr. Castell tells me my portfolio is also being considered in the county-wide Arts Council awards. One student from all six schools will be awarded a $500 scholarship. I try not to think about it. Instead, I ride my bike to the beach, write a few pages every day, and I tell the rhinoceros it must have been some other boy who got hurt all those years ago.

42

STATUTE OF LIMITATIONS

I wish there was a statute of limitations on my mother. Why is it the people you rely on the most to come through for you instead turn everything into something about them? This is not about my mother or my father. This is about me. Not that I want the attention—I don't. *But why is my mother the victim here?*

It happened to me, and I myself have no interest in waving the victim flag. I don't want to throw a "poor me" party or demand everyone feel sorry for me for the rest of their lives. Sadly, however, this is what my mother intends. It's so pathetic. I can't even hate her for how childish she's acting.

This is what I think about, rather than respond to the selfish crap blaring out of the telephone in my ear.

I came home from school, and Grandma followed me into my room to talk to me. I think she's been concerned since the police visit and the revelation that I was abused by Steven Jacobs. She sat on my bed while I was at the desk.

"How are you doing, Joel?" She wasn't asking out of courtesy but out of genuine interest in my well-being. Tears crowded in the corner of my eyes. *How did I manage to keep a grandmother who's actually normal?*

I swallowed the urge to cry and clenched my jaws, teeth on teeth, until it passed. Instead, I chewed on my lip. I couldn't lie to her.

"Some parts are okay, some are pretty tough. Dad showing up, the police, and now all of you knowing, I can't hide from it like before." I had to look away, in case.

"Maybe you shouldn't… have to hide it. When terrible things happen, family and friends are meant to help you through it. God doesn't mean for us to walk it alone."

"Where was God when all this happened? Dad left, my mother was too busy to notice, but shouldn't God have? I thought He was 'all-powerful' and 'all-knowing.' Why didn't He stop that from happening to me?"

My grandmother nodded, thinking about what I'd said. She knew I was serious, that this wasn't a joke.

"Joel, I do have an answer to your question. But it's one best held until you are ready to receive it. God didn't forget about you. It broke His heart to see you suffer. No one should have to go through that. He was there then, and He's still here now. He will wait until you're ready to ask Him yourself."

I try to ignore the precipitation sliding down my cheeks and plopping onto my shirt. I stare out the window. The neighbor's children ride pedal cars up and down the sidewalk, unaware of the conversation happening next door.

"I wish I weren't so angry all the time." I turn toward her, wiping my face. I think of the wall I smashed up in the hallway. It's been repaired, but I feel the ghost of that hole every time I walk by. I'm glad my dad never saw it.

"Feelings aren't wrong. That's what makes us human. It's what you do with those feelings that can be good or bad."

"I'm so… ashamed. Confused. Tired. Angry. And lots of other things. It's like this well that keeps bubbling up inside me. I had to crawl my way out. I don't know how to contain it sometimes."

"You go ahead and feel whichever way you need. Maybe I'll start dancing around the house and wail right along with you."

"You won't be angry? Ashamed?"

"I couldn't be ashamed of someone I love, Joel. And I'm not angry, not about this. I'm surprised you never heard me outside your door. Praying. Too many nights to count."

I sat in stunned silence for a minute. My grandmother walked over to me.

"Joel, do you want to go back with your mother and your brother when the school year is over?"

"I miss Jonathan. It's weird being away from him this long, but my mother and I don't get along."

"I thought you might say that. I was hoping you might stick around a while longer. I could use the company and the help, to be honest."

"Is Dad staying? I'm not ready for that. I haven't even figured this out. Why is he even here?"

"Joel, you'd be surprised how similar you two are. What you've been through. Maybe you could help each other through the rough parts."

She left me to my thoughts but returned when the telephone rang. It was my mother. She talked to Uncle Brandon and now wants to know why I didn't tell her myself.

"That was a very difficult time for me, Joel. Your father had just walked out on me leaving the two of you to take care of, and I had to go to work. We couldn't just freeload on his family forever and a day. I can't believe you'd make all this up, like some desperate cry for attention. It's ludicrous, Joel. What kind of counselor are you seeing that puts these thoughts in your head? I can't even imagine—"

After a while, I let my mind wander again, until she gets it all out. I know this means an end to our relationship, for now. At least until I can get a better handle on things. *Parenting her through this? Not a chance.* I let her rattle on from the inside of a cage I have constructed in my mind. I think the sign "Don't Feed the Animals" would be redundant at this point.

When the call is over, I take my bike ride to the beach and return home to write. *Home. I like the sound of that. Now it's more like home.*

I receive a call from Officer Newborn. She informs me that the statute of limitations does indeed affect this case, and currently a judge is reviewing it to determine whether the psychological trauma present would rule out the rights of the accused. She said it may take as long as six weeks or longer, if Steven Jacobs provides his statement, before a determination can be made. All I know is it's up in the air. All I can do is wait.

I receive a letter in the mail from Princeton University. When I open it, it's from the head of the English department. This year's contest received more than 5,500 entries. My poems were among the top 20 in the nation.

I run screaming through the house, because I can, to share the news with Grandma. She is elated. At school the next day, I show the letter to Mr. Castell before class. He takes it to the principal, who asks me if he can read it over the morning announcements. I am lauded throughout the day by my teachers.

Princeton University! Do I have a real chance of making it in? I'm not even a junior yet. I cannot believe it. The validation definitely helps, considering the invalidation the statute of limitations has given me, like it never even happened. I must have made it all up, like my mother said. Trust me, no one asks for this, and if they've lived through it, they certainly never effing made it up.

I'm completely unprepared when Mr. Castell announces in English class that I am this year's recipient of the county arts council writing award. I will receive my scholarship at the awards ceremony. *Maybe I am supposed to be a writer. Maybe I have found my voice.*

I am significant.

It's like the book we're reading to close out the year: the main character is a piece of work, Holden something-or-other... Caulfield. He and I have a lot in common. We've both been in and out of a lot of schools. We've both run from our lives in some way for a long time. Then there's the obvious thing we both share.

If he were alive today, I think we could get along. Of course, maybe we'd rub each other the wrong way. I guess I couldn't say for sure, unless I knew him and could talk to him.

"...What really knocks me out is a book that, when you're all done reading it, you wish the author that wrote it was a terrific friend of yours and you could call him up on the phone whenever you felt like it. That doesn't happen much, though..."

I wish I could call up Holden on the telephone. I know what I'd ask him first. Heck, I'd settle for Amber in a heartbeat. I miss my friend.

***

My butt has an indentation of the front porch embedded in it, but I can't seem to move. If I sit here long enough, maybe it'll become permanent. I hear the door open behind me. It's Grandma.

"Whatcha doing out here all alone?"

"Turning to stone. It's a slow process."

"I see. Well, it's nearly time for dinner. Any ideas?"

"I'm not really hungry."

"Or talkative, but here we are."

"Yeah."

"I'm not going to go away until you tell me, so you might as well spill what's got you bummed out on my front porch."

"I was supposed to go somewhere but decided not to."

"Suit yourself. We can have dinner whenever you're ready." Grandma retreats back inside.

I pull my hoodie more snugly around me, as if I could wrap myself in silence. Nothing works. When I look up, I see Padma and her entourage—Marques Bellamy, Shanae Moody and Osita Quiñones—exit Marques's sedan and head up the sidewalk, eyes fixed on me as my skin hardens in anticipation. Ezra Kingston isn't with them, since he's the one with mono whose spot I filled.

"Joel, did you forget the slam's today? C'mon, we don't have much time to get downtown," Padma beckons me, twirling the ends of her head scarf.

"Get it in gear or we'll use your porch to stage an intervention." Shanae cocks her hip to the side and juts her chin way out. It goes perfectly with her purple-and-black fauxhawk. "We haven't got all day. Grab your portfolio, and let's move."

"That's the thing. I've decided I'm not going."

"What? Are you serious? Joel, there's no time to find someone else. Without you, our team will forfeit."

"And I refuse to go down like a chump," Padma adds.

"You'll be fine. Let's go. You're just having last-minute jitters," Osita says.

"Happens to the best of us. Don't sweat it, Joel. C'mon, let's roll," says Marques. "My engine's still on."

As I stand, coldness spreads out across my posterior. Maybe my ass did turn to stone after all. It's like the time I had that nightmare in study hall and the whole school found out. Part of me wants to just slink into the background and disappear. But the part of me that agreed to take Ezra's place knows silence gives only a false sense of security. The truth is in finding the right way to speak and the right path for sharing what happened on my own terms.

FISH OUT OF WATER

From the journal of Joel Scrivener, his first public performance at the Poetry Slam

"You have made men like fish in the sea… The wicked foe pulls
all of them up with hooks…"
—Habakkuk 1:14, 15

In sleep, I fear water's weight, pressed down, drowns me
each time the air seeps out. Stunning, the stab
of throat, accustomed to lightness of air, darkness of water.
Down dream's womb, panic to plunge back, shock of air,
rebirth, exquisite death of consciousness, knowing darkness,
myself, a harbored shadow thrown against the wall.

What remains in shade but the drowning truth of light?

Hardened hands in earth at 5am rout out the fatted meat,
dirt passed through flesh, worms in black soil.
Softened by deliberate work—take in filth, attain purity—
their bodies baited, opened, cast into dark waters;
air leans in, cuts through current, another dying. He clutches
the stringer, stripping basket, dressed to receive the feast.

What is fishing to me now—the practice of his hands thread
pieces of me on hooks—thrusts beneath the surface of the water!

The clustered claustrophobia presses in, tightens, clench of teeth,
tensing up, rigid rigor mortis, tiny death in wakefulness.
His sweat an urgent haste, skin thrusts to satisfy, gratified, I die.
Laden, laid in graves clothes, I pass from stringer's chain
to stripping basket, casket stokes the choke of light, weight of sight.
My unlived life a fathomless dream;

seamed by the death I live with him;
worn revelation of shame mourned, torn in water, reborn.

43

PHOENIX RISING

I am still angry. Every day, I am irascible. I burn so long from my anger, the coal bed has turned to white ash while I blink and tear in the smoke. My clothes are singed, wisps curling up throughout the day. I try to extinguish the fury—this fire—but it burns on blindly before me. Every morning, it's there again, from the moment I rise, phoenix-like and terrible, until I fall into bed at night, smoldering. Molten. Oil and wick. I'm struck by the fact I don't know how to contain it; like it will, at any moment, implode inside me from its sheer potency and force.

Steven Jacobs took from me my childhood, my manhood and nearly my life. I never offered those things to him. He simply reached out and took them.

"…But every time he burnt himself up he sprang out of the ashes, he got himself born all over again…"

Yet, I'm still here, alive and breathing, born again. Every day, I keep coming down to the beach. And, every day, I place my anger like a hot brand into the ocean; hear the hiss as it sinks beneath the waves, swallowed by its depths. It's big enough—the ocean, that is. It can take all of my anger. I am not big enough to contain it.

The ocean is like a mirror, reflecting back what I miss or need to sort through. I spend time thinking here. I used to run from my life, from even the simple, ordinary little things. Learning people's names. Listening to their interests. Realizing it's not all about me. There's more past the end of my nose.

"…Among other things, you'll find that you're not the first person who was ever confused and frightened and even sickened by human behavior…"

I've remembered how to dream. I don't have to let nightmares overtake me or drag me down to the depths anymore. Now, I control them—I can risk dreaming again—allow my heart to take chances and harbor hope like something lost, now found at sea.

So, I keep coming.

Expectant. Waiting. I want to hear from someone, something. God, maybe. Once, I thought the ocean would stand up from its stone valley and talk to me. I think things like that sometimes. They seem important, like shells under beach sand that only I can find. I should write them down. They have meaning, significance, even when I don't understand it all yet.

So, I write.

Writing, too, helps me to calm down. When I get so angry I can't breathe or see straight, everything is tinted, edged in red. Then I know I have to write. Sitting at my desk, pen in hand, I know I can get my head around it, reshape it, hammer words onto a page until they change, transform into something beautiful.

"…'I was getting to where I could see the truth. Someday I'll be brave enough to speak it.'…"

Like now, at sunset.

I realize I'm not alone. I wonder how long she has been watching me. I turn and see Amber standing behind me, sandals dangling from the hook of her finger. Her arms are crossed and her lips are pursed, like she's trying to figure something out. She scrunches her eyes, holding her hand up to block the sun.

"You came," I say.

"Well, I didn't leave, if that's what you meant," she replies.

I turn back and lean my head on my knees, wrapping my arms around my legs for warmth. It got cold suddenly, sitting on the sandy beach. Amber sits down next to me, I'm not sure why. We stare in silence for a while, watching the sun start to dip in the sky, like a paintbrush streaking pink and orange over the blueness. Amber turns to me.

"Why didn't you tell me, Joel?"

"Tell you what?"

"About what happened to you all those years ago? I was there at the poetry slam. You took the breath right out of me. And I'm not the only one."

I want to yell at her for coming to the slam and leaving like that, but I'm the one who left her in the dark. Instead, I take a deep breath and sigh. I might have growled also, I'm not sure.

"It's still pretty new for me. I only just remembered it myself," I say.

"I didn't know it was something private—you chose a pretty public way to share it."

"The last time, I didn't get a choice. The whole school found out. My brother posted it online. It got out of control pretty quick."

"And now? After the slam?"

"Better. I feel more in control this time."

"I've missed your writing. You've got such a talent. I could never write like that. Believe me, I've tried."

"Do you mean that?" I ask. "I've never read anything you've written. Why haven't you shared anything with me?"

"You've read my letters."

"Yeah, but they don't count. It's not the same thing."

"Fair enough. Tell you what. Come with me this summer on our youth trip, and I'll bring my best writing."

"It's not all churchy, is it?"

"The trip or the writing?"

"Both."

"No, we rent a beach house and go out on a boat. One year, we saw a whale. You should give it a try. As for the writing, you'll have to be the judge."

"I don't know. That's asking a lot just to read your crummy writing."

"It is not!" She punches me hard in the shoulder.

"Prove it," I say, taunting her. "You've never had trouble speaking your mind before. What's stopping you?"

"Fine. Maybe I will. You come out here to be alone, but you're not the only one who's ever been broken." Then, almost to herself, she adds, "I realize that now. You know, I could have shown it to you if you were still coming to the Writing Center. Why'd you stop?"

"I don't know. It was crazy a few weeks ago. I wasn't exactly good company for anyone. It's a hell of a deep well. Sometimes, I'm still not okay."

"That's understandable."

Amber pulls her jacket on. For a moment, she looks like she's on fire, the orange sun shimmering behind her as it descends toward the horizon. I stretch.

We watch the waves for a few minutes.

"It's funny how things never seem to turn out the way you expect."

"Tell me about it," she says, wrapping her arms around herself. "The things… I thought I knew…" She looks at me, and I can see something shift.

"Joel, I have to tell you something."

"Okay, I'm listening."

"You heard my parents separated, right?" I nod. "They're probably getting a divorce."

"Wow. I never thought that would happen."

"Me neither."

I wait and watch as she gathers herself, collecting her thoughts, maybe deciding if she's going to let go of the last of her secrets.

"My father was arrested, Joel. He's done something, and it only just came out. I almost didn't come tonight, but I had to find you. It was your poem that brought me here." She's holding my hands and looking at me with such fear, it nearly breaks me in two. *Now it all makes sense.*

"Not you, too," I say, pulling her into an embrace before tears take hold and neither of us can speak.

Amber takes a step back, sliding her arms along the sides of my upper arms. "No, Joel. Not the same. He rigged a way to watch me through the air vent in the office. The vent shares a wall with my bedroom. Mom found him holding a candle up to the vent, gawking at me, and he was so startled, he couldn't lie his way out of it."

"That's horrible. Your own father. How are you feeling?"

"It's surreal. Like it happened to someone else. I don't know how to make any sense out of it."

"The good news is you don't have to. Remember the trip to the lighthouse, when your mother made you wear that dress?"

"Yeah, that makes me feel so old."

"You're not that old yet. Although I never realized how similar your feet are to my grandmother's. Yikes!"

"Joel!" She shoves me away from her, trying to be mad, but she's laughing, too.

"Well, at least we're laughing. I haven't had much to laugh about, myself." There won't be a more perfect time than now I realize, so I stand up and pivot around until I'm facing her. I reach down to take her hands, and she's already reaching up to take mine. "Wait here a sec, okay?" I give her hands a squeeze and try to let go, but her eyes are pulling me in like the tide tugging at the shore. Still, I break away and grab my backpack.

From inside I pull out flameless pillar candles and light them, twisting them down into the sand in a circular space. Amber stands at the edge, waiting for me to complete the circle. I turn on the MP3 player my aunt and uncle got me for passing my sophomore year and offer Amber an ear bud while I put the other one in my ear. I slide my hand around her waist and take her other hand in mine, and we dance at the edge of the world, the sky and the sand. My heart hammers in my chest like a fierce bird on fire, freed from its cage, ready to rise.

I haven't felt freer than this moment in my entire life.

If we wanted to, I think we could dance off into the clouds. Instead, we turn circles inside our candles that give just enough light before the stars emerge in the darkening sky above.

Amber stops, the flicker of a question crossing her face. She tilts her head.

"How do you do it?"

"What do you mean?"

"The candles. The music. Us dancing. How do you separate all that you've gone through from right now?"

"Well, you've owed me this dance since you walloped my shoulder all the way back at the lighthouse."

"No, I'm serious, Joel. It's got to be tough. How are you doing?" Her eyes are searching, penetrating.

I don't know how to put it into words. Until you're broken, you cannot be healed. Until you're empty, you cannot be filled. Until you catch yourself holding your breath, you don't realize you're no longer breathing.

I can't answer her right away. My throat is too tight for some reason. I have such a desire to kiss Amber right now, but I'm scared to act on it. Would she let me? Then I remember she asked me a question.

"Okay, I guess. Although the police came and told me I might not be able to press charges."

"What? Why?"

"There's this 'statute of limitations' thing that protects the accused. Apparently, I took too long remembering. It happened more than ten years ago."

"So, what are you going to do?"

"They're still checking into it. It's up to a judge what I can do at this point. They haven't even found him. The hardest part for me is it's like it never even happened. Like it's not real or I made it up."

"You can't make up something like that, Joel. You know it's real. No matter what a judge or a court says. Maybe you should fight it."

"I don't know if I'm up for a fight. I get so angry. And I hate myself for feeling that way. That's why I come here. I need to get rid of it before it consumes me. Also, writing helps. If only I had a friend who could console me in my hour of need."

"You're such a dork," she says, grabbing sand and throwing it in my direction.

I laugh, not because I think it's funny, but in surprise. I'm sharing things that are deeply felt, personal things, and she throws sand?

I grab wet clumpy fistfuls and throw them right at her, from point-blank range. I scramble after her and chase her down the hill toward the water, grabbing sand ammo along the way.

Amber has already armed herself and tosses spurts of sand like tiny clouds that shower down all over me in grainy rain. I don't care. I ignore the sand and push myself to close the distance between us. I empty my hands of ammunition all on Amber and move in for the tackle.

We're splashing in the water, clothes getting soaked, but the heat between us is warm and intoxicating. Our eyes lock. I'm swimming in golden flecks, her brown eyes. My hands find the small of her back, tracing the indentation along her spine, nudging her closer. She smiles, sidling nearer. I hold her hips and pull her to me, fingers hooked in her belt loops.

We allow our bodies to press together like dancers then follow our instincts, lips touching with electric crackling energy—we've put this off far too long. We are crashing waves like the ones pooling at our feet. I lose all sense of time, nothing else matters but this moment. She kisses me back as much as I kiss her. I find myself gasping to catch my breath. She lets out a faint sigh.

I no longer notice the sun, large and fiery, sinking into the horizon.

The water has risen to our hips. We come to our senses and realize the sun has gone from yellow to orange to a deep crimson red and the sky has deepened to the blue of twilight.

We laugh, two drunk swimmers who have found a sunken treasure, traveling far to reach land and air again. This finally seems right to me, I know it in my gut; the stomach-flutter quivers of two stones crashing together, the beginning spark of love. We climb out of the water and head up the beach, stumbling but happy to have found new hope together.

***

That night, when I push away from shore in the boat of sleep, I travel to the middle of the lake. I have been here before. This lake.

This boat. It is as familiar to me as blank lines on a page waiting to be filled. But something has changed.

When I look to the shore, expecting to see him, no one is there. My younger self is no longer there, either.

I return to the shore and see signs of a scuffle in the dirt. I know we've been here, but somehow I got away. As I start to walk away from the pond, I am surrounded by darkness, then a flicker, a flame far off. I head in that direction. Something draws me toward this light.

Then I sense the ground has changed.

I walk on stone. Before me, a corridor juts out; torches are ensconced at regular intervals. I follow the passage until it reaches a corner. When I turn, I realize where I am.

The stairwell.

I start down. As I begin to go down the stairs, it occurs to me I don't have to keep going. I can turn around and head back up. Only I don't. I want to know for sure. I reach the bottom and turn the corner into the crypt. The two rooms are dark, empty.

I am alone here.

I finally do what I should have done long ago. I head back up the stairs and keep walking. I don't look back.

***

On a day just like any other, I head to the grocery store to grab a short list of things for Grandma. Amber is joining us for dinner. I head down the soup aisle, checking over my list written on a Post-it. My radar goes off. I hear a scuffle in the next aisle over. Some parent must be wigging out on their son.

"C'mere, once-et. I said c'mere!" A voice I would know anywhere. I don't even think. I start to run down the aisle. The sounds of their conversation recede toward the back of the store.

But when I get to the end of the aisle, I can't find him or the younger voice I heard with him. I turn this way and that, but I'm dizzy, disoriented. I falter in my steps.

They've got to still be somewhere in the store. I take off for the front and start scanning the lines, checking each register for Steven Jacobs and companion. Nothing.

I still don't have a cell phone. I turn to the nearest cashier.

"Call the police. A child has been kidnapped. I'm not kidding. Call them, now!"

I make for the door and hope I'm not too late. I frantically scan the parking lot.

And then I see it. His pickup truck is unmistakable: A 1986 Ford F150 with a stupid blue cab and a scratched-up navy blue bed, his bright orange Adventurer tackle box careening around the back of the truck as he turns left out of the parking lot onto the road. And the one thing I'm staring at as I absorb each detail like it's part of a police report: the boy-sized baseball cap bouncing with the lilt of the truck in the passenger seat.

ACKNOWLEDGMENTS

I have carried the seed of this book for much of my life. It is a heart book, and so it took me awhile to open my hands to the possibility I could write it down and share it with you. Now it is yours, and I hope it finds its way into your heart and life and lives on. Maybe it is also my wish book.

One of my first conceptions of this book was from the perspective of Joel's mother. I wrote a short story in high school with the same title, and it was published in the *Crossed Sabers Literary Magazine* at Loudoun County High School. It was also a part of the writing portfolio submitted to the Loudoun Arts Council Writing Award for my graduating year, 1991, for which I received a $500 scholarship. But it wasn't until I discovered there was much more to the story if I told it from Joel's perspective that I sat down with him, took a drive, and just listened as he spoke and shared his secrets with me. Once I tuned my ear to his point of view, the story took shape and grew.

Start to finish, it took about two and a half months to write. The editing, revising and crafting process took five years. Many times, I came very close to trunking the book and giving up. I share this with those of you who carry the seeds of books around with you. It is my hope you will dare to consider the possibility you can plant it on the page and use words to grow it into a book, even if you come close to giving up, as I did. Share it with us. We need to hear your stories. Your voice matters. Speak up. It is worth the risk.

Along the way, I have been supported and helped by many. Much of Joel's life is familiar to me. And despite having a tumultuous childhood, I found my way to the library and to books that were like a map to the way out. Thank you to the authors who shared their stories, so that I could find my way out and survive so many of life's challenges. Of course, I've still got many challenges left to manage, which means I have many more books to read. Thank you to Roald Dahl, Norton Juster, Diana Wynne Jones, C. S. Lewis, S. E. Hinton, Robert Cormier, Laurie Halse Anderson, Cheryl Rainfield, Daisy Whitney, Kevin Craig, Barry Lyga, Mike Mullin, Carl Deuker, Matthew Quick, Benjamin Alire Saenz, Christa Desir, Trish Doller, Corey Ann Haydu, Courtney C. Stevens, Adam Silvera, Brendan Kiely, Jason Reynolds and at least a thousand others who have caused my soul to shudder in response to reading your books. Joel's story would not have been written without you.

To my first readers, the Betas: Joanne Uppendahl, Helen Ross, Lydia Sharp, Kevin Craig, Kendra Kilbourn, Kelly Said, Adrien-Luc Sanders, Amy Hill, Niki Moss, Nina Allen, Gerry Crete and Sandy Figley, thank you for the tender way you held my heart, kept it beating, and gave it back to me with the encouragement I needed to finish it and stop all the bleeding.

To my fellow writers who joined me and offered sage words of wisdom, lines, edits, or who talked me down off the ledge many a time, shaping this book into something I'm incredibly proud of: Georgia McBride, Kelly Hashway, Natalia Jaster, Jennifer Million, Jessie Harrell, Gabe Cole, Monica-Marie Vincent, Helene Keough, Tymothy Longoria, Cameo Renae, L M Preston, Dahlia Adler, Nicholas Potts, Tye Tyson, Kimberly Sabatini, Jill Hathaway, Sheena Frietas, Ilsa Bick, Summer Heacock, John Hansen, Andrea Hannah, Andrew Bundy, Jenny Shickley, Eric Pinder, Missy LaRae, Jeanne De Vita, Marci Clark, Julie Rau and Madhuri Blaylock. Shout out to the members of Christ Community Church Writer's Group, my weekly writing group and workshop: thank you all for your support!

To the incomparable Crystal Smalls Ord for the stunning commissioned art that gave life to Joel and Amber and the demons that haunt them both. Thank you.

To the agents who read and either passed or requested a read, to those who took the time to add a personal note or sent me a form rejection, all of these helped immensely, and I remain grateful to each of you.

To many others who supported this book in the making: Brandon Harper, Rolando Ponce, Jr., Tim April, Cindy Strachan, Kathy Szczytko, and the high school students who read a chapter and wanted more while I subbed in your classroom, thank you.

To my incredibly talented team at Booktrope: April Gerard, Jessica West, Greg Simanson and Kathryn Galán, and the Team April Authors: it's an honor to work alongside you crafting amazing stories and sharing them with the world.

To my family, especially my wife and four boys: thank you for the support and patience through the lengthy process this project took. Each of you sacrificed the most in allowing me time to write and edit these words until I got it right. You also held me close or gave me space when I found myself triggered and reeling from what these words had brought to the surface. Thank you for being patient and loving with me. Your love made all the difference.

The journey through the planting, pruning and cultivation of this book has taken many years, but along the way, I also gained the skills needed as a writer to craft a story. What I've learned is that mine is not the only story that needs to be told. There are others out there. It is my hope that readers will find inspiration to discover their voices and use them to share even more stories with the world. We need them all. Please speak up.

Abuse, as depicted in this book, survives and grows in our culture and in our world through silence and looking the other way. The best way to eradicate it from our history is by shining light into dark places and speaking about it, no matter how uncomfortable we may feel. May this book help further that conversation. Right now, one in four girls and one in six boys experience child sexual abuse before they turn 18. The statistics are not getting better. They are moving in the wrong direction, toward one in three girls, and one in five boys. We can and must do better for ourselves and for our children.

Finally, thank you to Christopher Anderson and the folks at MaleSurvivor.org who have graciously partnered with me to establish a scholarship fund for men who cannot otherwise attend "Weekend of Recovery," a retreat and workshop for male survivors of child sexual abuse to gather together and, in the strength and unity of fellow survivors, face those dark places and find healing together. Find out more at their website. A portion of each book sold will go to this scholarship. I thank you for joining me in this ministry for men by purchasing a copy of this book. Together, we can make a difference.

I have been significantly blessed throughout the writing of this book. Not only has it given voice to my own childhood sexual abuse experience, but it has led to self-discovery, post-traumatic growth (PTG), illumination, and profound teaching about CSA, recovery of a lost and important friendship, progress toward overcoming in my own healing journey, and the determination to help others do the same. I will no longer be silent. I welcome those of you who will join me.

BIBLIOGRAPHY

Scripture quotations taken from *The Holy Bible,* New International Version®, NIV®.

Copyright © 1973, 1978, 1984, 2011 by Biblica, Inc. ®; Ecclesiastes 1:2, 1:5a, 1:7b, 1:9c, 1:11; Psalm 37:8, 9

Bradbury, Ray. *Fahrenheit 451.* (New York: Del Ray Books, 1953), 163.

Cormier, Robert. *The Chocolate War.* (New York: Random House, 1974), 129.

Hinton, S.E. *The Outsiders.* (New York: The Penguin Group, 1967, 1995), 35.

Salinger, J.D. *Catcher in the Rye.* (New York: Little, Brown and Company, 1945, 1946, 1951), 18, 189.

The Outsiders. Zoetrope Studios/Fox Broadcasting Company. Based on the work of S.E. Hinton. 1990.

RESOURCES FOR ALL SURVIVORS

Rape, Abuse, & Incest National Network
http://www.RAINN.org
1(800)656-HOPE (4673)

Trauma Recovery University
http://traumarecoveryuniversity.com/

TRU: Weekly video podcasts:
http://nomoreshameproject.com/

No More (Domestic Violence and Sexual Assault)
http://nomore.org/

The Joyful Heart Foundation
http://www.joyfulheartfoundation.org/

Darkness to Light (D2L)
http://www.d2l.org

1(866)FOR-LIGHT (367-54448)

#SVYALitChat Project (School Library Journal, via Teen Librarian Toolbox)
http://www.teenlibrariantoolbox.com/2014/02/svyalit-project-index/

RESOURCES FOR MALE SURVIVORS

Male Survivor
http://www.malesurvivor.org

1 in 6
http://1in6.org

The Bristlecone Project
http://bristleconeproject.org/

1 Blue String
http://www.1bluestring.org

ABOUT CHERISH EDITIONS

Cherish Editions is a bespoke self-publishing service for authors of mental health, wellbeing and inspirational books.

As a division of TriggerHub, the UK's leading mental health and wellbeing organization, we are experienced in creating and selling positive, responsible, important and inspirational books, which work to de-stigmatize the issues around mental health and improve the mental health and wellbeing of those who read our titles.

Founded by Adam Shaw, a mental health advocate, author and philanthropist, and leading psychologist Lauren Callaghan, Cherish Editions aims to publish books that provide advice, support and inspiration. We nurture our authors so that their stories can unfurl on the page, helping them to share their uplifting and moving stories.

Cherish Editions is unique in that a percentage of the profits from the sale of our books goes directly to leading mental health charity Shawmind, to deliver its vision to provide support for those experiencing mental ill health.

Find out more about Cherish Editions by visiting cherisheditions.com or by joining us on:
Twitter @cherisheditions
Facebook @cherisheditions
Instagram @cherisheditions

Cherish
EDITIONS

ABOUT SHAWMIND

A proportion of profits from the sale of all Trigger books go to their sister charity, Shawmind, also founded by Adam Shaw and Lauren Callaghan. The charity aims to ensure that everyone has access to mental health resources whenever they need them.

You can find out more about the work Shawmind do by visiting shawmind.org or joining them on:

Twitter @Shaw_Mind
Facebook @ShawmindUK
Instagram @Shaw_Mind

Your Local Mental Health & Wellbeing Charity

DISCUSSION QUESTIONS FOR
THE PACKING HOUSE

1. If you lived in Joel's world, what name might he give you and why? (Shampoo Girl, Skaterdude, Math Punk, etc.)

2. If you were in Joel's place, would you run away? Why or why not?

3. Joel uses reading and writing as a way to cope with the stress and trauma from his life. What strategies or coping tools would you use to manage the stressors you deal with?

4. Having discovered the underlying cause of Joel's nightmares, reflect on the underlying meaning in each of the nightmares. What else might they represent?

5. Explain the significance of each of the main relationships in Joel's life (mother, Jonathan, Amber, Grandmother, Uncle Brandon, father). How does each help or hinder Joel's recovery from his past?

6. Animals are symbolic throughout the novel. What significance do they play in relation to Joel and his journey? Consider school mascots (Panthers, Ravens, Sharks) and salamanders, among others.

7. What role do the intra-chapter poems play in Joel's story? Do they tell their own story? Why or why not?

8. Discuss the theme of communication as shown in both positive and negative ways throughout the novel. What role do letters, a phone booth, a TracFone, telephones, and recorded conversations play in supporting positive communication, or perpetuating a lack of communication?

9. Based on the clues and references throughout the book, compile a list of books Joel read throughout the story. In what ways might these books correlate with *The Packing House*? What insights can you draw from Joel having read these books?

10. Do you feel the traumatic content (child sexual abuse, PTSD, hallucinations, dissociations, domestic violence) of the book was gratuitous or helpful in grounding the story in reality? Support your reasons with examples from the story.

11. What is the significance of fishing and worms in the poems and the story? How might this relate to Joel?

12. Secrets are a big part of the story in *The Packing House*. Were they more helpful or infuriating for you as a reader? Why or why not?